My Off-Limits Single Daddy

AN AGE GAP DAD'S BEST FRIEND ROMANCE

ANNA PIERSON

CHAPTER 1

Ashley

"**E**xcuse me, ma'am, what can I get you?"

How about some perspective?

That's what I *really* need right now. Not an overpriced drink in a fancy-ass restaurant bar that I had no business coming to in the first place.

Who the hell do you think you are, Ashley Elinor Payne?

The thing is, there's just something about the fancy places that fascinate me. Now what is it? Oh yeah, that's right—the fancy people.

Observing them, listening to them, watching them walk through the world gives me something to aspire to. It makes me believe that anything is possible. Surely, one of these beautiful creatures was once a lost twenty-year-old with zero savings, no income, and absolutely no plan for the future?

No one figures out their life at twenty anyway, right?

On the bright side? I'm starting a new job tomorrow. I'm going to be PA to the CEO of Ackerman Corp. I have *no* clue how I managed to land the job in the first place, given that I'm currently rocking the college drop-out status, but by some miracle, I did get the job.

Now, I just have to figure out how to do it.

I look at the bartender and force a smile onto my face. One that is hopefully confident enough to make him believe that I belong here. "Can I get a Negroni, please?"

His smile tightens just a little. "Of course, ma'am. But first, I'm gonna need to see some ID. I do apologize, but it's bar policy."

I don't hesitate. I pull up the new purse I'd purchased right after landing this job (it was on sale at Macy's), grab my ratty old wallet and produce my ID.

He stares at the picture, then at me, then back at the picture. "One Negroni coming right up," he says as he hands back my ID. "Thank you, Wendy Peters."

I can't help but shake my head at the slightly awkward picture of 'Wendy Peters' staring back at me. God help her, I'd learned to love that picture. I remember the exact moment I'd received this card. Most teenagers have to lie to their parents, pay a ton of money to get the older brother of a friend to hook them up with a decent fake ID.

Not me.

I was gifted my fake ID by my father on my seventeenth birthday. "*I'm not encouraging drinking or anything,*" he'd told me, "*I just know you're gonna go out and drink with your friends, and if you're gonna do it, you might as well do it right.*"

My father was a legend in the town of Scottsdale, Arizona. He never had to try to be the cool Dad. He *was* the cool Dad.

He was laid back and open-minded. He didn't care who I hung out with or what I did as long as I was honest with him about all of it. I was the first of my friends to ever be in a club because my Dad took me to one when I was fourteen years old. I tried beer when I was fifteen because my Dad handed me his bottle and told me to have at it. I was allowed to have boyfriends over as long as I introduced them to him first.

His parenting approach was criticized by many, appreciated by some, revered by others. But whatever your opinion on his parenting was, one thing was undeniable—it was unusual.

That might have been because he had no female counterpart reigning him in. It might have been because he was just a free spirit who marched to the beat of his own drum.

It might also have had a little something to do with the fact that my father and I are almost exactly sixteen years apart, give or take a couple of months. We were basically the Gilmore Girls if Lorelei had taken off and Christopher had been the one to stay and raise Rory.

Except we don't have a show.

Just one loving but often dysfunctional relationship. Which is par for the course really.

"Here you go, ma'am." The bartender sets the Negroni down in front of me. It's in a square crystal glass, complete with a fancy silk coaster. "Enjoy."

"Thanks."

As I sip my drink, I partake in my favorite pastime—people-watching. There's an older couple sitting by the window, having their dinner and not talking. There's a family sitting at the table next to theirs. Every single member is on their phone, texting.

On the other side of the restaurant is a couple who look like they're on a first date. She's definitely got a fresh blowout for this dinner and he's looking a little too stiff in his Burberry coat.

Next to the first date couple is a table of girlfriends, knocking back drinks in their Sunday best and generally shooting the shit. Adjacent to them is another couple and they hold my attention because of how shiny the two of them are. She's wearing a skin-tight dress, high heels and a haughty expression and he—

Whoa.

My eyes focus on the man and I feel my heart kick up a couple of notches. I've never seen anyone with a presence that powerful. Or a face that ruggedly handsome.

Jesus, I can tell his eyes are blue from here.

Then suddenly—we both lock on. His gaze isn't just blue; it's direct as hell. And he doesn't look away. Which is why I do—quickly and guiltily.

Cringing inwardly, I focus on my drink and try and remember that I did not come here to be distracted by a handsome face. I came here to take the edge off my nerves. I came here to give myself a much-needed jolt of courage.

Nothing does that quite as fast as a Negroni in a fancy city bar.

That's another reason I like these kinds of places. They make me feel like I can be someone else for a little while. I don't have to be the awkward, insecure, shy Ashley. I can be someone who's confident, ambitious and unapologetic. I can be someone who has her life figured out. I can be someone who goes out into the world and gets exactly what she wants. I can be someone who *knows* exactly what she wants.

I finish my Negroni slowly over the course of the next half an hour. Then I flag down the waiter to ask for the bill. While he brings it over, I check my phone. I have a couple of texts. One from Sandra and two from my father.

Sandra: *Just wanted to wish you good luck tomorrow, girl. You're gonna fucking kill it! Hope there's tons of cute boys at the office to pick from. *winking emoji**

Smiling, I shake my head and heart Sandra's message. She was the only other high school friend who ended up staying in Arizona for college. The rest got out the moment they could. She stayed because she has aging parents and a great love for the home state.

But me?

I stayed because I was too scared to leave. And if I'm being totally honest, it was also because I have a *slightly* co-dependent relationship with my father.

I mean—I was sixteen and still walking around calling my father my best friend.

Who does that?

This numb-nut, that's who.

Which is why when I turned twenty a couple of months ago and realized that I had no interest in the business degree I was studying at Arizona State, I figured the best way to figure out who I was and what I wanted was to take myself out of my comfort zone.

Which brings me back to this city. In this bar. Facing a new job that has me sweating from the armpits every time I think about it.

But that's *exactly* why I did this. Because I can't rely on my father for everything. I have to grow up. I have to be independent. I have to learn how to be a Goddamn adult.

Dad: *Remember, you are Ashley fucking Payne. You can do this.*

Dad: *Love you kid.*

I'm in the process of replying when the waiter appears in front of me. "Um, sorry, ma'am. But your card was declined."

What!!!

"Declined?" I gasp. "How is that possible? This card's *never* been declined before."

The waiter holds up the card for me. "It's expired, ma'am."

That's when I realize—I *knew* this card was expiring

5

months ago. I'd even applied for a new one, which I'd received in the mail a few weeks before my big move to California. Problem is, somewhere between dropping out of college, second-guessing all my decisions and actually moving, I'd completely forgotten to swap out my old card with my new one.

Operation *Become an Adult* was off to a great start.

"You can pay by cash," he says helpfully. "It's fourteen dollars and fifty cents, ma'am."

Jesus! Almost fifteen freaking dollars for ONE drink!? I *really* was not in Kansas anymore. And this Dorothy had to remember that she didn't have the money to be throwing around on frivolous stuff anymore.

Daddy's all the way in Arizona now.

Clearing my throat, I pull my wallet open and immediately, my heart sinks. I have a five-dollar note and maybe two more dollars in change. If I were a half-way decent flirt, I'd think about turning the charm on to get out of paying for this drink, but honestly, I'm way too self-conscious a person and the stakes are too high.

"I'm so, *so* sorry. But I forgot my card expired and I didn't bring enough cash. I can totally give you what I have and—" the bartender's face has soured but still I keep going out of pure desperation, "—and I promise to come back tomorrow and pay for the rest of this drink."

"Ma'am, I'm sorry but I can't allow you to leave without paying for the drink."

I'm noticing a few eyes shift my way. My cheeks redden but I keep my attention focused on the bartender. "Listen, I know you probably hear this all the time but I'm good for the money. I *will* come back tomorrow and—"

"Hey, Charlie." A dark shadow falls over me and I freeze as a twenty-dollar note slides across the counter towards the bartender. "This should cover it. Leave the young lady alone, will you?"

God, is this embarrassing.

"Thank you. That's really nice of—" I turn on my stool to face my knight in shining armor. My eyes nearly bug right out of my head.

It's him. He's even *more* gorgeous up close. Those eyes of his are the most piercing blue I've ever come across. His nose, cheekbones and jaw are perfectly symmetrical, and those lips of his are turned up in a slight smile.

"Don't mention it."

I glance behind him, trying to figure out where his date went. "You really don't have to do this."

"Do you have another alternative?"

He has a point. Which means all I can do is blush deeper and say another fervent "thank you."

"Like I said—don't mention it."

"I'll pay you back."

He raises his eyebrows. Which are thick and decidedly masculine. Somehow, they frame his face perfectly. "That's really not necessary."

"Of course it is," I say with my father's voice blaring in my ears. "I don't take handouts."

He smiles. "How about you do me a favor in return and we call it even?"

My eyes go wide. "Really?" He nods and I'm instantly suspicious. "What kind of favor? If it involves getting naked, then I'm out."

He looks shocked for a moment. Then he snorts with laughter. "You're direct."

Jesus, now why had I gone and said that? Why would a man like him possibly be interested in someone like me?

"Have a drink with me and we're square. You get to keep your clothes on and everything."

Trying to keep the blushing in check, I fix him with a quizzical expression. "Um, you want to buy me *another* drink?"

"Yes."

"How would that make us even?"

"It's poor form to question other people's favors."

I can't help but smile. He's not just handsome, he's charming too. It's a double whammy. One that I'm seriously not prepared for. I don't have the skill or the experience to handle a man like him.

Judging from the shiny silver Rolex on his wrist and the fact that he has ready cash in his wallet, it's clear that this man is an adult. A proper one. He's definitely older than me, but not by more than a decade or so. If I had to guess, I'd probably peg him at around twenty-nine, maybe thirty. Closer to my Dad's age than mine. But with a face like his, that's easy to overlook.

"I have a question first."

"Go for it."

"Where's your date?"

His smile gets a little wider. "She took a cab home."

"Oh." I'm feeling really squirmy under that gaze of his. "So… it didn't go well?"

"It was pleasant enough but we're not soul mates."

I lift my eyebrows. "How do you know?"

"Because she believes in soul mates and I don't."

"Maybe that's because you haven't met her yet."

He chuckles. "So—what do you say to one more drink?"

"I get to keep my clothes on?"

His eyes twinkle. "Definitely. Unless, of course, you specifically request me to remove them."

Jesus. I've never been so aware of my... *ahem* nether regions before. I can feel this throbbing down there that I've honestly never felt before. Of course, all the men I've dated so far have been teenage boys.

And the man sitting next to me is definitely not a boy.

So, I make the decision to be someone else for tonight. Someone interesting and funny and worldly. Someone who can sit in a bar like this and command the attention of a man like him. Tonight, I'm not gonna be Ashley Payne.

Tonight, I'm gonna be Wendy Peters.

"I'd love to have a drink with you."

CHAPTER 2

Tobias

S he's a blusher.

That's clear in the first two minutes of our conversation. She's also having trouble looking me in the eye. Which is incredibly endearing. And incredibly telling.

She's young. She's not used to being in a place like this, which is why she acts as though she doesn't belong. I'm hoping to hell that she's here because she's freshly twenty-one and not as a result of a fake ID.

"What brings you here this Sunday night?" She stiffens immediately and I raise my eyebrows. "Wow, and I thought that was the icebreaker question."

She smiles. "I'll be honest. This isn't my regular haunt."

"No?"

She shakes her head. "I come to places like this when I want to be someone else," she admits. "Pretty silly, huh?"

"Not at all. I get it."

Her eyes go wide. "Really?"

I nod. "Of course. Whenever life gets to be too much, it helps to slip on someone else's skin. Pretend that you come from a healthy, loving family with a golden retriever with some cutesy name."

"Peanut?"

"Or Bubbles."

Her eyes brighten as she relaxes a little. "I had a friend who named her dog Doughnut."

"Poor dog."

She bursts out laughing. *Fuck, is she pretty.* She's pretty in a way that feels familiar. She laughs and talks and moves in a way that feels familiar. Maybe that's why I'd noticed her the moment she walked into The Blue Canary's bar.

But she also moves like she doesn't want to take up space. She doesn't demand attention the way most people who walk into this place do. She swerved her way through people, took the stool in the farthest corner of the bar and sat there like she wanted to disappear.

She tucks a strand of auburn hair back behind her ear and gives me a shy glance with eyes that are a deep caramelly hazel. Even now, it feels like she wants to make herself smaller.

"So… you pretend you're someone with a healthy family, huh?"

Hmm, I gave myself away there.

"Not necessarily. I was just giving you an example."

She cocks an eyebrow at me. "You came up with that example pretty fast."

I smile. She's not quite as mild-mannered as she comes off. I like that. "At this point, I'd settle for having any kind of family," I admit.

It's trippy saying it out loud. I'm really not sure why I did it, but perhaps it's because she's a stranger.

"Oh…" her expression gets really sad. "I'm sorry."

She doesn't say it in that generic way that people do when

they hear you've lost a loved one. She says it with her eyes, like she really, truly, deeply feels for me.

"It is what it is."

The crazy thing is, if she asks about my childhood, I just might tell her. But she doesn't. She takes another sip of her drink and offers me an uncertain smile. "I like to pretend to be someone well-traveled. Someone who's seen the world and isn't shocked by anything anymore."

I raise my eyebrows. "That's what you wish for?"

She nods. "I've never even been out of the country. Moving to California is my one big flex in all my life."

I raise my eyebrows, curiosity getting the better of me. "All your long life, huh?"

She blushes self-consciously and shifts in her seat. It really does look like she's uncomfortable in her skin. "You're still young. Far too young to talk as though you've wasted your life. Especially when you haven't even started it yet."

She purses up her lips and her eyebrows rise. "I'm older than I look."

"Oh yeah?"

"I'll be twenty-six on my next birthday." She seems to sit up a little taller as she informs me of her age.

Twenty-five. Somehow, that's a relief. Ten years is still a big age difference, but somehow, it feels less of a mental leap.

"I'll tell you what? Why don't we pretend to be our alter egos? Just for tonight. See what it's like to live in someone else's skin."

Her eyes pique with interest at the suggestion. Then a slow smile spreads across her face. "That's a great idea."

I offer her my hand. "I'm Oliver Bryant."

Her smile gets wider as she slips her hands into mine. "I'm Wendy Peters."

"It's a pleasure to meet you, Wendy."

"And you, Oliver."

We're still clasping each other's hands long after the introduction is over. For whatever reason, I don't want to let go.

She looks down at our linked hands and blushes deeply before pulling away. She hides behind her drink for a second.

"So Wendy, what brings you to California?"

"I wanted a fresh start somewhere new," she says simply.

"Funny, that's the same reason I moved to this city too."

"Yeah?" she asks eagerly.

I nod. "The town I grew up in was small. So small that there was nowhere to hide."

She raises her eyebrows. "You came here to hide?"

I chuckle. "I suppose I did. But somewhere in the midst of everything, I figured out what I wanted to do and who I wanted to be."

Her eyes widen and something tells me I've struck a nerve. I've stumbled across some sort of inextricable connection with her that has her leaning in towards me.

"That's… amazing."

I shrug. "It's sink or swim when you're on your own. And that's not necessarily a bad thing."

"I'm counting on it."

We raise our glasses and cheers together. "What was her name?" Wendy asks, gesturing over to the table I'd been sitting in with Alicia.

"Alicia Appleton-Statham."

"Wow, she's a hyphenate," I smirk while Wendy continues. "She's beautiful."

"She's extremely intelligent too. She's a lawyer for her father's firm."

Her eyes pop. "What kind of law?"

"Family law."

"Wow, I can't compete with that." Something tells me that she doesn't mean to say that out loud because the moment she does, her cheeks go bright red.

"Wendy," I say, leaning in a little closer to her. She smells of cinnamon. "I'm gonna be honest with you. Alicia and I *were* on a date. But it was a date with no strings attached. It's more of a casual relationship."

"As in… friends with benefits?"

Jesus, she is young.

"I suppose you could say that."

Her cheeks get even redder. "B-but… then why did you come over here?"

"Because I realized that I'd rather talk to you than sleep with Alicia." Her eyes pop open and for a long time, she doesn't say a word. It makes me wonder if I've overstepped a personal boundary for her. "Just to be clear, I don't expect anything from you tonight. Like I said, I just want to talk to you. You don't have to be nervous."

She shakes her head. "I'm not. I guess I'm… flattered."

"May I be so bold as to make an observation about you?"

Her eyes go wide. She looks terrified for a moment. "Um… sure?"

I smile. "You're not used to attention."

She exhales sharply, clearly having expected a different question. "I'm not used to men like you," she admits.

"Men like me?"

She blushes. "Let's just say that the men I've dated in the past are the kind that like to hang out in their Mum's basements, sleep till noon and play video games for hours."

"Oh *God*."

She nods. "I know."

"Why on earth would a woman like you waste time on men like that?"

She shifts in her seat. I'm making her uncomfortable again but I don't care at this point. It's criminal that a woman as beautiful and interesting as she is wouldn't think she deserves more.

"Lack of choice?"

"Is that really it?"

She looks at me through her eyelashes and sighs. "Maybe. Maybe it's just the pitfalls of small-town living. I'm trying to figure that part out. I'm trying to figure a lot out."

"Don't be in such a rush. Sometimes finding yourself ends up being an accident."

She laughs. "Is that what happened to you?"

"What makes you think I've found myself at all? Just because a person looks like they've got their shit together doesn't mean they have."

Her eyes go wide as she takes that in. "I spend a lot of time with privileged, powerful people with more money than God. What people tend to see are the designer clothes and the statement jewelry, the fancy cars and the material wealth. What they don't see are the addiction issues, the mental health issues, the infidelity and mistrust that plagues their marriages and the number of people they've cut in order to get to where they are."

She sighs. "I guess when you grow up poor, it's easy to fall into the trap of believing that money equals happiness."

I shake my head. "Money equals opportunity. But happiness... that's another beast entirely."

"When was the last time you were truly and wholly happy?"

I raise my eyebrows but she doesn't rescind the question.

"Jesus, when was the last time I was happy?" I repeat, thinking back to my childhood in Scottsdale.

There were moments in the midst of all that growing up when I can say I was truly happy. "Probably around fourteen and fifteen."

Her eyes soften. "Can you tell me why?"

I've never had to tell anyone why. The people who know my story were there for it. The people who don't know it, I've never had any inclination to tell.

Until now.

"That was the last time my mother, brother and I were together as a family."

There's a thin film of moisture coating her eyes. How is it that this stranger could feel so much after knowing me for only a couple of hours? My father had never managed to muster up even half that emotion after a lifetime.

"Thanks for sharing that with me."

I clear my throat gruffly. "I honestly don't know why I did."

She shrugs, "Chemistry." The moment the word is out of her mouth, she blushes. Then she tries to cover it up by looking at the antique bronze clock on the bar's back wall. "Oh *shit,* is that the time?" She jerks off her bar stool. "I hate to just run off now but… I have work tomorrow and I can't be late." But once she's standing, she hesitates. "Um… it feels weird. Not knowing your real name."

I smile. "How about we meet here a week from now? Same spot, same time. And we exchange real names then."

Her smile is bright and brilliant. "I'd love that."

"Thank you for everything."

"No, thank *you*," I say as I lean in. The thought of watching her walk out of here feels… unnatural. But I can sense that asking her to accompany me back to my place would just spook her.

"So… next week then?"

I reach out and put my hand on hers. She freezes, clearly startled by the contact. "I hope you'll forgive me. But I can't wait a week to kiss you."

Then I kiss her.

CHAPTER 3

Ashley

I was twelve when Jimmy Nelson kissed me. It was sloppy and wet, and it's the reason I didn't kiss another boy for two more years.

By the time Matt Helsby made his move, I hadn't just forgotten about Jimmy Nelson's kiss, I was *ready* for what I considered my first 'real' kiss. Turned out that all that expectation and all that anticipation was for nothing. Matt Helsby's kiss was clumsy and awkward as hell.

The first kiss I had that I actually enjoyed came a year later from Nathan Gould. I later described that kiss as 'fairy-tale perfect.'

Until some months later when I started kissing Victor Smith and I had to bump Nathan off his pedestal.

My point is—I thought I had a great roster of kisses to look back on fondly. I thought I had experience. I thought that in the world of kisses, I had some skin in the game.

Turns out—I have *never* been properly kissed.

Because none of those kisses felt like this one.

And this one feels like—I'm flying. I'm not surprised by how confident a kisser he is. Everything about him just exudes that intoxicating sense of self-assurance. His lips are firm but soft, passionate but gentle. He holds my lips firmly against his and takes the kiss like it belongs to him.

In the back of my head, a tiny little thought echoes softly. *He's just ruined me for other men.*

My lips part of their own accord. His tongue slides into my mouth and I tremble violently, desperate for more but conscious about the fact that we're still in public. The second our tongues meet, it's game over.

My head is spinning manically.

My pussy is throbbing so hard it feels like a ticking time bomb.

And somewhere in the midst of this intense, mind-boggling, transformative kiss—I find a little confidence.

When we break apart, I'm panting softly and I'm pretty sure he is too. "I'm sorry," he says in a deep whisper that sets my heart racing all over again. "That went too far."

Not nearly far enough.

"Don't apologize."

He's still holding my hand, his deep blue eyes fixed on me with the kind of hunger I never believed existed in real life. *Why the hell didn't I move to this city sooner?*

I take advantage of my newfound confidence and say something I'd never have said if I were just plain old Ashley Payne. But Wendy Peters? Now that girl is wild.

"I don't want to say goodnight just yet."

His eyes widen. "What—"

"I want you." The moment those words escape me, I feel the panic come on. *What if this is too forward? What if he's not interested? What if I've just made a giant fool of myself?*

Panic.

Panic.

Panic.

"I want you too."

Relief floods through my pores so hard that it feels like it has the power to knock me over. *Thank God.* I glance around the restaurant. It's emptied out a little but there are still a couple of tables that are occupied.

I've never been *that* girl. I've never been the confident, forward one. I've never made the first move in my life. And yet here I am, contemplating a real femme fatale kinda move. "Meet me in the bathroom in five minutes," I whisper to him.

Then I get off my bar stool and walk towards the restrooms, trying to look as cool and sexy as I can. I haven't glanced back once, but I can *feel* his eyes on me, watching me walk away.

The moment I get into the ladies' room, I splash cold water onto my face and take a couple of deep breaths.

"You can do this," I tell my reflection in the mirror. "This is the beginning of the new you. Ballsy and brave. The kind of woman who knows what she wants and goes after it."

In this case—it's the handsome stranger from the bar.

I'd opted to pair my black leather mini with my only silk white blouse; a blouse that I'm planning on wearing tomorrow on my first day. If I'd known I was gonna have torrid sex with a stranger in a public bathroom, I'd have picked something less expensive that I didn't mind getting ruined.

But as it stands, I'm gonna have to risk it.

The bathroom door opens and I spin around. He's standing there in all his glory, looking at me with eyes spiked with lust.

Oh, he's definitely worth ruining a white silk blouse for.

Neither one of us speaks. We move towards each other, meeting in the middle, our bodies crashing together like a storm. He's kissing me and touching me and I'm returning fire, throwing out all the boundaries that I've spent a lifetime building.

Whatever.

Any rule that would have prevented this is not worth following.

He grabs me by the hips and pushes me up against the bathroom counter, pulling my skirt up in the process. I can't remember what panties I wore underneath this outfit. It doesn't really matter though. I already know it's not a sexy pair. I don't really own any sexy underwear.

Oliver doesn't seem to care as he pulls my panties off in one steady swipe. He kisses his way up my body, pulling at the buttons of my blouse with his teeth.

RIP silk blouse. Your death was worth it.

He hoists me onto the counter so that I'm in a sitting position. Then he parts my legs and settles between them. I've never been so aware of my lady parts before. It's like I'm being introduced to my body for the first time.

My experience of sex has been so vastly different at this point that it feels almost laughable. I'm not being poked or prodded. I'm not being groomed or convinced. I'm throwing myself in because I've finally met a man who knows his way around a woman's body.

My whole body tingles when I hear the sound of his zipper. I can't look down but I feel him against my thigh. I'm not sure but it definitely feels big. Not that I'm surprised. Men are not capable of walking around with that much confidence and a small dick. But if there was a man who could do it—this man's probably the one.

His lips run down my neck as he presses his cock against my pussy. *Oh God.* He kisses me hard before pulling away. He meets my gaze, those blue eyes of his are blazing. "Are you sure?"

I've been with only two other men up until now. Had either one of them asked me if I was ready beforehand? Had either one of them even *looked* at me beforehand?

"I'm sure." It comes out as a gasp.

Then he pulls out something from his back pocket and steps back. I get a full, unadulterated view of his cock and *swoon*—it is a sight to behold. Big, sure. Beautiful, definitely. All mine? It is for tonight and I'm gonna make the most of it.

He brings the tiny blue wrapper to his mouth and tears at the top of it with his teeth. That's when it hits me. Condoms! How had I not even thought about protection up until now? Me? The girl who never does anything without thinking it to death.

I can mark the exact moment when I became a cautious person. It was when I was twelve and my father had sat me down to have 'the sex talk.'

Don't have sex until you're emotionally and physically ready. But if you do, use condoms. Cause I'm too young to be a grandfather and I don't have the money to raise another kid.

Those were his exact words. And they had haunted me through my entire adolescence.

I watch in awe as Oliver rolls the condom over his massive cock. Then he steps back towards me, his heat engulfing me once again. He grabs my ass and kind of pulls me onto his cock. I'm so wet that he slides right in. But even the extreme moisture down there isn't enough to distract from the fact that he feels even bigger inside me.

"Oh *God*," I moan.

"You okay?"

I nod fast. "Mmm…"

He starts thrusting but it's slow. It's almost as though he's scared to hurt me. I might have been worried about the same thing if I weren't so desperate for release. I grind myself against him, trying to spur him on.

Then I hear a dark chuckle in my ear. "Someone's eager…"

I don't even have it in me to blush anymore. I just want him to fuck the hell outta me. "Take me," I moan. "Just fucking take me."

He pushes me back, forcing me to grip the counter that dips into the sinks that are sitting on either side of us. One hand lands on my exposed right breast as his eyes lift to meet mine. He doesn't stop thrusting into me but he doesn't increase his tempo either.

"Look at me, baby," he growls through gritted teeth.

I do. And boy, does that kick things up a notch. We maintain eye contact the entire time he's fucking me. And even though he doesn't go faster or harder, the pressure builds, the intensity kicks up a couple of notches.

He's teasing me.

He's making sure I know who's in control.

I'm not prepared for how much I like it, which is when I decide to stop trying to make things happen. I decide to just *let* things happen.

And ironically, *that's* when he starts thrusting harder.

My eyes flutter as he keeps pumping, his hips jerking so hard against my pussy that the sound of flesh on flesh echoes through the bathroom.

"Yes," I exclaim, trying to dampen my moans. "Fuck *yeah*!"

"Is this what you want, baby?" he asks.

I nod desperately as my hair flies over my face. I can already feel the orgasm coming and it strikes me that this is the first time I'm experiencing one *with* a man. It's the first time I can honestly credit an orgasm *to* a man.

"Harder," I gasp. "Please... harder."

And by God, does he deliver. He fucks me so hard that at one point, I'm afraid we're gonna break the mirror that my back is currently slamming into. His jaw clenches, his thrusts become faster, more pronounced. My eyes roll back in my head as my body erupts with the wave.

Is this what I've been missing my whole life?

Three thrusts after I've cum and his body spasms slightly, his jaw clenches even tighter and I feel him release. His lips land on my shoulder for a moment and I start to count heartbeats. His or mine? I have no fucking clue at this point.

We kinda feel like the same person right now.

That thought catches me off guard. It fills me with this weird aching kind of heat... the kind that requires friction.

He pulls out of me and the emptiness he leaves behind is something I've never experienced before. He definitely notices the shiver running down my body because he starts pulling my blouse back around me.

"I think I ripped a button or two."

...Aaaand cue the blushing. Apparently fucking him hadn't quite obliterated that reaction like I'd hoped it would. "That's okay. I have more blouses like this at home." *I wish.*

We put ourselves together in silence and as our clothes come back on, the self-consciousness starts to edge into the space between us. Had I played right into the hands of a practiced ladies' man? Was he going to disappear on me now that he'd gotten what he wanted? Is this what he was after the whole time?

I remind myself that *I* am the one who had asked him to meet me in the bathroom.

Then again, *he* was the one who kissed me.

Oh God...

"Wendy." His voice pulls me out of the rabbit hole I'm

close to jumping into. "I want to see you next week." *Joy!* "But—" my happiness dies a quick death, "—considering what just happened—" *please don't say what I think you're gonna say,* "—maybe we should just exchange our real names right now?"

Ah, sweet relief.

I'd been almost certain he was gonna tell me that he wasn't interested in seeing me again now that we'd had sex.

But nothing he's said or done tonight suggests that he's the kind of man who would lead a woman on. He could have lied to me about his beautiful date. But he had told me exactly what they were to each other.

He'd treated me with nothing but respect and kindness.

Even now, he's giving me the choice to decide the next move.

I offer him a shy smile. "If it's all the same to you—I'd like to stick to our plan and meet here a week from now."

His eyes twinkle softly. "Yeah?"

I nod. "Yeah."

"Can I ask why?"

My smile goes from shy to confident under his gaze. This feeling in my stomach is new. It's butterflies but dialed up to a thousand. It's this floaty feeling of freedom and possibility and passion. It's the new dream I was chasing. It's the new start I was hoping for. It's the new me I was desperate to find.

"Because… I trust that you'll show up."

CHAPTER 4

Ashley

I've got cheesy old romantic melodies playing in my head the whole way back to my one-bedroom apartment at the very edge of the city.

As much as I try not to think about next week and seeing him again, that's exactly what I end up doing. The whole freaking time. My head is pinging with questions, alternate scenarios, vague doubts and the very real fear that he might not show up at all despite my earlier confidence to the contrary.

No, he's gonna show up.

No man looks at a girl that way and then doesn't show up. That just doesn't commute.

On the bright side? This little adventure tonight has successfully distracted me from the fact that I will be starting a new job tomorrow morning. One for which I'm woefully underqualified.

You'd think that being a PA would be no sweat. But as it turns out, being the PA to one of the wealthiest men in one of the most reputable and successful businesses in the whole of California requires more than just your basic secretarial skills.

Don't think about that now. Hold on to this feeling. Hold on to this night for as long as you can.

By the time I get back home, it's just a little past twelve. I'm still so preoccupied with thoughts of Oliver that it doesn't even register that my lights are on. At least not until I'm halfway into the apartment before I realize that I *definitely* did not keep the lights on before I left.

I freeze. *What the—*

"Hey, baby girl."

My hand slams against my chest. "*Jesus*, Dad! You scared the living shit outta me."

He chuckles. "It's a good thing I sent you for those Tae Kwan Do classes then, huh?"

I roll my eyes and drop my bag onto the only 'sittable' chair in the living room. "It was five classes. That hardly qualifies me as a black belt."

"It was six classes and that's all you needed."

Laughing, I walk into his outstretched arms. He still hugs me like he used to when I was six years old. Sometimes, I feel like he's on the verge of lifting me up and spinning me around. But as annoyed as I am that he's here at all, an equally big part of me is glad.

Nothing says comfort and safety like my father. "What are you doing here?" I ask accusingly into his shoulder.

"You didn't sound so good the last time we spoke, kid."

I cringe. "I was just... having a tiny little meltdown. It happens. You didn't have to come all the way down here just to check on me. A call would have sufficed."

He lets go of me but he keeps his hands on my shoulders. "I texted *hours* ago and never got a response." *Oh shit.*

He's got an eyebrow raised as he turns the accusation back on me. His hair is in its usual disheveled mess. But the rest of him reads respectable small-town mechanic. I can't blame people for assuming he's my older brother. He definitely doesn't look like the father of a twenty-year-old.

"What happened?" he asks pointedly.

"Um well…" I can't exactly tell my father that my head was turned by a handsome face. Or that I had torrid sex with the owner of said handsome face. "I just went for a walk in the city and I guess I got distracted."

"Hmm…"

I pull away from him, laughing. "Stop it. I'm fine."

"You're not telling me something."

That's the thing about being *too* close to certain family members. Sometimes, they know you better than you know yourself. "I'm telling you just enough."

"Did you use protection?"

"Dad!"

And that was the thing about having a father who could easily be grouped into the higher end of *your* generational bracket. He was brutally open about everything. Including the stuff you wished he would just pretend he didn't notice.

He holds his hands up in surrender. "Just checking."

My eyes go straight to the duffel bag in the corner of the living room slash kitchen slash dining room. Of course, at the moment, since it's completely empty, it just looks like one big room. "You really didn't have to come all the way down here."

"It's the first time you've been away from home. You're starting a new job tomorrow. It's no shame to need a little help in the beginning." He looks around the room pointedly. "Look at this place. You have *no* furniture. You told me you had it covered."

I sigh. "Because I didn't want you to send a bunch of money my way. You're already taking care of the first three

29

months of rent. I'll buy furniture when I can afford it. For right now, this chair works fine."

"Ash, I know you want to be independent. But independence isn't like addiction. You don't have to quit cold turkey."

I smile. "Dad, you're not buying me any furniture. I'll take care of it the moment my first paycheck hits. Ackerman Corp. pays really well. So well, in fact, that you don't even need to cover more than the first month of rent."

He waves that away. "It's what I promised you. It's what I'm gonna do." He's already circling the room, clearly making a mental note of everything he's going to buy for me.

"Dad, seriously." I don't wanna go there but he's not leaving me much choice. "You can't afford to do this."

His light blue eyes get just a tiny bit darker and I notice his jaw twitch slightly. "I'm not destitute, Ash. It's just been a rough year, that's all."

"It's been a rough couple of years, Dad," I point out. "And it's time you let me fend for myself. Let's face it, I'm the one who's been draining your resources."

His eyes narrow. "Don't say that."

"It's true though. And anyway—"

"How about a drink?" he interrupts abruptly. "I brought a six-pack but the grocery store around the corner had some great brews too."

I raise my eyebrows and walk around to the open kitchen that flanks the right side of the living space. "You went to the grocery store already?" I open the cupboards and of course, they're now fully stocked. "Jesus, Dad."

He smiles sheepishly. "You need to eat."

Suppressing a sigh, I turn to him. "Beer?"

"Please."

I grab a can and hand it to him. Then I fill a glass of water for myself. Since there's no real place to sit, we just lean against the counter towards one another.

"So… how long are you staying?" I ask, conscious of the fact that there's exactly one single bed in this apartment.

He smirks. "You don't have to worry about having your old man here cramping your style. There's a decent motel around the corner."

My eyes go wide with horror. "That place looks like a crack den. You're not staying there."

"I can also crash at Toby's place. He won't mind. It'll give us a chance to catch up. It's been a while since we've really hung out."

"Oh right," I say with a nod. "Toby lives in Cali."

He takes a long swig of his beer. "Been here for almost two decades now. Somehow, it feels like longer."

I can't say the same. I've heard about this Toby all my life but I've never actually met him. I haven't even seen a picture of him. Sometimes, I think Dad regrets that more than the fact that I've never met my own mother. But their relationship is unique. I guess you could categorize it as one of those 'boy' friendships. There's not always a lot of contact or conversation. But when they are together, it's like old times.

"Does he even know you're in California?"

"Thought I'd surprise him actually."

"Like you did me?"

He mock-punches me in the arm. "Listen, it's late, so I figure I'll crash on the floor in my sleeping bag and go over to his tomorrow."

I shake my head. "Dad, seriously. You're more than welcome to stay here. It's not a problem. We both know you're gonna go out tomorrow and buy a nice, comfy sofa bed anyway." He snorts and I know I've hit the nail on the head. "And I can use the sleeping bag. You take the bed."

He leans in and kisses me on the forehead. "You're a good kid, Ash." I feel like I'm ten years old when he speaks to me like that—but in a good way. "But I'm happy in my sleeping bag. Now, why don't you get to sleep? You've got a big day tomorrow."

I frown. "You're not going to bed right now?"

"I thought I'd try giving Toby a call."

I nod. "Does this mean that the two of you aren't fighting anymore?"

Dad gives me a smile that's bordering on guilt. "It was never a fight exactly. We had issues but they happened a long time ago. We're both adults now. We don't need to talk it through to get over it. That's the thing about good friends, kid. You can go years without seeing or speaking to each other. But when you do meet—it's like no time has passed. Toby knows that I have his back no matter what. He calls me asking for a favor, I'm there. Same with him."

"Must be nice…"

Dad smiles. "He's a good guy. You'll meet him soon."

"I'm looking forward to it." I head into my room, which is separated from the main living area by a paper-thin wall. I probably should, but I stop at the threshold and look back over my shoulder at him. "Dad?"

"Hmm?"

"So… Toby?"

"What about him?"

"Did he know my mother too?"

The moment I mention her, Dad's face drops. It's the reason I try not to mention her as much as I can. "Yes."

"Were they… close?"

Dad clears his throat and turns away from me as though the conversation is already over. "We all were," he admits. "Until we weren't."

Those words carry weight—a lifetime before me that constructed the man my father became. A past that he was never able to truly get over. His gaze turns towards the tiny window above the sink that overlooks the street.

I know from experience that he's done talking. He fists his beer and I nod with resignation. "Good night, Dad."

"Good night, kid."

CHAPTER 5

Tobias

The high wears off the moment I step foot inside my four-bedroom penthouse.

The carpeted foyer leads me to the main living room, which boasts wooden floors and panoramic views of the city. It's a view that stopped 'wowing' me years ago though. Somehow, looking out into the twinkling lights of the sprawling metropolis just puts into perspective how alone I am in this big city.

Why does a thirty-five-year-old bachelor require *three* extra bedrooms? I don't have a partner. I don't have a child. I don't have family who sleep over occasionally and I certainly don't have guests. Sporadic or otherwise.

I barely spend any time in this apartment myself.

I go to work early, I come back from work late. When I do socialize, it's with colleagues who frequent fancy restaurants or exclusive clubs. It had held a certain appeal once upon a time but I'm quickly becoming bored with the predictability of it all.

Even my dates with Alicia had taken on a predictable routine. Dinner. Light flirting. Dessert. Back to hers for sex.

I've never brought a woman back to my place and I don't intend to start anytime soon. As I round the sofa and walk towards the floor-to-ceiling windows that make the fourth wall of my living room, I realize that my current loneliness has less to do with other people and more to do with me.

I turn my back on the view to face my large living room. You'd think the way the bar was stocked that I had company over all the time. But I just like variety and accessibility. Apart from the paintings on the walls, every surface I have is empty. No pictures, no personal touches. I might as well be in a hotel room without the benefit of room service.

Sighing, I head over to the bar and pour myself another drink.

My current state of restlessness wouldn't be as pronounced right now if it weren't for the young woman I'd collided with this evening.

I say collided because that's exactly how it had felt like she'd *happened* to me.

There was just something about her. She was a break in the routine—a little jolt of unpredictability in an otherwise formulaic life.

I pour myself a shot of gin and walk it over to the sofa. I hadn't chosen this sofa. I'd chosen Miriam Stacey and *she* had chosen the sofa. The furniture. The marble countertops for the kitchen and the painted cabinets for the kitchen. I didn't know shit about interior design or aesthetic quality. All I knew was that if I were to dabble in this world—I needed to look the part.

Dark and ugly as the sofa may be, it's fucking comfortable. I sink into its soft leather cushions and kick off my shoes.

My shirt still carries a whiff of her scent. Cinnamon and hope. That's what she smelled like. I drag in another breath, hoping that a part of my brain will commit it to memory. Of course, there's always next week.

I'm not sure what prompted me to make the suggestion in the first place. It was far too romantic a move, far too starry-eyed a proposal. Who the fuck do I think I am? Ethan Hawke? Leonardo DiCaprio?

I shouldn't have told her I'd meet her there again.

Let's face it; she's too young for me. Too beautiful. Too full of life and hope and possibility. She deserved a man who wasn't so jaded with life yet.

And even as I consider the possibility of not showing up next week, I know it's never gonna happen. I have to be there just to see if she shows up. Now that I've started it, I have to see it through and risk the chance that *she* might be the girl who turns things around and changes my perspective.

"Wendy," I whisper out loud.

I know it's not her real name and I'm glad. It doesn't suit her at all. She's far too sexy for a name like Wendy. Not that she seems to know that.

Ping.

I look down at my lock screen. The message is from Alicia.

Alicia: *Was she worth ditching me for?*

Tobias: *Thanks for understanding, Ally. You're a fucking queen.*

Alicia: *Agree. But you still haven't answered my question.*

Tobias: *She was worth it.*

Alicia: *Damn boy. That's cold. But I'm happy for you. Try not to scare this one off, will you?*

Tobias: *How the hell would I do that? I don't come on too strong and I keep shit to myself. Always have.*

Alicia: *Exactly. If you want this to go somewhere,*

you're gonna have to let her in. I've known you for almost two years and I know next to nothing about you.

Great. I'm screwed.

Tobias: *Goodnight, Alicia.*

Alicia: *Aw, that's the politest* fuck-you-and-leave-me-alone *I've ever heard. Good night to you too, handsome.*

I put my phone face-down on the sofa beside me. There was a time when I thought Alicia and I could be something more. But she was too deep in love with her ex-boyfriend and I was too worried about protecting my secrets. It would have been doomed from the start.

Luckily, we were both smart enough to see it. And mature enough to set the rules and leave out the emotion. Sex without strings. It had worked so far.

Except that lately, I found myself wanting more.

I'm not even sure what *more* means in this context. I just knew that something had to give. And soon.

Ping. Ping.

I'm expecting more texts from Alicia, but instead, I see Daniel's name on my lock screen. I sit up and grab my phone. We'd been texting regularly for months now and somehow, we'd fallen seamlessly back into the relationship we used to have.

Before everything went to shit.

Daniel: *Hey man, I know you're probably sleeping but I just wanted to let you know that I'm in town. Will be for a few weeks.*

Tobias: *Couldn't cut the cord, huh?*

Daniel: *Still an asshole, I see.*

Tobias: *I swear. I'm a changed man.*

Daniel: *I'll decide that for myself.*

A part of me is hopeful. If we can joke about our past, surely it means we've healed from it… right?

The truth is—I'm excited.

When was the last time I spent any real time with Daniel? When was the last time we really hung out, talked, soaked up old memories, laughed at the old versions of ourselves?

Tobias: *Fuck, how long has it been?*

Daniel: *Since the last time I visited California. That was six years ago.*

Tobias: *Has it been that long?*

Daniel: *Pretty sure that's your fault. It wouldn't have killed you to visit from time to time, you know.*

Tobias: *Guilt tripping me already. Feels just like old times.*

The three little *typing* dots appear. *Typing... typing... typing...* then they disappear altogether. It forces me to consider the possibility that my current state of loneliness is self-inflicted. After all, I might have had more people in my life if I wasn't so adamant about pushing them all away.

Daniel was the one person I thought I'd never lose. And I hadn't.

But I'd come close once.

I referred to those years in my head as the Dark Ages. When I felt as though it was me against the world, it took me a solid decade before I started to realize that it was never me against the world.

It was me against myself.

Sometimes, it feels like that's still a battle I'm fighting today.

Ping.

Daniel: *I'm not here to guilt-trip you, brother. Honestly, I just wanted to thank you.*

Oh fuck no.

Tobias: *Don't even go there, okay? You've already*

thanked me a hundred times. It's fucking enough. Thank me one more time and I'm rescinding the offer.

Daniel: *Okay, okay.*

Tobias: *You'll be in town for a while, right?*

Daniel: *Yup.*

Tobias: *Awesome. Then we can catch up soon.*

Daniel: *On one condition: I'm buying.*

Tobias: *Still proud as fuck, huh?*

Daniel: *It's all I've got at this point.*

Tobias: *That's not all you've got, man. You have a family. Do you even realize how fortunate that makes you? That's not something I can claim anymore.*

Daniel: *I'm family, Toby.*

It means a fuck ton coming from him. Especially considering how I left things when I moved to California. The years seem to shrink as we text and I'm reminded of the boys we used to be, living just two houses apart on a quiet suburban street with the rest of our lives ahead of us.

It's amazing how everything can change in the blink of an eye.

In some cases, it's a phone call. A death. An unnoticed red light. A college acceptance letter. In our case, it was two tiny pink lines and a woman with an oval birthmark under her left eye.

Tobias: *I know brother. I'll never forget that again.*

Daniel: *You better not.*

Tobias: *If you need a place to crash, you know my door is always open.*

Daniel: *No wonder you're so popular with the ladies. *winking face emoji**

Tobias: *Jesus, you finally found the emoji keyboard, did ja?*

Daniel: *Asshole.*

Tobias: *Laughing face emoji.*

Daniel: *Appreciate the offer. I'll keep that in mind. For right now, I'm gonna stay put. Hold down the fort.*

Tobias: *Of course. Family comes first. Always.*

Daniel: *You ready for tomorrow?*

Tobias: *I'll let you know tomorrow.*

Daniel: *I know I'm not supposed to thank you anymore so I won't. This is me not thanking you.*

Tobias: *Thin ice, brother. Thin fucking ice.*

Daniel: *Kissing face emoji.*

I put my phone away and lean back against the sofa so that I'm facing the ceiling. Tomorrow is about paying Daniel back for everything he was to me when we were growing up. Tomorrow is about being the friend I *should* have been for him all those years ago.

Tomorrow, I'll attempt to right the scales.

It might not be enough.

But it's a start.

CHAPTER 6

Ashley

S o my white silk blouse is a no-go.

The two buttons he ripped out with his teeth are glaring and noticeable. Not the first impression I wanna make on my first day at a new job.

Which means I'm left rifling through my half-organized closet at six-thirty in the morning, trying to find something that will make me feel as grown-up and confident as the white blouse had. Turns out—none of the clothes I own are close to grown-up looking or confidence-inducing.

"Why?" I groan out loud. "*Why* don't I have any decent clothes? Urgh!"

Knock, knock, knock.

"Honey? Everything alright."

I cringe. I've actually forgotten that my father is sleeping right outside my bedroom in his sleeping bag.

"Um… sure."

"Ash."

I throw open the door and gesture him inside. He takes one look at the mess of clothes on my bed and nods. "Ah."

"All my clothes are hideous!"

"What about that white blouse you bought at the Macy's sale?"

I groan. "I can't wear it today. I… um… accidentally lost two buttons in the washing machine. So I have to choose something else to wear."

Dad fixes me with his signature *let's-put-out-the-fire-together* look. "Honey. You're a beautiful girl. Anything you wear is gonna look great on you. What you really need is to take a deep breath."

"I hate it when you go all Zen master on me."

He chuckles. "Pants or skirt?"

"I have exactly one black pencil skirt so I'm gonna go with that."

"Corporate chic. Love it."

I roll my eyes. "*Dad.*"

He suppresses a laugh, grabs something from the bed and whips it at me. "What about this?"

"Um, this is a t-shirt."

"So? You'll be the cool new girl in a t-shirt."

"I'll be the small-town hick who thinks she can show up to work in a freaking t-shirt," I say adamantly, returning the t-shirt back to the bed.

"Wanna borrow one of my shirts?"

I'm in the process of scoffing when I stop short. "Wait…"

Dad's eyes go wide. "I was kidding."

"Did you bring any plain shirts?" I ask urgently. "The blue one. Or the white one? Please don't tell me that duffel bag is filled with plaids."

"Don't knock my plaids. They're chick magnets."

"Ew."

"Seriously, Elizabeth Kearney practically purrs every time she sees me in one."

"*Dad!* Did you not hear me say 'ew'?"

He walks out into the living room and I follow him there. He rifles through his duffel and pulls out the white shirt I had in mind. "Here you go."

"Dad, you're a lifesaver!"

He laughs. "Never thought I'd have to deal with my daughter stealing my clothes. Kinda thought that was a mother-daughter thing."

The words fly out of his mouth and I see the exact moment when he hears what he just said. His eyes go wide, his smile freezes, the color drains from his face.

"Dad…"

He clears his throat and pretends like he didn't just balk at the mention of the big bad shadow that's hung over most of our lives.

Namely—the first and only woman my father had ever loved. Aka, the mother I never had.

"Go on and get ready. I don't want you to be late on your first day of work."

He badly needs me to disappear. So I do. I take his shirt and retreat into my room. Half an hour later, I've showered diligently, applied copious amounts of deodorant and swapped out my bunny rabbit PJ's for the pencil skirt and white shirt combo.

I gotta say, from the slightly distorted reflection in my bathroom mirror, I look pretty good. The oversized shirt look really works with the slim fit of the pencil skirt. All I need now is a little lip gloss and a pair of heels that are flattering and office-appropriate. I find that in a pair of second-hand Kate Spade ankle boots that Dad had gifted me for my eighteenth birthday.

"Okay, Ash. You can do this," I tell myself fiercely as I step out of the bathroom. "Ta-da!"

Dad's behind the kitchen window with a cup of coffee in

hand. He sets down the mug and puts a hand to his heart. "My baby girl—all grown up."

"You really think I look okay?"

"You look amazing, kid. Seriously, you're gonna knock 'em dead today."

I force a smile onto my face but voice the very real fear that's been percolating in my brain since I got the job. "What if my boss turns out to be an absolute fucking nightmare?"

Dad just laughs. "I have a feeling he's gonna be great."

"I can't take anything you say seriously right now."

Chuckling hard, he walks me to the door. "Just work hard and be yourself, kid. It's worked for you in the past."

"Has it?" I demand. "Because as far as I can tell, I've been riding your coattails my entire life."

He stops short. "What is that supposed to mean?"

I shrug. "Let's face it. Everyone in that town *loved* you. And they loved me because I was your daughter."

"Not true."

"So true."

He actually looks kinda offended now. "Ashley Payne. They loved you because you were a lovable kid and you are a lovable person." He shuts down my eye roll with a very pointed glare. "You're honest, hard-working and kind. What's not to love?"

I like that he's not taking into consideration the fact that *he's* the one who got me my first job. Hell, he's the one who got me my second job too. I got onto the swim team in school because he convinced the teacher I had hidden talent. He got me into the debating club in junior high even after I'd missed the deadline. He was always there, ready to catch me when I fell, ready to push me when I lagged behind.

Sometimes, I loved him for it.

Other times, I resented him for it.

But right now, I'm just grateful he's here, cheering me on. As much as I want to walk into Ackerman Corp., all confident and ready, the nerves are starting to kick in and it's not even eight o'clock yet.

"Okay, Dad, thanks for the pep talk. I gotta go."

"Do you need to be there this early?"

"No. But… better to be early than late."

He gives me a wink. "That's my girl." He presses a kiss onto my forehead. "You're gonna do great. Just don't second-guess yourself. You have the smarts and the ability. Just trust that."

Easier said than done. But I just nod and wave goodbye.

It takes me twenty-eight minutes to get to Ackerman Corp. and I'm still ridiculously early. By one hour and twelve minutes to be exact. So I grab a cup of coffee from a kiosk down the road and sit outside the massive fountain in front of the intimidating skyscraper.

There are five different companies in this building but Ackerman Corp. occupies the ten highest floors. I crane my neck back as far as it will go but I still can't quite see the top. Maybe that's how you know you've made it when you're literally so high that you can look down on everyone else.

Once my coffee is finished, I take a deep breath and head into the building with my special employee lanyard at the ready. I'd received it with the personal orientation I'd gotten from Mr. Ackerman's previous assistant. She was a kind older woman named Julianne who was leaving her position to enjoy an early retirement.

She'd had nothing but positive things to say about Mr. Ackerman but she did stress the fact that the job was much too 'high stress' for her to keep up with.

He was too polite to ask me to leave, my dear she'd told me last Friday, *so I thought I'd save him the trouble and just hand in my resignation. He pays so well that I can afford to retire early.*

It was mostly positive.

Which is probably why I'm so damn suspicious. It just sounds a little too good to be true.

By the time I get to the seventieth floor, I'm winded. Even taking the elevator up there is a trek. On the upside, the place is pretty empty, considering I'm here so early. It gives me a little time to scope out the place before my boss comes in. Apparently, he's always here at nine a.m. sharp, which gives me just over twenty minutes till I'm officially on the clock.

I walk down the broad corridor that leads to the CEO's wing. I kid you not. It's actually called that. If I thought the name was intimidating enough, nothing prepares me for the awe I feel walking into the massive foyer of sorts that precedes the glossy black door that leads to Tobias Ackerman's office.

My desk sits just outside it, with views flanking the East and West side of the city. I sit down at my generous desk and pick through the stationary that's been organized into each cabinet. Even this freaking desk is intimidating as hell.

Ping.

I almost jump out of my seat as a message appears on my lock screen. Of course, it's my father.

Dad: *You can do this.*

I can't help but smile. I put my phone on silent and take a couple of deep breaths. *You can do this,* I tell myself. *It's all about hard work and determination.*

Despite my little internal pep talk, my palms are already sweaty. Dad's not a nervous sweater, which means I probably inherited that trait from my mother.

Urgh.

She always pops into my head at the most random, most inconvenient of times. I've spent too many days, too many nights obsessing about a woman who spent no time thinking about me. Which is why I'd promised myself that it would stop with this move to California.

Still—old habits die hard, I guess.

As the office starts filling up a little, my nerves kick up a notch. But I busy myself, trying to memorize the schedule my new boss has going for this week. It's no joke. He's got board meetings, Zoom meetings, client meetings. He's got a call from China at this time. A call from Russia at that time. I'm tired just looking at how much he's got going on.

"Good morning, Mr. Ackerman."

I jerk to my feet as confident footsteps echo down the hall toward the CEO's wing. *This is it, Ashley. Don't fuck it up.*

He emerges from the corridor into the foyer. His navy blue suit catches my attention immediately before my eyes veer up to his face. And then—

No.

No.

No. no. no. no. no. no. no.

His eyes land on me. His jaw clenches tight. Those piercing blue eyes are just as intense as they were last night. But the expression behind them leaves me grappling... and unsure.

"M-Mr. Ackerman," I stammer, aware that there are people milling around down the corridor. "I'm your new PA."

His eyes never leave my face. He swallows. His jaw doesn't unclench.

This cannot be happening. Honestly, how is it possible that someone as young as he is, is the CEO of a major international company?

"You're Ashley? Ashley Payne?" I remember his voice

being that deep. But last night, it was warm, gentle… inviting.

Today, however, it's cold as ice.

"I am… sir."

I cringe. Calling him 'sir' feels even weirder, considering he was literally *inside* me last night. He glances back over his shoulder as though he's ashamed to be seen with me. When he glances back my way, he doesn't make eye contact.

He definitely doesn't acknowledge that we met last night.

He nods and starts walking towards his office door. After a moment's hesitation, I start to follow him. He stops so abruptly that I nearly walk right into him.

"Stay at your desk."

I get that he's just as shocked as I am at this cruel twist of fate, but honestly? Why does he sound so cold? Why does he look so *angry*?

"B-but Julianne told me that I'm supposed to shadow you for the first—"

"*Stay* at your desk," he snaps harshly. "If I need you, I'll call you."

He walks into his office and shuts the door in my face. I stand there for like five minutes trying to process what just happened.

Wow. First day and I'm off to a great start.

So much for not fucking up.

CHAPTER 7
Tobias

W hat.
      The.
Fuck!!!

It's been half an hour since I shut the door in her face and I've been pacing furiously ever since then. I've also missed my nine o'clock appointment with Tokyo and my nine-thirty call with France. I'm pretty sure I'm gonna be absolutely useless for the rest of the day, considering the fact that my heart is pumping like a runaway train.

What fresh hell is this!?

How? How had this managed to happen? It felt too fucking cruel to be coincidental. Of all the fucking gin joints in all the world, she had to walk into *that* one.

And I had to notice her?

And fuck her?

"Oh God," I breathe as the cold reality of my situation sinks in slowly.

I've fucked up. I've fucked up colossally. The irony? I didn't even know I was fucking up when I was doing it.

I had gone to sleep with a smile on my face because I

actually believed I'd met a woman I could actually fall for. I'd woken up this morning with the same idiotic smile on my face. I was actually looking forward to this damn day. I was looking forward to the whole damn week because it meant counting down the seconds until I saw her again.

Who would have thought that seeing her face again so soon would have caused my hopes to die a slow and painful death in the three seconds it took me to realize *exactly* who she was?

Personal assistant was bad enough.

But the other thing… *Jesus*.

I really thought that life was done screwing me over. I'd had my fair share of pain, right? Sad childhood, asshole father, enough loss to fill a lifetime. Hadn't I been through enough?

There's a knock on the door. It's shy—tentative and I know exactly who it is. "I told you I didn't want to be disturbed!"

There's a moment of silence. "Uh, sir…" I fucking *hate* that she's calling me that, "… there's a call for you on line two. Harry Stiller."

I walk over to my desk and check line two. Harry Stiller from the accounts department. I can handle an internal call. That won't take up too much brain space.

As it turns out—it does.

I miss almost all of what Harry was trying to tell me and when I realized that I wasn't actually processing anything he was saying, I made a lame excuse and hung up on him mid-sentence. I was fucking losing it. On the job. For the first time since I started this company.

And after everything I've been through to build it—*this* is what's gonna take me down?

A one-night stand in the bathroom of a restaurant bar?

It wasn't just a one-night stand.

The thought rips through me like a bucket of ice water. I push away the regretful thought and try to recalibrate. It's going to have to be a one-night stand because what happened last night can *never* happen again.

I ignore the incessant *ping* of my cell phone as I sit down and take several deep breaths. I'm not sure how but I have to find a way to get through this day. I have to figure out what to do about my brand-new PA.

Didn't she say she was twenty-five last night?

She did. But she also told me her name was Wendy. Right before I'd kissed her. Right before, I'd followed her into the bathroom and fucked her on the counter. *Damn it, had I worn a condom? Yes, yes, I did.*

There's a sharp *rap, rap, rap* against the door that jolts me back into the present. When I ignore it, the handle turns and she walks right in, her face blazing with determination. She looks different from last night. Maybe it's the baggy shirt, pencil skirt combo that's throwing me. Maybe it's the fact that she kinda looks pissed off.

"Listen," she starts, "I know this is a shock to us both but I don't see how avoiding each other is going to solve anything."

Her directness is vastly admirable, especially considering what a fucking pussy I'm being right now. Of course, *she* doesn't know everything yet.

"Last night happened and there's no pretending otherwise. I didn't know who you were. You didn't know who I was. We had sex." I cringe and I'm pretty sure she flinches too. "But all I can say is, we were two consenting adults and—"

"Adults?" I interrupt hotly as I rise to my feet. I'm intensely glad that there's a whole table between us right now. "Did you just say adults?"

Her eyes go wide. "I'm—"

"You're nineteen fucking years old! You're a Goddamn teenager!"

She's clearly not expecting my outburst because she takes a few steps back. "I… what are you talking about? I'm *twenty*, not nineteen."

Is she?

I've completely lost track at this point. But I won't lie. Hearing that she's out of the teenage years does make me feel slightly better. Not by much though.

"Why would you think I was nineteen? And anyway, what does it matter? I'm an adult. And just so you know, what happened last night—"

"Ashley." Somehow, I feel as though I've lost the right to say her name. "Please don't."

"—I don't regret it."

Fuck me.

"You don't know what you're saying."

She frowns, her cheeks coloring instantly. She looks away from me as she shuffles from one foot to the other. "I… um… that was probably really inappropriate, huh?"

"You have no idea."

She blushes a deeper shade of pink and I hate that I'm making her feel so self-conscious. I should just come right out and say it but the truth is that once I do, there'll be no going back. I'll be drawing a line in the sand that we can't cross.

"I'm sorry…"

"No, *I'm* sorry. Last night should never have happened."

Her eyes jerk up to mine. They flood with hurt. "Why would you say that?" she asks and her voice is actually trembling. "We had a genuine connection." She stops short. "Unless… that was just me."

I have no fucking clue how to handle this situation. "Ashley—"

"Was it just me?"

It's a question that demands an answer. And I want to give it to her but if I do, I'll be betraying the one person in my life that I swore I'd never hurt again.

"Ashley. I'm your boss. And in any case, I'm way too old for you. You told me that you were twenty-five!"

"I also said my name was Wendy," she snaps. "And *you* told me your name was Oliver. We agreed to be different people. I didn't think lying about my age was that big a deal."

"I'm thirty-five, Ashley."

She doesn't flinch. Something that surprises me, given what I know about her. "I don't care about that. A connection is a connection." Boy, do I wish it were that simple. She seems to sense that I'm drumming up a list of reasons why this is not a good idea because she plows ahead. "Listen, I get that this is complicated but I also want this job. I *need* this job."

Tell her. Just fucking tell her. "I'm not going to fire you over this."

She takes a deep breath but she doesn't look altogether relieved. "Really?"

"Really. But as for last night, we need to bury it. Pretend like it never happened."

Her eyes go wide. "Are you serious?"

"Yes."

She shakes her head. "Because I'm your PA?"

"No, Ashley," I say gently. "This is not about you. This is about me. Trust me, you're gonna feel differently once you know who I am."

Her eyebrows pull together. "What do you mean? I know who you are. Tobias Ackerman, CEO of Ackerman Corp."

Man up and do it.

I take a breath and pull off the damn band-aid. "Ackerman is my mother's maiden name. I changed it when I moved to California... from Scottsdale, Arizona."

Her head twists to the side. "Scottsdale... I'm from—"

"Growing up, I went by my father's last name. Mason." I pause slightly but I can see that she's still processing. "My friends knew me as Toby Mason."

That's when it hits her.

The truth.

The reality of who I really was.

Her eyes go wide. Her jaw drops. Her cheeks pale. She actually takes a step back as though I've just grown horns. "No," she breathes. "No, no, no, no... this can't be happening."

"I'm so sorry, Ashley. If I'd known who you were, I never would have—" *Jesus.* I literally have no idea what to say to her. "I'm sorry."

She opens her mouth but only a sob comes out. "Toby Mason," she whispers. "You're Toby Mason?"

"Yes."

There are tears sparkling in her eyes now. "You're my... father's best friend?"

Except if Daniel ever found out about this, I probably wouldn't be his best friend for very much longer.

CHAPTER 8

Ashley

I't's probably *super* melodramatic to say it but—I'm pretty sure my life is over.

After a lifetime of chasing different identities, I finally meet someone who makes me feel like I can be myself. Whoever the hell that is. I meet a man who makes me feel confident and powerful and beautiful and important.

In short, I meet the man of my dreams.

And it turns out—he's my boss.

That's bad enough, right? Wrong. The universe has a little extra screw you to throw my way. Not only is the man of my dreams my boss, he's also my father's *best friend.*

This cannot be happening.

"Ashley."

I flinch, my eyes glancing up at him for a moment before I shift them away again. He takes a step towards me and I back away instantly.

He sighs. "I'm sorry."

"So… I didn't get this job on my own, did I?"

He looks startled for a second. "Um…"

"My father called you. Asked you to hire me out of pity."

"That's not what happened."

I cock my head to the side. "I'm a college drop-out with no internships and no work experience under my belt. You're telling me that those are the credentials you want your PA to have?" I snort derisively. "Honestly, I should have known."

"Ashley—"

"*God*, this is so embarrassing."

"Listen, your father loves you so—"

"*Don't*," I hiss. "Don't talk about him… like that."

"Like what?"

Jesus, I don't even know at this point. I'm literally sweating now. "Like… like you know him."

He fixes those too-blue eyes on me. "I know this is a lot to take in. I'm just as thrown as you are. But like I said, you don't have to lose your job over this."

"Really?" I demand. "Are you letting me keep this job because you really want me to work for you or is it because you don't want Dad finding out about any of this?"

His hesitation is all the answer I need. I twist around and make for the door. "I can't believe this—"

The door is halfway open when it slams shut again. I gasp when I realize that Tobias… Toby… whatever his name is at this point, is right behind me, holding the door shut with an extended arm. He's so damn *big*.

And he smells of coffee and pheromones.

"Ashley, please."

I turn around slowly and look up at him. He's close. One could argue he's a little *too* close. "What are you asking me?"

Those beautiful blue eyes are burning but there's a definite question in them. He doesn't know any more than I do.

"I'm sorry…"

I shrug. "What exactly are you sorry for?" I ask him

sadly. "Sleeping with me last night or trying to act as though there's nothing between us?"

He shakes his head and backs away quickly. "I won't lie. Last night was... special. But it can't ever happen again. You are my best friend's *daughter*. Jesus, Ashley. I've seen you as a baby. I've carried you. I was there in the hospital the day you were born."

I cringe. "That was a long time ago."

"Twenty years," he says softly. "Even if you weren't... who you are... you and I—" he sighs. "—I don't know if we'd have made sense together."

My jaw drops. Is he really trying to re-write what happened last night? "Are you trying to say that my *age* is a problem?"

"You're *fifteen* years younger than me, Ashley."

"Which is only five years younger than the age I gave you last night. What's the difference?"

"There's a big difference!"

"Bullshit. You're making excuses."

"Yes!" he explodes. "You bet your ass I'm making excuses. Did you not hear a word I just said? I grew up on the same street your father did. We went to school together, entered adolescence together, messed around with girls together!"

"I get it. You're my father's age. Big freaking whoop."

"That doesn't bother you?"

I stop short, biting my bottom lip. "I mean... I'll admit, it's weird. But I can't just forget what happened last night."

"Well, you're gonna have to try. Because this—" he gestures between us, "—this is wrong. And it's over."

My heart sinks. Even after everything he's just told me, I can't find any relief or acceptance. All I feel is the aching sting of disappointment. I may be only twenty, but I know how hard it is to make connections. And the one we'd established last night was real. It was important. And I hated that he was trying to make it seem like a cheap one-night stand.

I swallow. "Okay, so… what's the plan? I just go back to being your PA and you go back to being my boss?"

"Yes."

"And if I wanted to quit?"

His eyes go wide. For a long time, he doesn't say anything. Then— "If you wanted to quit, I would accept your resignation and give you a great recommendation letter."

"Even though I haven't even lasted a day?"

"It was quite a day."

I shake my head and look down. He *wants* me to quit. Quitting would make things a lot simpler for the both of us. I'd find another job, I'd work for another man—one who wasn't my Dad's friend, one who I hadn't slept with. It just made sense.

Except that, I don't want to do the sensible thing right now. I wanted to… stay. Even if it meant seeing him every day, knowing that I could never have him.

"If it's all the same to you, I'd rather keep this job."

His eyebrows rise. "Okay. If that's what you want."

Now, he's the one who looks disappointed. I can't say it doesn't hurt but for whatever reason, I can't quit either. Maybe one day I'll figure out why but for right now, I just turn my back on him and march back out to my desk.

My bottom lip quivers the whole way there but I refuse to cry until I'm in the privacy of my own space. I spend the rest of the day doing my job, trying to prove to Tobias that I *could.* Not just in the general sense of competency but also in the uniqueness of our situation.

Sure, we've ended up in a colossally fucked up situation, but that wouldn't get in the way of me doing my job.

Because I'm smart, I'm responsible, I'm real fucking mature. And I'm going to prove that to him.

He manages to avoid me for the rest of the day, which is an amazing feat, considering I'm tasked with shadowing him for at least the first few weeks. But he makes sure there are always other people with us. And if by chance we happen to find ourselves alone, he finds some little errand to send me off on.

I take every note, task and directive with the enthusiasm of a true-blue professional. And when I'm finally dismissed at the end of the day, with nothing more than a nod and a curt: "You can go home now."

I feel drained.

And sad.

And really fucking betrayed.

Which is why when I get back home, the adrenaline is pumping and I'm ready for the fight that's been stewing since the moment Tobias told me who he *really* was.

"Hey, baby girl! How was the first day?"

"How *could* you!?"

I turn to him furiously and he comes to an abrupt stop in front of the brand-new coffee table that's sitting between a comfy-looking armchair and a sleek three-seater sofa.

Of course, he went and furnished my whole apartment. He's even bought me a little chocolate cake with '*congratulations*' written across the surface in pink frosting.

But today, I don't care that he's a great Dad. Today, I don't care that he's blown a bunch of money on furniture for my apartment. I don't care that he's driven all the way down here to help me through this transition.

I'm pissed and I want him to know it.

"Honey, what—"

"I told you I wanted to stand on my own two feet. I

wanted to be independent. I wanted to work my way up on my own merits!"

His face pales. "I know that—"

"No, you don't. You don't know that. Because if you did, you'd never have called up your best friend and asked him to give your charity case daughter a job."

"Ashley, that's not—"

"I should have known. I should have *known* that I could never have gotten this job on my own. I'm a freaking college drop-out for Christ's sake."

"Hey now—"

"Do you know how embarrassing it was for me to walk in there and figure out that Tobias Ackerman, my *boss,* is also Toby Mason, the man I grew up hearing stories about most of my childhood? I felt like a complete idiot, Dad!"

He just stands there, not interrupting me anymore. He swallows. Looks at me, looks away again.

"Well?" I demand. "Say something!"

He sighs. "I don't know what else to say except I'm sorry. I should have told you but you were just so excited and I didn't want to ruin your first day." He takes a step towards me. "But I just want you to know, honey, Toby would never have hired you if he didn't think you could do the job."

"Yeah, I'm sure that's precisely what *Toby* felt when you asked him to hire me."

"I did not ask him to hire you. I merely made a suggestion—"

"You know what? You need to stop interfering in my life!" I snap. "I can't do anything without you getting involved."

"Hey, that's not fair."

"Isn't it?" I ask. "It's no wonder I couldn't get through

college. You've made me feel like I can't do anything without you. You've made me feel like I'm not capable on my own."

"Honey—"

"You need to stop, Dad! My whole life, you've been over-compensating for the fact that I don't have a mother, and you need to stop!"

The air turns cold. The silence stretches on for miles and I stand there, feeling angry, hurt, frustrated and guilty all at the same time.

I clear my throat once it becomes clear that Dad's not gonna say anything. "I'm going to my room." I glance at the cake sitting on my new coffee table in front of the sofa that I'm pretty sure folds out into a sofa bed. "Thanks for the cake but I've lost my appetite."

I head to my room and close the door. *It's going to be okay,* I tell myself, *it's going to be okay.*

But today, of all days, I can't bring myself to believe it.

CHAPTER 9

Tobias

"**Y**ou seem distracted tonight, baby."

I glance over at the willowy blonde sitting next to me on the velvety sofa that's comfortable to sit on but hideous to look at. It's a deep royal purple that changes color depending on where you are in the room.

She cocks her leg and the slit of her dress slides up a little further. It's a skin-tight, flesh-colored mini that has the appearance of making her look like she's naked. Not that I haven't already been there, done that. But the animal part of my brain is still noticing things. I'm just waiting for the rest of my body to catch up.

But despite the fact that she's clearly dressed to seduce me, despite the fact that she's looking sexy as hell, despite the very obvious fact that she's more than willing—I can't bring myself to get in the mood.

Worrying about whether you've lost your best friend will do that to you.

Although, if I'm being honest, I've spent most of today thinking about Ashley, not Daniel.

"Tobias?"

I force my neck to swivel in her direction. "Sorry, Emma. There's a big merger coming up at work and I guess I'm just a little preoccupied."

She gives me an understanding wink. "Let me fix you a drink. What would you like? Vodka? Gin? Bourbon? I have a fully stocked bar."

It's a nice perk of coming to Emma's place. Her being a successful lingerie model and a party girl means that she loves entertaining and she has the money to do it.

"Gin, please."

"Coming right up."

She gets off the sofa, making sure to move as slowly and seductively as possible. My eyes take notice but my cock remains disinterested as ever. *Well.* That's the first fucking time that's happened. And it really bothers me.

I force my eyes to the view and try not to let my thoughts fall back onto Ashley. Considering this was her first day on the job and she'd just discovered she'd slept with her father's oldest friend, she'd done a great job. In fact, she'd maintained an air of professionalism far better than I had.

She was definitely way more mature than her twenty years suggested. But then again, I shouldn't be surprised; she was raised by a single father who was only sixteen years older.

Still, it's a mind fuck I'm still trying to unravel.

How the hell do I make the division in my mind now? Daniel's daughter is one thing. The smart, sexy, beautiful woman I'd met in that bar is a totally different one.

The worst part?

Even after realizing who she was—my attraction to her is still going strong. You'd think it would have shriveled up and died an instant death. You'd think it would have disintegrated the moment I found out. But no. It's still alive and well,

66

distracted me every so often with completely inappropriate thoughts.

It doesn't help that I have the memories to back them back—that first kiss. The way she looked when I'd walked into that bathroom. Her moans as my hands slid over her breasts. Her little gasp when I'd thrust into her for the first time…

Jesus, stop!

"Here you go." Emma offers me a glass of gin and sits back down next to me with one of her own. She sidles a little closer so that her leg is practically draped over mine.

Her cleavage is on full display tonight but again, I can't bring myself to get excited about it.

"Cheers," she says, clinking her glass against mine.

"Cheers."

"I'm glad you called me. That was unexpected."

It's been a minute since I'd last seen Emma. The last time we'd slept together was probably five months ago. Maybe more. She had a busy life and so did I. Also, last I checked, she was also not interested in settling down and that worked for me. I didn't want the pressure.

Which is ironic considering that, especially lately, I'd decided I wanted more.

"It's been a busy quarter."

"Isn't it always?" she asks with a wink.

"How've you been?"

"Been traveling a lot lately. I've been in Milan and Paris for the last couple of weeks. It was glorious."

"That's nice."

She waits for me to offer up something more but I just sit there, sipping on my gin, hoping the alcohol will take the edge off. Usually, it's sex that does the trick for me, historically speaking. But tonight, the thought of touching Emma is making my stomach drop.

"It is nice," she says, putting her hand on my leg and sliding it up to my thigh. "But a girl gets lonely on the road."

That's my cue to make my move but I just stiffen in response. "I'm sure those French and Italian men kept you company."

Her eyebrows rise. "I suppose they did…"

She sounds uncertain now. I know I'm throwing her for a loop. We usually have a drink together *after* we've fucked.

"Tobias? Is everything okay?"

Ping. Ping.

I turn immediately towards my phone, which is sitting on the coffee table far enough away that I can't see who's texted or why.

Is it Ashley? Daniel?

"Hello? Tobias?"

"Sorry," I mumble, turning back to Emma. "It's just…"

"Yes?" she presses.

She's starting to look a little offended at my lack of attention. Maybe that's why I start talking. "It's just been a weird day."

She raises her eyebrows. "A weird day?"

"My oldest friend called me weeks ago and told me his daughter was moving to California. He asked if I could find a position for her in my company."

"You gave her a job? That was nice of you."

"She's now my PA."

Emma looks confused. "Okay? And that's bad because…?"

"Did I say that was bad?"

"Your tone and expression imply that it was bad. Am I reading that wrong?"

I clear my throat. "She's just not what I expected. I expected someone… younger." I'm aware that I'm making no sense right now. "I don't know, I just had her stuck in my head as a little kid, you know?"

Emma frowns. "I'm assuming you didn't believe that you had hired a five-year-old as your PA."

"Of course not."

"Then what were you expecting?"

"I don't know. Just someone younger, less… mature. Less capable. Less—"

"Attractive?"

My eyes snap to hers. "I didn't say that."

Emma's eyes narrow. "How old is she?"

I'm sensing that I've entered dangerous territory here but somehow, I can't seem to stop talking. "Twenty."

Her eyes go wide. "Is *that* why you're so distracted tonight? Because you're thinking about your friend's hot daughter?"

Okay, I definitely fucked this conversation up. "No, that's not—"

"Oh my God," she gasps, jerking up to her feet so fast that she almost sloshes gin over her dress. "*That's* why you called me tonight. You weren't interested in seeing me. You wanted a distraction from your dirty thoughts about your friend's kid!"

I wince as I get up. "She's not a *kid*, okay? Don't say it like that."

Emma glares at me. "Is that why you're here in my apartment?"

Jesus, she's right. It's exactly why I'm here in her apartment.

"Answer me, Tobias!"

"Emma, listen—"

"You know what? Just get out. Get the hell out of my apartment and get the hell out of my life while you're at it."

I stand my ground. "If you wanted to throw that gin in my face, I'd understand."

She stops short. She stares down at the gin she's holding and then back at me. Then she snorts with laughter.

"*Goddammit.*" Shaking her head, she puts the gin down. "You were always a charming devil."

"I'm not trying to be."

"That's what makes it so attractive," she sighs regretfully. "You know I was really excited when you called tonight."

"Fuck, Emma—"

She holds up her hands. "Don't. It's okay. We've never exactly been exclusive or anything. It's just that a woman wants to know that she's the only thing on a guy's mind when he calls her up and asks to see her."

"Which is completely fair. I'm the asshole here."

She sighs. "I wish that were true. It'd be so much easier to hate you."

I smile. "You're a class act, Emma. Seriously."

She rolls her eyes. "So… what are you gonna do? About your friend's daughter?"

"I'm going to be a good boss and a good friend and keep my distance."

She raises her eyebrows. "Is that what you want to do?"

"Honestly? At this point, I don't know what I want. But I know one thing; I can't lose my friendship with Daniel."

"That close, huh?"

"He's the brother I never had. We've been through a lot together."

I can't even begin to count how many nights I climbed out of my room to sneak into his. It wasn't just the thrill of doing something I wasn't supposed to. It was self-preservation. I needed a break from the turmoil that was my family. And Daniel's family was so much more stable. They were the kinda family I wish I had been born into.

"I guess you know what you have to do then."

"Right," I say confidently. But the truth is, I have no fucking clue what I have to do. Apart from getting through each day without crossing another line with Ashley.

"I'm gonna go."

She nods. "I think that's best."

"I'm sorry, Emma. Truly. I should never have called you tonight. You're much more than just a distraction."

She gives me a shaky smile. "Thanks for saying that."

I grab my phone, leave my half-finished gin on the coffee table and head towards the door. Emma walks me out with an air of resignation. I refuse to look at my phone until she's shut the door on me.

"Hey, Tobias?"

I turn on the spot right in front of the elevators. "Yeah?"

"Don't feel like you can't call me for a good time, okay? We have had fun together. We can keep having fun. I just… I want to be the only girl you're thinking about that night."

I smile. "Fair. I'll be seeing you, Emma."

She returns my smile and shuts the door. I get into the elevator and pull out my phone. Two messages from Daniel. Immediately, my palms start to sweat. Are these just innocent text messages? Or has Ashley told him what happened between us?

No, she wouldn't have.

And in any case, if she had, he wouldn't be texting me at all. He'd show up on my doorstep ready to punch my lights out.

I open our conversation thread.

Daniel: *Okay, I totally fucked up.*

Daniel: *She came home really upset and now she won't talk to me. Call me when you're free.*

So the takeaway is—Daniel still doesn't know. But I feel guilty calling him and talking to him, knowing that I'm gonna have to lie, at least in part, about the whole situation. It feels counter-intuitive, lying to your closest friend.

I'm really not relishing this conversation but I call Daniel anyway.

"Hey."

"I knew she'd be annoyed," he says, jumping right in. "But I didn't expect her to be *that* upset."

I sigh. "You should have told her."

"I know but I knew I'd get pushback and I just wanted her to have a good job, something stable. With someone I trust."

Jesus, it's like a knife to the heart.

"She's not gonna quit," I say regretfully. "I gave her the option."

"Yeah?"

"Yeah. It was only fair. But she said she wanted to stay on as my PA."

"Ashley's not a quitter."

I walk out of Emma's building but stop by the curb where I've parked my BMW. There's a crisp chill in the air that's making me wish I'd walked. It's quite a walk from here to my place but I feel like I need it.

"Listen, Toby, if she wants to stay, that's a good sign. I guess I'm just gonna have to let her be mad at me for a while."

"Um… you know, if this is too awkward for her, I'd understand. I can get her a job in another department, another company even—"

"No, don't do that. She'd take that personally. I don't know why but her self-esteem has always been really low and

I don't want the first thing that happens to her in this city to be that she loses her job."

"She wouldn't be losing her job. I'd get her another one."

"She'd see that as more charity. That's why she's so pissed off about me pulling strings with you to get her this job."

I bite my tongue. "Right…"

Daniel sighs. "This is my fault."

"It's not your fault. You were just trying to be a good Dad."

"She was right…" he mumbles.

"What was that?"

"She accused me of overcompensating tonight."

"Overcompensating for what?"

"For the fact that she doesn't have a mother." I freeze the way I always do whenever Kristen is mentioned. "And you know what? She's not totally wrong either."

"Daniel—"

"I said I don't know why she has low self-esteem. I was lying. I do know why. It's because of Kristen."

"Do you think that's fair?"

"Fair?" Daniel repeats bitterly. "Maybe, maybe not. I don't know. But I *do* know that it's not fair that my daughter had to grow up without a mother because Kristen just couldn't be bothered to be a parent."

"Kristen was sixteen, Daniel," I say gently.

"So was I!" he says, his voice rising just a little. "So was I, Toby."

"I know."

He exhales sharply. "Sorry. Didn't mean to go down that road."

"It's okay…"

"Listen, I think it would be helpful if we had dinner together. All three of us."

My body goes cold with dread. "Oh, I don't know about that, Dan. I think that might make it harder for her." *It would definitely make it harder for me.* "Maybe we should just give her time… lay low for a while."

"Lay low? You're her boss. No, I know my daughter, Toby. I think a dinner might help to calm her down, show her that there's nothing to worry about. You can be her boss and my friend and it's not a big deal."

Except it is. It's a big fucking deal.

"Please, Toby? You'd really be helping me out."

I don't know why—call it guilt, call it loyalty, call it fucking stupidity—but I find myself nodding the same way I did the last time Daniel called me up and asked me for a favor. "Yeah, okay, whatever you need."

Right.

That's exactly the kinda talk that got me into this mess in the first place.

CHAPTER 10

Ashley

I 'm up at the crack of dawn.
Thinking about my hot boss, who I might—no—who
I *definitely* have feelings for. Not to mention the fact that said
boss also happens to have been the same man my father grew
up with. The same man who was at the hospital when I was
born.

How weird is that?

I can't deny that I'd spent most of last night trying to
think myself out of my feelings for Toby Mason aka Tobias
Ackerman.

*You can't have feelings for him. He carried you in the
hospital right after you were born.*

*You can't have feelings for him. He used to chase girls
with your Dad when they were teens.*

*You can't have feelings for him because he's clearly not
interested in you anymore.*

Didn't really work the way I hoped it would. Which is
how I'd ended up wide awake at five-thirty in the morning
with another day of work ahead of me, trying to pretend that I

wasn't feeling completely hurt and betrayed by the entire situation.

I mean, I get that this is not Tobias's fault. He didn't know who I was that night. The moment he knew, he made it clear where he stood. Wouldn't I have done the exact same thing in his position?

But still, irrationally, I do feel let down.

The connection we had was real. In only a matter of hours, we'd talked, laughed, found common ground and had amazing sex.

That was not nothing.

I drag myself out of bed and head to the kitchen to grab myself a cup of coffee. I move quietly so that I don't disturb Dad but when I open the door to my room, I realize he's already awake. Sitting up on his new sofa bed with a cup of coffee in hand. I can smell it from here.

He twists around when I shut the bedroom door.

"Couldn't sleep either, huh?"

I clear my throat. "Not really, no."

"Coffee?" I made a fresh pot.

I glance over at the counter. "You bought me a coffee maker too?"

"It's the cheap kind but it makes decent coffee. I thought you could use it on days you didn't feel like paying a ton for a cup in one of those Bohemian chic cafes they've got all over the place."

I head to the kitchen, pour myself a cup, and then walk it over to the armchair that's sitting directly opposite the sofa bed.

"Honey, I'm sorry."

I sigh. "I know."

"I should have told you about Toby before you went in yesterday."

"You should have."

"I didn't think."

"No. You didn't."

He raises his eyebrows. "You're not gonna go easy on me, are you?"

"Nope." But then my mouth twitches and I give him a small smile. "I know you meant well. You always do."

"It's not because I think you're not capable, you know?"

"I know."

"But what you said yesterday—"

"I'm sorry about that. I shouldn't have said it."

"No, you were right." Dad sighs deeply and sips on his coffee. He winces at the bitterness and nods. "I do try and compensate... in some cases, overcompensate for the fact that you don't have a mother."

"Dad, I'm twenty. I don't need a mother anymore." He raises his eyebrows and I sigh. "I mean... it would be nice to have one obviously. But this is what I have—a very loving, very protective, slightly over-the-top father."

He laughs. "Thanks for saying slightly."

I sip my coffee. "You never told me that Tobias... I mean, Toby changed his name to Ackerman."

I'm trying to be super casual about my questioning but I already feel stiff and awkward asking at all.

"Oh well... I don't think he's legally changed his name or anything. It was just a way for him to revamp his image after moving here."

"Revamp his image?" I ask. "Why would he need to?"

Dad raises his eyebrows. "I... well, it's complicated."

It makes me realize that apart from *I had a best friend named Toby*, I don't really know a whole lot about him. Small things, sure. Like the fact that he lived a few houses down and they went to the same schools. But that was it. Nothing concrete. Nothing too personal.

"What's complicated?"

Dad adjusts in his seat uncomfortably. "That's Toby's story to tell, honey."

I suppress my disappointment. "You don't really talk about him all that much outside of your childhood."

"Well, our friendship was formed and forged in our childhood. And after that, lots happened. It took Toby here to California and I stayed in Scottsdale… we kinda grew apart right after he left."

I frown. It feels like there's more to the story but I know I'm not going to get it from my father. "So, he knew… Kristen then?"

The moment I mention her name, his face changes. His jaw clenches, his eyes kinda contract in and he looks like someone's just punched him in the gut. The fact that he still looks that way every time her name comes up, even twenty years later, makes one thing very clear to me—he really fucking loved her.

He clears his throat. "We were all friends. You knew that."

"Was Tobias close with her?"

"Yes."

I raise my eyebrows. Dad usually isn't the one-word answer kinda guy unless he *really* doesn't want to talk about it.

"He must have felt pretty betrayed when she skipped town too, huh?"

Dad's looking pained now. "You'd have to ask him." The moment he says it, he pales. "I mean, I wouldn't ask him. It was a long time ago. Ancient history really. We're all moved on."

But considering Dad's face is as stark white as his knuckles, I'd say that he hasn't moved on at all.

"Listen, honey. Kristen…" he winces imperceptibly, "… she's in the past. And that's where she's staying. Toby and I haven't heard from her in twenty years and I doubt we ever will. We just need to focus on the here and now. And to that end, I've suggested we do dinner sometimes—the three of us."

"The three of us?"

He nods. "Toby's a good man, Ashley. And I think you'd be better off knowing him." If only he knew how deeply I agree with that. *Which is the problem.* "I know he's your boss now and you have no reason to want to, but I'd really like for you to get to know your uncle Toby."

I flinch violently. "Urgh, no, Dad. No."

He raises his eyebrows. "Honey, it's just a dinner. If you—"

"No, I'm not talking about *that*. I'm talking about the 'Uncle Toby' thing. He's not my uncle anything, okay? He's your friend—fine. He's my boss—I'll deal with that. But he's not my uncle by any stretch of the imagination."

Dad looks momentarily taken aback by that, but then he nods. "You know what? Fair enough. It's unfair of me to expect you to be so attached to a man you only ever saw when you were a baby."

If he only knew…

"Thanks," I mumble into my coffee cup.

"So… you're okay with dinner?"

I sigh. "I'll make an effort."

"Thank you, honey. It means a lot to me."

I nod. "All this—" I gesture to my furnished apartment, "—means a lot to me too. You didn't have to do all that. I know that—"

"Hey now, you don't have to thank me for this. I'm your father. It's what I do."

"You don't have to do quite so much, Dad. At some point, I'm gonna have to stand up on my own two feet."

He seems to be really listening. "I get it. And I hear you. Which is why I'll be staying with Toby for a few nights until I find a motel in the area."

"You're not gonna stay with me?"

"I want to give you your space."

"Dad—"

"Like I said—I hear you."

I sigh. "Dad, seriously. You're only here for a short time. You've gone and bought the sofa bed already. It would be a shame for it to go to waste."

He narrows his eyes at me. "You're sure?"

"Positive."

"You're a good kid, Ash."

I shrug. "You're a good Dad, Dan."

He chuckles. "I really lucked out with you, kid." As I move to the kitchen to wash out my coffee mug, I hear him mumbling something under his breath. It sounds a lot like, "her fucking loss."

≈

He keeps me so busy at work that our conversations are limited to schedules, meetings, appointment cancellations and appointment bookings. I take it all in my stride, refusing to give him a reason to think I'm half-assing the job.

My father may have got me hired but that doesn't mean I'm not gonna give it my all.

Of course, when I start noticing that Tobias aka the boss

man, seems determined to avoid me, I start getting a little frustrated.

I started noticing it with the messages. He doesn't call me into his office to give me a directive. He either sends me a message or sends it through someone else. I can tell it's a weird set-up because every time Lillian or Bob or some other director's PA walks over to me, they do it with a slightly superior air of *clearly-someone-can't-hack-it-with-the boss*.

By the time three o'clock rolls around, I feel fully prepared for the company meeting that's happening in a board room around the corner. I know I'm supposed to be there taking notes; all the other PAs on the floor have been gearing up for it all morning.

It's the whole reason I've worn my black pumps, pencil skirt, white shirt combo (and yes, I sewed the buttons back on).

When Tobias appears from his office cave, I get up, notepad at the ready. He stops short and meets my eyes for only a split-second.

"Ashley, there's no reason for you to accompany me to this board meeting."

My stomach drops. "I… I was under the impression I had to be there."

"Usually, yes. But today—no."

He doesn't offer me any other insight before he walks away, all tall and sexy. It's still not enough to distract from the sting of rejection. When I glance down the hall, I can see the other PAs sneaking peeks down here, whispering about the boss's new PA.

I spend the next two hours sitting at my desk, looking out the window and doodling on the same notepad I'd bought especially for this board meeting.

When Tobias does eventually show up again, he glances

at me with an expression that suggests he's completely forgotten about my existence.

"Ashley, you're still here?"

My eyes pop. "Um, yes. It's my job to be."

"You can leave early if you want. I don't have anything more for you to do today."

Before I can respond, he walks into his office and slams the door in my face. I turn around on the spot and catch two interns staring down the corridor at me, their heads pushed together conspiratorially.

That is it.

Without bothering to knock, I open the door and walk into his office without an invitation. He's already in his intimidating black swivel chair. His eyebrows rise when he sees me.

"Am I being punished?" I demand.

He fixes me with that cool blue gaze that could make the most hardened spy spill all their secrets. "Excuse me?"

"Am I being punished for something? Because it sure seems that way."

"I don't understand."

"*I'm* your PA. You realize that, right?"

"Of course I—"

"Then why does it feel like I'm simply an ornament? Why is it that every other PA on this floor has been doing the grunt work while I sit at my desk and take down meaningless notes that you'll never read? Why wasn't I at that board meeting just now? Because every other PA in the building was."

"Ashley—"

"Do you not think I can do the job? Because you should at least give me a chance before you decide that. Did you even think about how this would make me look to everyone

82

else? You're acting as though I'm incompetent. And I assure you I'm not. I can do this job and I can do it well."

He opens his mouth to say something but I'm on a roll now and I can't seem to stop. "I get it, we had sex and you'd rather not face that fact. But it did *happen*; there's no sense pretending otherwise. Because all that's doing is making me feel like I'm being punished *because* we had sex. And if that's the case, then I'd really rather quit now and save us both the drama."

Jesus. I'm actually winded after that little speech. He stares at me; those blue eyes are indecipherable.

"Um… I'm putting away my soap box now."

He raises his eyebrows just a fraction. "You're right."

Umm… What?

Whatever I expected him to say, it wasn't that. "I am?"

He stands up and nods. "I have been treating you unfairly today. You haven't given me any reason to believe that you're not a perfectly competent PA and I apologize."

"Umm… okay. Thanks."

He nods. "I'm going to send you some briefs. I'll need you to read and annotate them. Once you're done, you can leave them on my desk and head home."

"I'll do that."

"Goodnight, Ashley."

"Goodnight, Tob—umm… goodnight, Mr. Ackerman."

His eyes meet mine and they sparkle brilliantly against the Californian skyline. I wish he didn't make me feel so unmoored on the inside but even now, that's exactly how I feel.

Unmoored.

Like my whole world is off its axis and he's the reason.

I'm almost at the door when he stops me. "Ashley?"

"Yes?" I ask, turning on the spot.

"It feels strange for you to refer to me as Mr. Ackerman, don't you think?"

I'm not sure what I'm supposed to say to that. "Well… you *are* my boss."

He hesitates. "That's not all I am to you."

I draw in a sharp breath, wondering what he's going to say next. Hell, what am *I* going to say next?

"I-it's not?"

"I'm also your father's friend." *Oh. Right. How could I forget?* "Let's keep it simple, shall we? Just call me Tobias."

"Are you sure?"

"Yes," he nods with a small smile that makes my heart beat race higher. "I'm sure."

CHAPTER 11
Tobias

I t's been about four days since Daniel suggested the idea of a dinner. But since then, he hasn't really put pressure on me to make it happen.

A part of me hopes that he's forgotten. Honestly, it's hard enough that I have to see Ashley at work every day. Worse still, she's fucking amazing. Not only is she smart, competent and efficient as hell, she's got a way with people.

It's barely been a week and already she knows everyone on this floor and the three floors below it. She's friendly and accommodating and always ready to take on someone else's task if it makes their day a little easier.

I caught her looking up autism support groups for Joan Manning down in accounting because she found out her second child was diagnosed only weeks ago. She brings Douglas Perry a decaf coffee every morning because she found out he quit caffeine recently and he's having trouble making it stick. I passed her in the hallway yesterday when she was comforting Mirabel Ruiz because, apparently, she'd recently gone through a bad breakup.

Her bleeding heart might have been annoying as hell

if it weren't for the fact that her work was always on point. She never missed a deadline or dropped a call. She ran my schedule like a well-oiled machine and she never once complained about the fact that she was forced to come in early on some days and stay late on others.

Horrible as it sounds, I kept looking for ways to find fault with her and I kept coming up blank.

I'm snapped out of my reverie when one of my internal lines starts beeping. It so happens to be the one directly connected to my PA's desk.

"Yes, Ashley?"

"Sorry to disturb you, Mr. Ackerman. I have an Elaine Peiris here to see you."

That was the other thing about her. She was smart. Despite the fact that I'd given her permission to call me Tobias at work, she didn't flaunt her connection to me. She referred to me as Tobias when it was just the two of us. But whenever any other person was around, it was always Mr. Ackerman.

Was I a total perv for finding that kinda… a turn-on?

Yes. Yes, it was.

Urgh, kill me now.

"Send her in."

A few seconds later, the door opens, and Elaine walks in, in her signature pantsuit look. She's one of the more senior members of my board of directors and, by far, one of my favorites. She clicks her way into my office in her Prada heels and sits down before I invite her too.

"Are you about to become a cliché, Tobias Ackerman?"

That's what I've always loved about Elaine. She doesn't pull any punches. She's a straight shooter and when it comes to tough business decisions, that definitely comes in handy.

Of course, when it comes to personal decisions—not so much.

"What does that mean?"

She raises her eyebrows. "The *very* pretty new receptionist you've hired…"

It hits a little too close to home but I pretend to be clueless. That was the other thing about Elaine. She'd had two different husbands and raised two sons who were both grown men now. If anyone knew about men—it was her.

"What about her?"

"Come on, you can't pretend you haven't noticed how attractive she is."

"She's also young."

She cocks her head to the side and gives me a smirk. "That's never stopped you before."

I sigh. "Not that I don't love our little chats but are you here for a reason, Elaine?"

"Ooooo, did I hit a nerve?"

"She's my closest friend's daughter."

That definitely gets a reaction. Elaine looks at me with beady-eyed curiosity. "How old is this friend of yours?"

"A year older than I am. Ashley was born when he was sixteen. I was there in the hospital when she was born."

"Well, she's certainly not a baby anymore."

"Elaine."

She giggles. "I came to tell you that the financial reports for the last year came in this morning. We've done spectacularly well." She pushes the files towards me. "I think you'll be pleased."

I open up the file and scan through the figures. "This is very good."

"We have you to thank for that."

I wave away the compliment. "It was a team effort."

"For a handsome man, you certainly are modest."

"What is this?" I ask, looking down at the notes made at the bottom of the page.

Elaine shifts in her seat, looking mildly uncomfortable. "Some of the members of the board feel that, given the profits we've made last year, a salary hike is justified."

I snort. "The salary hikes seem to apply to the board only."

"Well…"

I push the file back to her. "I see. They sent you in here to negotiate with me because they know you're my favorite."

"Am I?" she asks coyly.

I smirk. "You may be my favorite but I'm not playing this game, Elaine. You can take this file back to those arrogant blowhards and tell them that their six-figure salaries are more than ample. The profit we made last year is going towards salary hikes and bonuses for our support staff. The PAs, the drivers, the security staff, the cleaning crew."

Elaine raises her eyebrows. "I told them that's what you'd do."

"Do you have a problem with that?"

She smiles. "Would it matter if I did?"

"No."

She nods. "Then I think you're doing the right thing." I give her a wink and she gets to her feet. "And don't worry about the others. I'll get them to see the light."

She heads out of my office and I stare at the freshly prepared schedule that Ashley put on my desk an hour ago. She's started color-coding stuff so that it's easier to read. I have a meeting in twenty minutes and then a bunch of calls with our international departments. But I have no motivation for any of them.

Why is it that work has felt like such a fucking drag lately?

I push down all my reluctance and power through the day. I attend every meeting. Take every call. Entertain every employee who walks into my office. And by the time eight o'clock rolls around, I'm feeling reasonably good about my productivity for the day.

Knock, knock, knock.

"Come in."

Ashley pokes her head into my office. "Hey."

I raise my eyebrows. "What are you still doing here? I told you that you could go home an hour ago."

She pushes the door open and walks in with a bunch of files. "I had some work to finish. I wanted to get it all done today." She sets the files down on my table. "There you go. I've marked the urgent ones with red tacks so you know to get to them fast."

I eye her tentatively. "You should go home, Ashley."

"Are you going home?"

I raise my eyebrows. "Not right now."

She shrugs. "Then I'll stay too."

She's about to turn towards the door when I stop her. "You're not required to stay as long as I do. That's not part of the job description."

"I know but I'm gonna stay anyway."

I'm actually getting kinda worked up about this. "You're just gonna sit out there until I leave?"

She narrows her eyes. "Um, I'm not gonna just sit out there. I'm gonna organize tomorrow's schedule and revise the minutes from today's board meeting."

"No PA really does that."

"I do."

There's definitely an air of pride when she says that.

Annoyingly, it reminds me of Daniel. "Well, I just have a couple more things to do and then I'm leaving."

"Good to know."

I suppress a sigh. "Anything that needs signing?"

She nods and pulls up a vanilla-colored file. I expect her to hand it to me over the desk but instead, she walks around my desk and stands at my shoulder. She opens the file and leans in a little when she points down to the blank space where I'm supposed to sign.

Jesus, she smells like rain and grass and hot chocolate on a rainy day.

Her blouse billows slightly as she leans, which means if I turn my head to the side by an inch, I'm going to be able to see her cleavage.

Keep your head down.

"I heard you're giving the support staff raises this quarter."

I put my pen down and look up at her. "Jesus, is it already going around the office?"

She winces. "Afraid so."

"Fucking gossips."

The side of her mouth twitches up a little. "People are thrilled."

"Um, I hope you know that the salaries only take effect for permanent employees who've been with the company for two years or more."

She frowns. "I know that. I wasn't saying I was thrilled. I was saying *people* are thrilled."

"Right. I just wouldn't want you to get your hopes up."

She rolls her eyes. "I'm not angling for a higher salary on my second week at the job, Tobias." As always, I feel a strange little thrill when she says my name. "I'm just saying that I'm happy for your staff. And I also think it's really cool that you would do that. Most CEOs just keep lining the pocket of the big execs."

"I'm not like other CEOs."

She nods. "Yeah… I see that." Despite my better judgment, I meet her gaze. Those beautiful, sad eyes are bright and electric. "You really do care about your employees, don't you?"

I clear my throat. "A true leader *should* care about his or her employees."

She smiles. "Dad always did say you had a big heart."

I raise my eyebrows. "Does he?"

She smirks. "Don't tell him I said so. He'll probably deny it."

I laugh. "He probably would." My laugh subsides fast though. "Daniel's wrong though. I haven't got a big heart. I'm just pretending."

She frowns. "Why would you pretend?"

I shrug. "I think I'm overcompensating."

"For what?"

"For being a shitty person most of my life. Being a shitty son, a shitty brother and a shitty friend."

Her eyebrows rise. "I don't believe that's true."

I give her a small smile. "That's because you want to see the good in people. I choose to see people for who they really are. Saves you a ton of disappointment down the line."

Jesus, why am I talking so much?

I suppose the honest answer is that she's easy to talk to. There's just something about her that makes me want to spill my guts, lay myself bare and deal with the consequences later.

"That's a very pessimistic view of things."

"You say pessimistic. I call it realistic."

She rolls her eyes. "Dad used to say that to me all the time."

"He probably learned it from me."

Her jaw clamps shut and her eyes grow a little wary. She rounds my desk again and I get the feeling that she wants to put some distance between us.

"I'm gonna head home now if that's okay?"

"Of course it is."

She nods and turns towards the door. Then she freezes, turns back around and fixes me with a searching expression that I can't quite decipher.

"Ashley?"

She shakes her head. "Sometimes I forget that you and my Dad grew up together. It's… weird."

"Believe me. It's as weird for me as it is for you."

She nods. "I still want this job."

Her jaw is set with determination and that move reminds me of Kristen. My chest throbs painfully. "The job is yours for as long as you want it, Ashley."

I'm just not sure if that's me being generous or selfish.

CHAPTER 12

Ashley

He knows everyone by name.

Even the cleaning crew comes in late after everyone has left for the day.

I'm hiding behind the water cooler when he emerges from his office at last. Matilda is cleaning out the trash can by my desk while the city lights twinkle outside the massive glass windows.

"Tilda, how are you? I haven't seen you this week."

"I switched shifts with Juan, sir," she says in a quiet voice. "My son's been sick."

Tobias's face immediately shifts into seriousness. "Is it serious?"

"I... well, no. I mean, it's pneumonia. He had to be hospitalized. We were so scared that we made the mistake of going private and now it looks like..." she trails off self-consciously.

"You're looking at an enormous hospital bill."

She nods, her cheeks coloring slightly. "My husband is picking up extra shifts too, so we'll manage it. The important thing is Jacob is alright."

Tobias puts a hand on her shoulder. "It can't be easy, I'm sorry. You should have come to me."

She shakes her head. "Oh sir, I wasn't asking…"

"I know you weren't. I'm offering. What hospital is Jacob checked into?"

"Sir—"

"Matilda. If you don't tell me, I'll pull strings and find out anyway. You're just saving me a step."

Her chin quivers. "Saint Mary's."

He nods. "I'll take care of the bill. And you can have next week off with pay. Jacob will need someone to stay at home with him and help him recover."

Her eyes go wide. "M-Mr. Ackerman… I can't possibly…"

"That's an order, Matilda. Consider yourself fired for the next week. I'll see you the Monday after next. Goodnight."

He doesn't even let her thank him properly. I slip into the lunch room so he doesn't see me hiding, and I watch as he walks down the hall toward the elevators. His dark brown hair ripples under the golden lighting. Is that a halo I'm spying or am I just seeing things?

Only when the elevator doors close do I step outside of the lunch room.

"Ashley?"

I turn on the spot to find Matilda staring at me with raised eyebrows. It's slightly awkward, considering I met her only half an hour ago. "Hey, sorry. I swear I wasn't eavesdropping. I just wanted to get some water and I… also didn't want to interrupt."

She gives me a watery smile. "It's okay."

I take a step towards her. "I am glad for you though."

"I feel bad."

"Why?"

"Because Mr. Tobias has done so much for me and my family already. He's the one who got my husband hired at Hanson and Sons, and last February, he helped my daughter get a scholarship into Sarah Lawrence."

My jaw drops just a little. "That's amazing."

"He's a good man. It's not something you can say about a lot of rich and powerful men."

"No," I whisper, looking towards the elevator.

"What are you still doing here, by the way?"

"Oh… um… I was just on my way out too. Goodnight, Matilda. Hope your son feels better soon."

She waves me out and I take the elevator down. I walk part of the way back home and then take a bus the rest of the way. The apartment smells like beef stew when I walk in.

"Ash? Is that you?"

"Well, a burglar wouldn't have a key, now would they?"

"Ha-ha," Dad says from the kitchen. "Come over here and park it. Dinner's almost ready."

I glance at the time. "It's almost nine o'clock."

"Uh-huh. And?"

"How did you manage to time it so perfectly?" I ask curiously. "I didn't tell you I was going to be late."

He gives me a weird little smile and pretends to busy himself with ladling the stew into one of the new bowls he'd bought to 'fill out my kitchen.'

"Dad."

He sighs and turns around. "I may have texted Toby."

"You did what!?"

"Relax, honey. I just asked if *he* was still at work and he just mentioned that you insisted on staying back as long as he did. He told me he'd text me when he left and I didn't tell him not to."

"Well, *tell* him then. This is ridiculous."

"Ash—"

"Don't you *Ash* me. You do not get to exchange or compare notes on me. There has to be some boundaries. There have to be lines in the sand and I'm drawing the first freaking one."

Dad sighs. "It was purely a coincidence, okay? I just happened to text. It wasn't like I was texting *about* you. Toby and I are friends."

"Urgh, don't remind me."

He raises his eyebrows. "I thought we were over this."

"Just because we talked it out doesn't mean I'm not still annoyed, Dad. Especially when you go around gossiping about me behind my back."

"Oh hon, it was hardly—"

"You know what? Never mind. Can we just have dinner already?"

He pursues his lips up into a tight line and nods. "Of course. Beef stew and rice for dinner. Are you hungry?"

I nod and he serves me a big bowlful. We sit down at the kitchen window, him on one side, me on the other and eat in silence for the first few minutes.

"What was he like in school?" I blurt out.

Dad stops short. He looks at me with raised eyebrows. "Um… he was a quiet kid. Introspective, thoughtful, and perceptive as hell. And he was smart as a whip, even back then. He was the kind of smart that meant he never needed to try at all. He just remembered things."

"*That* kind of smart, huh?"

Dad laughs. "He was good at everything he tried too but he didn't really do any sports in school. Every team tried to poach him but he just wasn't interested."

"Why not?" I ask, leaning in a little.

"He um… he had a lot going on at the home front. He

took on a part-time job when he was eleven years old. And by the time he was thirteen, he had two to juggle."

"Wow."

Dad nods. "Yeah... he made it look easy. But only the two of us knew how hard it was for him to juggle everything."

"The two of us?"

Dad pales a little when he realizes his slip. "Um, Kristen and I," he says reluctantly.

"What kind of troubles did he have on the home front?" I ask, partly to gloss over the fact that he mentioned *she-who-must-not-be-named* and partly because I was just that curious.

"They're not my troubles to speak of, honey," he says gently.

I suppress a sigh. Sometimes, it was annoying how principled my father could be. "What about girlfriends?"

Dad frowns. "What about them?"

"Did he have any?"

I'm probably being a little too enthusiastic with my questions but I'm too adamant to take notice of the little furrow in Dad's brow. "I mean... sure. He was a good-looking guy. And he had the whole tall, dark, broody thing that girls go nuts for."

I suppress a smile. "But he didn't really have a serious girlfriend. I love Toby but he's never really been a one-woman kinda guy."

It's annoying how quickly my heart sinks when I hear that. I try and keep my expression neutral though. "So he... was a player?"

Dad raises his eyebrows. "You're certainly curious today."

I try my best not to blush. "Yeah, well... he's my boss now. And I have an inside source. Why listen to idle gossip around the water cooler when I can get the real scoop straight from you."

Dad chuckles. "Is there a lot of gossip around the water cooler?"

Just about how great of a boss he is.

Which is *so* not the kinda information I'm after. "Um, sure. Everyone's got their different theories about Tobias. Apparently, he does date a lot."

"Then that hasn't changed."

Heat flashes across my skin. "So he *was* a player?"

Dad clears his throat uncomfortably. "Just so we're clear, he never lied to girls. And he never cheated. He was always upfront about the fact that he was really interested in monogamy." I raise my eyebrows and Dad starts looking even more nervous. "I mean… I'm guessing about that. It's just that for all the time I've known him, Toby's had dates, not relationships. They're two very different things."

Sadly, I agree.

"How come he's never come back to Scottsdale? Even for a visit?"

Dad takes pains to avoid my gaze. He takes this moment to carry the pot of chili to the sink. "You'd have to ask him. I think maybe… it was just too much for him."

It's the vaguest answer he could possibly have given me. "Dad?"

"Hm?"

"Why didn't *you* ever visit him?" I ask. "I mean… you claim that he's your closest friend. Your best friend, in fact. So, how come you two never really made the effort to see each other? Arizona and California aren't that far apart."

"I visited him twice."

"That was just in the last few years. I'm talking about *before* that."

Dad sighs. "There was a period when... we didn't talk that much."

"Why was that?"

He looks at me warily. "Honest truth?"

"Please."

"I was a fucking idiot and I behaved like one."

I stare at Dad in disbelief. "I can't imagine that."

"Because you've only ever seen me as your Dad. But with Toby... sometimes it's easy to fall back into the person I was *before* you. Not a responsible parent but a stupid teenage kid."

"Something had to have happened though."

"He left. That's what happened."

I frown. "What do you mean? You were pissed at him for leaving Scottsdale?"

"Basically—yeah. It wasn't fair to him and it was arrogant and selfish of me, but I resented him for leaving town. He saw a new start and all I saw was... that he was abandoning me."

"Aw... Dad..."

He shrugs. "Like I said, I'm not proud of how I behaved back then."

"Well... you were young."

He smiles. "Thanks for always finding excuses for me."

"I've never really had to before now."

Dad gives me a wink. "In any case, with any real friendship, you can pick up right where you left off. When I finally grew up a little, I called Toby up and apologized. And, of course, he forgave me because he's just that kinda guy. The rest is history."

"He just forgave you... just like that?"

"There was a lot going on in his life at the time. He needed a friend as much as I did."

I desperately want to ask what was going on in his life at the time but I know Dad's not gonna tell me. So I bite back the questions and concentrate on finishing my chili.

"By the way, I'm heading out tonight."

I take a sip of water. "Where are you going?"

"Just out."

I raise my eyebrows. "Why do you look so guilty?"

He frowns. "I don't."

"Are you going out on a date or something?"

He actually blushes. "Of *course* not."

"Why do you say it like that?" I ask. "There's nothing wrong with going out on a date. You're thirty-six years old. You should be dating. A lot."

"Are we seriously having this conversation?"

"Dad, your whole life can't revolve around me, ya know? You have to get out there and meet people."

He starts doing the dishes and he *hates* doing the dishes. It's a surefire sign that he wants to avoid this whole situation. "I'm fine."

"When was the last time you went on a date?"

He groans. "Ash."

"Answer the question."

"I can't remember."

"Lucky for you, *I* remember. It was right before my nineteenth birthday. That was over a year ago."

"The women in Scottsdale aren't my type."

"Then maybe you should try the women in California?"

He throws me a self-conscious smirk. "It's sweet of you to worry about me, kid. But I'm okay. Really, I am."

When I was younger, I was happy to believe that. But now—I'm not sure anymore.

"You know, there's no reward without risk sometimes, Dad," I say gently.

"What's that supposed to mean?" he asks, somewhat defensively.

"It means you can't be so scared of being hurt that you close yourself off to every possibility that comes your way. That's no way to live."

He meets my eyes for a fraction of a second. "I haven't done a lot right in my life, kid. But at least I can rest easy knowing I did a good job with you."

"Does that mean you're gonna take my advice?"

I can see the corners of his mouth rise in a small smile. "We'll see."

I'll take it.

CHAPTER 13

Tobias

B *uzz. Buzz. Buzz.*
　　What the fuck?

I've lived in this building for five years and never once has my doorbell buzzed without prior notice. I figure maybe it's just the security guard who comes to notify me about some new building regulation or a misplaced letter or something.

But when I open the door, I find myself face to face with—

"Daniel."

"Hey, friend."

"Jesus," I breathe. He looks good. The laugh lines around his eyes have gotten more pronounced and he's lost some weight since I last saw him but he looks every bit the hand-some high school jock he used to be. "What the fuck are you doing here?"

He walks into the apartment, and we embrace like we used to. It's full body, hard slaps on the back. "I came to clean the gutters. Why do you think I'm here?"

I snort. "How'd you get past security?"

Daniel rolls his eyes. "Come on. Getting past security was child's play. I didn't want to risk buzzing up and having you pretend not to be in."

I glare at him. "I'd never do that."

"So you're trying to say that you haven't been avoiding me?"

I cringe inwardly. I'd assumed I'd been more subtle than that. "I haven't been avoiding you. It's just that things have been busy at work, that's all."

Daniel rolls his eyes. "Come on, brother. I've known you a long time. I know when you're being shady."

"I'm being shady now."

Daniel turns towards the apartment and his eyes go wide. "Jesus Christ. Look at this place. It's a fucking palace in the sky."

Seeing Daniel in this place makes me strangely self-conscious. "I know… it's a little much."

"How many bedrooms?"

"Uh… four."

"Fucking hell."

I run a hand through my hair. "It's obnoxious, isn't it?"

Daniel walks over to the floor-to-ceiling glass windows and gazes out at the Californian skyline. "What are you talking about? It's fucking epic. You've done well for yourself, Toby."

Toby. It brings me right back to that street in Scottsdale. I haven't been Toby in so many years that it feels almost confronting to be faced with that name now. Daniel turns to me slowly. "You shouldn't be ashamed of that."

I frown. "I'm not."

"No? Because I've been to this city three times now and this is the first time I've seen where you live."

I sigh and sit down on the sofa facing the view. "Sometimes I think I don't deserve all this."

"You think I'm gonna resent you for moving up in life?" Daniel asks, and he kind of sounds a little mad. "Are you fucking serious?"

"No, of course not. I guess…"

"I was there from the very beginning," Daniel reminds me. "You remember that, don't you?"

"I remember."

He nods. "You deserve all this, Toby. All this and more."

I shake my head. "You deserve this too, you know."

"Don't even go there."

"Why not?"

"You know why you deserve all this?" Daniel demands. "Because you've *earned* it. That's why. That's nothing to be ashamed of."

I shake my head at him. "We always jump right back into things, don't we?"

Daniel smiles. "It's why this friendship has lasted so long. You gonna offer me a beer or something?"

"Shit. Sorry." I get back to my feet and head to the kitchen. Daniel follows behind me, his neck swinging from side to side like an oscillating fan. "Damn this place… I can't get over it."

"I *do* have four rooms. You're welcome to one if you need it."

"I appreciate that but I think I'll stay with Ash for a little while longer. I think she could use the support."

I have no idea what he means by that and I'm desperate to know. I just don't want to be too eager with my questions unless he maybe suspects something.

Please.

There's no way he's ever gonna suspect that I've slept with his daughter.

As I pass him a beer from the fridge, I see a flash of Ashley. Not the polite and efficient young woman who brings me my coffee every morning or takes notes during meetings. But the vibrant beauty who had moaned desperately when I'd pushed inside her for the first time.

Stop it.

"It's nice to be out of Scottsdale, honestly," Daniel says, breaking through my thoughts. "Sometimes it gets a little claustrophobic in that town."

"Are you thinking of leaving?"

He shakes his head. "I've got the business all set up down there. I can't uproot right now. In any case, I can't follow Ash to California. She needs room to breathe, room to grow without her father standing over her shoulder all the time."

I nod. "Yeah… fair enough." I help myself to a fresh beer as well, just to get the edge off. I've got too many distracting images running around inside my head.

"Thanks again—"

"Don't thank me again. You've already thanked me enough times now. And in any case, I should be the one thanking you. She's a great PA."

"Yeah?"

"She's got your work ethic, for sure."

"Yeah, well, she sure as hell didn't get it from Kristen."

The name drops between us and I feel the air in the kitchen get heavy instantly. Daniel seems to realize the same thing because he winces. "Shit. Sorry… that sounded really fucking bitter, didn't it?"

I take another swig of my beer. "You're allowed."

"Am I?" he asks. "It has been twenty years. Shouldn't there be a statute of limitations on regret?"

"You'd think. I'm still waiting on mine to run out, to be honest."

Daniel smiles. "It is fucking pathetic that sometimes I still think about her."

I tense up immediately. I love Daniel. He's the closest thing I have to a brother. Which is why every time Kristen comes up, it feels like I'm betraying him all over again. A part of me just wants to come clean, tell him everything, *explain*. A part of me just wants to get it all out in the open so that we can finally have the kind of friendship we had *before* Kristen got pregnant.

But judging from the look on his face, this is not the right time or place.

"It's not pathetic. Not at all."

Daniel snorts. "You're just saying that."

"She was your first love," I point out gently. "She's also the mother of your child. It's natural to have regrets… hurt feelings. You're only human."

"That's what I tell myself about her sometimes," Daniel admits. "She was only human. She made mistakes. She was flawed. Why didn't I fucking *see* that before she ran out on Ashley and I?"

My head drops. I don't have the answers he's looking for despite the fact that I have a lot more clarity than he does right now.

It's not your fucking place to say anything.

"Because you were in love with her. You saw only the best in her."

"Even when there was none to see."

I shift uncomfortably on my kitchen stool. "You don't mean that."

Daniel shakes his head. "Fuck. That's the thing—sometimes I do mean it. How could she have held that perfect baby in her arms and left? How could she have looked at Ashley, kissed her, sang to her, loved her and then left her? It makes no fucking sense. Which is why I'm still trying to figure it out twenty damn years later."

"She was sixteen years old, Daniel."

"I was sixteen years old, Toby."

That's the thing with us. We reminded each other of our childhoods. When I saw Daniel, I saw the street where I grew up. I saw my parents, my brother. I remembered all those little things that made me a man.

When Daniel saw me, he saw all the little moments that made him who he is today. He probably saw the football pitch we used to crash at midnight. He probably saw the park where we used to drink beer out of cans. And I'm pretty sure he saw her too.

Kristen.

She was the point in our little triangle. And it wasn't until after she was gone that we both realized how much her leaving cost us.

"Not all of us can hack single parenthood at sixteen, brother," I say gently. "Sometimes you judge everyone else by your standards."

"What's that supposed to mean?"

"It means that not everyone is as strong or principled as you are. And not everyone is as lucky."

His eyes land on me, heavy and borderline angry. "So because she had shit parents, she's excused for running out on her kid?"

"That's not what I said."

"It's what you meant though."

I sigh. "Beer usually relaxes you."

"I shouldn't have come," Daniel says, slamming his beer

down on the table. "I'm gonna head out. This was a bad idea."

"Typical Daniel."

He twists around before he's even made it to the doorway. "Excuse me?"

"Every time we have a real conversation about Kristen, you choose to run away. Talking about her might actually help. Did you ever think of that?"

He frowns. His jaw clenches tightly and I remember that expression from when we were kids. He's trying to decide if he should stay or leave, listen or fight.

"Why does every fucking conversation always end up being about her?" Daniel demands.

"Maybe because you always find a way to bring her up," I point out. "You keep talking about what a shit person she was for running out on her kid but I don't think that's why you're really mad at her."

His eyes go wide. "Oh and *you* know why I'm really mad at her, do you, Doctor Phil?"

"She ran out on you."

His jaw drops. He looks like he may just punch me. Honestly, I would take the punch. I deserve it anyhow. Even if he doesn't quite know it yet. I do. It would make me feel better. I hope.

"Fuck," he mutters. And just like that, he deflates. He walks back to the island and grabs his beer again. He takes a long swig, enough to down the whole damn can. Then he goes to the refrigerator and grabs himself another one. "You may be on to something…"

I raise my eyebrows. "Wow, did you just admit that I might be right?"

"Don't get used to it."

I chuckle. "Just for the record… I think she made a huge mistake running out on you. On both of you."

Daniel sits back down and nods. "If only she thought that too… wherever she is."

My fingers tighten around the bottle. "Yeah… wherever she is."

"Will you come over for dinner tomorrow?" Daniel asks abruptly. "I think it might be nice to kinda… break the ice, so to speak… for all of us." I've been dreading this moment since I found out who Ashley really was. I'm trying to work out an excuse when Daniel meets my gaze. "It would mean a lot to me, brother."

Fuck me.

"Of course. I'll be there."

Daniel smiles. "Good man."

The thing is—I'm not so sure that I am.

CHAPTER 14

Ashley

It's five-thirty when Tobias comes out of his office, looking incredibly handsome in a navy blue suit that brings out the cobalt in his eyes.

I feel my stomach twist when his gaze lands on me. "You almost done over there?"

"Um, yeah…?"

He walks over to my desk, which he usually avoids like the plague. "I'm getting ready to head out for the day."

My first thought is—*why is he telling me?* My second thought is that h*e doesn't usually leave work this early.* My third thought is—*I haven't got nearly enough time with him today.*

"Okay."

"If you're ready, I can give you a lift?" The way he asks the question makes me think that he's waiting, maybe even hoping that I'll say no.

"You want to give me a lift back home?" I ask in confusion.

"Well, we are going to the same place."

It takes me a moment to process that. Then it hits me—
"Dad asked you to dinner?"

"He didn't tell you?"

I get to my feet, feeling goosebumps erupt all over my skin. I'm not sure if it's born out of panic or excitement. "He mentioned inviting you over for dinner sometimes. But it was just in passing. I didn't know it was happening today."

"If you're uncomfortable with it then—"

"It's fine," I say, cutting him off. "Dinner's fine. I'm ready to go."

We take the elevators down together and neither one of us breaks the silence. Not even when we're in his deep green Rolls Royce does he feel the need to talk to me, I wonder. I check my phone, realizing that it will take us at least thirty minutes to get to my apartment. And that's without factoring in traffic at this time.

Ten minutes into the city and no one has said a word. It feels… strange. The silence gets so heavy that I start to crack under the pressure.

"So um… are you always this chatty or am I just lucky?"

He glances at me out of the corner of his eye. "Sorry. Just preoccupied."

"With what?"

"Work stuff."

He descends back into silence and I sit there, pulling at my fingernails, wishing that I'd just done the sensible thing and turned down this ride.

Ping.

I glance down at my phone, thankful for a chance to focus on something other than the awkward silence.

Dad: *I'm making mushroom tagliatelle today. And apple pie for dessert. You're welcome. By the way, I've asked Toby*

to join us for dinner. Hope you don't mind. *smiley face emoji*

I roll my eyes and snort. We're stuck at a red light, so Tobias turns to me, clearly startled by my very unladylike snort.

"Everything okay?"

"Oh. Oh, yeah. Everything's fine. That was Dad. He's made pasta and pie for dinner."

"He's still cooking then?"

"Yeah, I think it soothes him."

"You know why he started to cook in the first place?" Tobias asks.

I glance at him curiously. "Is there a story there? I just assumed he liked to cook."

This time, Tobias is the one who snorts. "He barely knew how to boil an egg. He started cooking because I used to come around to his place hungry half the time. So he started reading up on different recipes so that he could cook for me."

"Wow, I didn't know that. How old were you guys?"

"I was probably nine. Daniel was a year older. It was right after Mrs. Payne started working again so we were mostly on our own after school."

"Mrs. Payne," I repeat. "Weird."

"I was really sorry to hear of your Grandma's passing," he says in a subdued tone. "I really loved her. She was like a second mother to me."

I swallow the lump in my throat. "She was the only mother I knew."

"It must have been hard for you... both of you."

I stare at him curiously without really acknowledging that. "Why didn't you come down for her funeral?"

He raises her eyebrows. "Um... what did your Dad tell you?"

I narrow my eyes at the windscreen. "Never mind what he told me. I'm asking you."

"Ashley—"

"Do *not* tell me it's complicated. If you do, I might just scream."

He sighs and I notice the way his hands tighten around the steering wheel. "Okay, honest truth? Your Dad and I weren't really talking at that point. I mean, we were... kinda. But there was tension. And I was a coward. I didn't want to come back to Scottsdale."

"Why?"

"Personal reasons."

That answer kinda shuts down the conversation but I'm not willing to let it die down just yet. "I always thought Dad and I were close. I used to refer to him as my best friend growing up," I say.

"Funny, he did the same."

I shrug. "Except it was clearly not true. Apparently, there's a lot about him that I don't know. There's a lot he hasn't told me."

"Probably because it's too painful."

"I get that when it comes to Kristen." *Did he just flinch?* "But what's the deal with you?"

He's looking really uncomfortable right now. He shifts in his seat and keeps his eyes fixed on the road. "The deal with me is—I left."

I raise my eyebrows. "That's it?"

He glances at me. "I know it seems silly, but after everything your father went through, it must have felt like a betrayal."

"Come on. It's not like you just disappeared on him like she did."

He's silent for so long that I look toward him. His eyes

are pinched together and his lips are pressed so tight that they've turned white. "Oh my God. *Did* you?"

He curses under his breath as we hit more grid-lock traffic. Then he turns to me. "I kinda did."

"Fuck," I breathe. "He never told me that."

"Because he's not the kinda man to go around talking shit about people. Even if they deserve it. I was a fucking asshole back then. I knew how much Kristen's leaving had hurt him. I knew how much it had hurt him the *way* she had left. And I did the exact same thing."

"You're right. That does sound like an asshole move."

He actually smiles. "Glad we agree on that."

I clasp my hands together, grateful that he'd told me. It gives me a little bit of the context that I've been missing all this time. "When did you guys start talking again?"

"When he showed up for my mother's funeral."

"Fuck."

Tobias nods. "Yeah. It was the nicest and meanest thing he could have done. It was an *I love you* and a *fuck you* all at the same time. But it was the right move. We talked *a lot*. And by the end of that night—it was like no time had passed."

"I remember him leaving when I was in middle school for a friend's funeral," I say softly. "He never mentioned that *you* were the friend."

Tobias frowns. "Why would he?"

"Well, because he spoke about you a lot."

Tobias's eyes go wide. "He did?"

"All the time," I say emphatically. "My childhood was filled with stories of your childhood."

"Jesus," Tobias breathes.

I have no idea what he's thinking right now and I wish I did. I kinda regret mentioning that at all now. All it probably did was remind him that our childhoods were a generation apart.

"Fucking hell, the traffic…" he mutters under his breath.

"We're not getting out of this for the next fifteen minutes at least."

"Why don't you text your Dad and tell him we'll be a little late?"

I send off a quick text as the skies darken above us. Despite the gridlock traffic we're in, I've never been more grateful for big city congestion. He may be forced to spend time with me but at least he's talking.

"Can I ask you another question?"

He tenses just a little but he gives me a slight nod. "Sure."

"Is there a specific reason Dad had to cook for you after school? Were you hungry because you had a big appetite or because… there was another reason?"

"Jesus, you clocked that, did you?"

I smile. "So there was another reason."

He sighs. "I didn't have the most idyllic childhood. My parents were busy. They didn't really have time for my brother or me."

"I didn't realize you had a brother."

He swallows. "Yeah, well—we kinda raised ourselves. It was sink or swim in our house." He clears his throat and I can tell from the far-off look in his eye that he's going back there… to his childhood. "Sometimes I think if it weren't for your father, I might not have survived it."

I desperately want to know more. I want to know it all. But I have a feeling that the more I push, the more he'll shut down on me.

"If it weren't for my father, I wouldn't have survived my childhood either."

He throws me a smile. It lasts a few seconds longer than

an innocent smile should. He seems to realize that too, because he looks away quickly. "Fucking traffic," he says again.

"You know you *can* talk to me," I say softly. "If you want to…"

"Ashley…"

"Don't say my name like that."

"Like what?"

"Like you're trying to let me down easy," I snap. "I'm not some random girl you hooked up at a bar."

His eyes snap to mine. "Oh, we're going there?"

"Yes, we are. I'm sick of sitting here and pretending as though nothing happened between us."

"Well then, as long as we're going there, it needs to be said. You *were* some random girl I hooked up with at a bar."

I shake my head. "So it was just meaningless sex then, is that it?"

"Yes."

His jaw is clenched so tight he's in danger of snapping it right off. "Is that why you suggested we meet again the next week?"

He clenches even tighter. "So? That doesn't mean anything."

"Except for the fact that you *wanted* to see me again."

"That was before."

"So you know my real name now. Big freaking whoop. I'm still the same girl you met that night. I'm still the same girl you kissed that night. I'm still the same girl you fuc—"

"That's enough. We're not doing this."

"I don't know if I can keep pretending," I blurt out before I can stop myself. "Especially in front of Dad."

"Jesus Christ, Ashley. What are you saying?"

My eyes veer to his. "Maybe it's better that we come clean and tell him what happened."

"Are you trying to get me killed?"

"I'm trying to be honest."

"No. You're trying to blow shit up. And I'm not about that kind of drama."

My eyes go wide. "That's not what I'm trying to do."

He shakes his head. "You may be old enough to fight for your country and vote. But that doesn't make you a grown-up, Ashley. I'm fifteen years older than you. I would know."

I stare at him with my mouth hanging open. How had I not seen this side of him before? The pompous, arrogant side? The side that looks at me and sees a child instead of a grown-ass woman.

"Oh, you know what, *Tobias,* fuck you!"

He sighs. "That's real mature."

Grinding my teeth, I take advantage of the fact that we're still inching down the road at snail's speed and unbuckle my seatbelt.

"Hey. What are you doing?" I ignore him as I open the door and get out of the car. "Jesus Christ. Ashley! Get the hell back in the car!"

I slam the door closed and start running. There's a park right across the street and I fly through the wooden gates, trying to run from his rejection, trying to run from my feelings.

Trying to run from all the things I know aren't good for me—

But I want to anyway.

CHAPTER 15

Tobias

*G*oddammit.

If I didn't think our age difference was a factor before, I definitely do now. Not that I was actually entertaining the thought or anything. It was just helping make my case for staying away from Ashley Payne.

She'd actually jumped out of a moving car. Well... it wasn't technically moving at the time. *Fucking traffic.* But still. The car wasn't on park mode or anything. We weren't even at a fucking red light. And she'd decided to just jump out of the damn car.

It's not like I can just leave her either. Quite apart from the fact that I'm not a total fucking asshole, she's also Daniel's kid. I'm not gonna let my best friend's daughter run off into the darkness on her own.

So I find a place to put my car about a hundred meters from the park and I start walking fast. It's completely dark by the time I get to the gate that she'd run through. I'm hoping that she hadn't exited the park through another exit. Otherwise, I'm gonna be walking around in circles until I get a call from her father demanding to know what happened.

What the fuck am I supposed to tell Daniel then?

Aw, nothing happened, buddy. I just fucked your daughter before I knew she was your daughter and now she works for me, which is horrible because it means I can never get her off my mind and I really want to because it feels like I'll go crazy if I don't.

Right. That's gonna go down really well.

I circle the park once and just when I'm starting to give up hope, I spot her. She's in a secluded part of the garden overlooking the pond. She's sitting under a valley oak, looking down at her hands as though she's trying to read her fortune. I approach cautiously so that she doesn't get spooked.

Doesn't matter. She jerks when I say her name despite how soft I say it.

"Jesus," she gasps, putting a hand over her heart.

I raise my hands. "I come in peace."

"I don't want to talk to you right now."

"You realize your father's waiting for us, right? He cooked us dinner and everything."

"I don't feel like pretending tonight."

She's got her legs crossed and her hair flying loose in the wind. Those bright eyes are fixed on me but it's like she's looking right through me. It reminds me a little of Kristen. The way she would get all quiet and pensive everything something upset her.

"Then why the hell did you agree to work for me, Ashley?" I demand. "Did you not think that taking on the role of my PA would require a fuck ton of pretending?"

Her eyes go wide. "You have a point."

I take a deep breath. "Got room under that tree for one more?"

She glances at me out of the corner of her eye. "Knock yourself out. It's a free country."

I sit down next to her and snort. "I've never understood why people say that. *Nothing* in life is free."

She glances at me with raised eyebrows. "Wow, and I thought I was the cynical one here."

I shake my head. "Nope, that was always me."

"I guess… we really don't know each other all that well, huh?" she says softly.

"You sound surprised."

She shrugs. "I guess I convinced myself that night that we *did* know each other." When I raise my eyebrows, she frowns. "What I mean is… it just felt like we had a real connection. The conversation flowed; everything was easy. And in my experience, that doesn't happen very often."

"You're only twenty, Ashley. Give it time."

She still looks skeptical. "So you're telling me you've experienced connections like that in your life?"

I open my mouth to reply but then I realize that my answer wouldn't prove my point at all. It would prove hers. "Well…"

"Ah-ha," she snaps. "So you *haven't* had that kind of connection often, have you?"

"That depends on what you define as a connection."

She rolls her eyes. "Dad told me you never had girlfriends in high school. You just had dates. Sounds like you weren't really into commitment."

"Your Dad needs to shut his trap."

She smiles and I feel my entire body shiver at the way her face lights up. "Was he wrong?"

"No," I admit grudgingly. "He wasn't wrong. I didn't have girlfriends. But that was high school. I wasn't naïve enough to believe in the whole high school sweethearts nonsense. I knew, even back then, that I was too young, too restless, too immature for a relationship."

"And since high school?" she presses. "How many girl-friends have you had since then? Because if I remember correctly, the night we met, you told me that the woman you were having dinner with was basically your fuck buddy."

I wrinkle up my nose. "Nothing so crass."

"What would you call her then?"

"A friend."

"A friend you have sex with? Because if that's the case, it sounds like nothing has really changed since high school for you."

My first instinct is to vehemently deny her analysis of me. But I'm self-actualized enough to realize that instinct is coming from a place of defensiveness. Because the truth is— she's right. Nothing *has* changed since high school. I still walk through my life trying to keep people at bay. And every time I try and get close to someone—it blows up in my face.

Case in point—the situation we've got going on right now.

I was excited the night I met Ashley. I was tentative—yes. Scared—definitely. Nervous—fuck yeah. But I was also ready to see her again. I was ready to accept whatever a second night might offer.

I couldn't even have dreamed up the kind of curveball that life was gonna throw my way. As far as I was concerned, it was a giant fucking sign from the universe—*you do not get a happy ending. You were not made for the healthy family dynamic. Your big, lonely penthouse is as good as it's gonna get.*

Message fucking received.

"It's okay, you know," she says gently. "I've spent my whole life pushing people away too. I can read the signs."

I meet her gaze. This is why I hadn't clocked her as younger right off the bat. Those eyes of hers are soulful; filled with the kind of experience and knowledge you only find in older women. Women who had really lived.

"I'm not saying you're wrong, Ashley. But the reason I pushed *you* away is because the reality of us being together would be disastrous."

"Because of my father?"

"To name just *one*."

"He would understand. If we explained the circumstances to him."

"Jesus Christ, Ashley. That's a suicide mission right there. He'd never speak to me again."

"You're making an assumption."

"I know Daniel. I may even know him better than you do. You're gonna have to trust me on this one. If there's one person in this world he would kill for—it's you."

She purses her lips together. I wait, wondering what she's going to come back at me with. But she doesn't say anything at all. In the end, she just sighs. "California isn't as bad as I thought it would be," she says softly.

It's a sharp pivot but I take the lifeline she's throwing me. "I hated it when I first moved here. But it grows on you."

"Why'd you choose to move here?"

I shrug. "It felt far enough away to give me some distance but close enough that I still felt like I could go back home if I really wanted to."

"So... you didn't actually want to leave Scottsdale? Is that what I'm hearing?"

"I didn't want to leave the people who cared about me. But I also didn't want to spend the rest of my life in that town. My parents both did and it didn't end well for either one of them."

"Dad's never told me anything about your parents."

I smile sadly. "Because he's a good man. And a polite one. He couldn't have spoken about them without saying that my father was a drug addict with a temper and my mother was an abused woman who suffered from depression and anxiety."

Her eyes go wide. "Jesus." *Why the fuck did I just tell her that?* "I'm sorry… that must have been awful."

I shrug. "It was all I knew."

"And… your brother?"

There was a time when I could barely talk about Tommy without wanting to punch something. Now, the anger has subsided, leaving only a dull ache. "My brother was a mix of my father and mother."

She doesn't push me for more information about him. "And you?"

"I suppose I am too, whether I like to admit it or not."

"I know this is probably poor comfort but at least you have no questions about who your parents were. You knew exactly where you came from, exactly *who* you came from."

I snort. "You're right. That is poor comfort."

She gives me a self-conscious smile. "I just mean… sometimes not knowing is worse. I've spent my whole life trying to figure out who I am. And I've always gotten stuck on the same questions over and over again."

"Like what?"

"Like the stuff that I know I didn't get from my Dad. My allergy to peanuts. The fact that I'm a left-hander. My dyslexia. The color of my hair."

My eyes go wide. "You don't know what color hair Kristen had?"

She gives me a glare that I have no idea how to interpret. "I've never even seen a picture of her. Dad claims that he burned the ones he had in a fit of rage one day after she left us."

My lips press together in a straight line. I should never have followed her here. Rookie fucking mistake.

"What is that look on your face?" she demands, eyeing me closely.

"What look?"

"You're not looking me in the eye."

"Ashley."

She puts her hand on mine and I feel like a fucking magnet being pulled in her direction. "Please," she whispers. "I know it's easier to shut me out. But if that's what you *really* wanted, you wouldn't be talking about any of this in the first place."

She has a point.

I take a deep breath. "Your Dad wasn't lying. He did burn all her pictures a couple of days after she left. I was there."

Her eyes go wide. "You were there?"

"We called it the Kristen Bonfire. Daniel was trying to erase her from our lives. And I suppose I was trying to be a good friend... you know, support him. So I stood there and I tossed in Kristen's pictures with him."

"Jesus."

"He was hurting a lot, Ashley. He wasn't his best self in the days after she left."

She lifts her eyes to mine. "I can't say that I blame him. If the love of my life walked out on me without an explanation or a goodbye, I'd probably want to do the same."

I nod. "I think he regretted it later. But he's never once admitted it to me."

"He probably won't either."

I smile. "You're probably right about that." She looks out

towards the pond and tucks an auburn strand of hair back behind her ear. *Fuck, she's beautiful.*

Maybe it's the quiet that surrounds us. Maybe it's the fact that she's making me feel something strange and foreign, something I've never felt before. Maybe it's because she simply deserves to know. But I make a decision then and there.

"Her hair was the same shade of autumn auburn as yours." Ashley's eyes snap to my face. "You have the shape of her face too. But your eyes—they're all you."

She swallows slowly. "What color were her eyes?"

"Dark blue. Really dark. You could almost mistake them for brown."

"What was she like?"

"She was… amazing," I hear myself say because Ashley deserves to hear that about her mother. But also because it's true. At least—it's true for me. "She was funny and bold and bright. She couldn't cook for shit but she could work wonders with a skateboard. She was really into heavy metal and alternative rock but she owned just as many records of Elton John and Sinead O'Connor. She was an amazing swimmer but she was scared of the ocean. She claimed she wasn't a singer but she could belt it out when she was drunk. She always rooted for the underdog and she hated bullies with a passion. And… she was allergic to peanuts too."

A single tear runs down Ashley's cheek. "S-she was?" I nod. "You've told me more about my mother in the last few minutes than I've found out in twenty years."

"I'm only sorry you didn't get the chance to know her like I did."

She blinks and two more tears roll down her cheeks. Seeing her cry fills me with this inexplicable rage that I can't quite process. It makes me feel like I would do anything to get her to smile; I would do anything to make sure she never has to shed another tear again for as long as she lives.

"Was she beautiful?" Ashley asks softly, turning towards me.

I know I shouldn't but I feel as though I don't have control over my body anymore. I raise my hand and cup her face. One of her tears slides right into my palm, and for one insane moment, I wonder—*what do her tears taste like?*

Her eyes are fastened on me with the kind of focus that feels like commitment. I should be scared but I'm not. I should want to run but I don't. Instead, I sit there, cupping her face in my hand, staring into those sad hazel eyes that exude warmth.

"Yes. Yes, she was beautiful," I say, letting my thumb run up and down her cheek. "But she wasn't nearly as beautiful as you are."

Then I do the stupidest thing I can do in this position.

I kiss her.

CHAPTER 16

Ashley

Ever had a kiss that feels like an out-of-body experience?

No—neither have I. I thought the first one was good. But it's nothing compared to *this* kiss. He doesn't hold anything back. He kisses me with the kind of passion that can only come from a place of urgency. A place of repression.

This kiss is proof that he's been pretending. Pretending that night meant nothing to him; that I was just some random girl he was hooking up with. There was no way he could walk it back now. Not after kissing me so passionately in the middle of a public, albeit lonely park.

I put my hands on his shoulders and climb on top of him until I'm straddling his lap. I can feel his erection against my thigh as I pull at the buckle of his pants. It's dark now. The only light we have is coming from the moon hanging above us and the streetlights around the corner.

I pull his cock free and fist him with my hand as I try and shimmy my skirt up my legs. His hands land on my ass and he sucks in a breath that has my pussy moistening fast.

"Fuck," he mutters. "Ashley…"

The sounds of traffic thunder in the distance but I'm completely dissociated from the world around us. All I can feel or hear or smell is him. The warmth of his skin as he grazes my breasts. The sounds of his heavy breathing. His deep oaky scent puts the trees around us to shame.

He fumbles into his pants and pulls out his wallet. For a second, I have no idea what he's doing. Then—I notice the shiny silver wrapper. *Of course. Protection.* I feel slightly embarrassed about the fact that I'd completely forgotten. Even worse, I would have gladly sunk onto his cock without anything between us. The very thought makes me tingle.

Stop it.

He slides the condom onto his cock and I lift my hips and position him right underneath me. I meet his eyes in the second before I sit back down again. His mouth is parted as though he has something important to say. I don't wait. I sit back down, landing on his cock.

"*Fuck*," he hisses through the teeth as he shoots deep inside me.

I start riding him slow, placing my hands on his chest, marveling at his sculpted perfection. His hands are placed firmly on each ass cheek, supporting me as I bounce up and down on his cock. His jaw clenches with every thrust and I just gain steam.

I've never felt this emboldened with a man before. I was the girl who always waited for *him* to make the first move. But somehow, it's different with Tobias. He makes me feel confident and empowered. He makes me feel like I could be the kind of woman that someone like him would be seen with.

My attraction to him was about so much more than his looks. Yes, he was handsome and tall and confident. But he also felt like a part of me. He knew things about my life and my past that I myself didn't know. When he looked at me, if felt like he really understood. I didn't have to pretend so hard. I didn't have to try so hard either.

I bend my lips down to his shoulder and kiss my way up to his ear. I swab his lobe with my tongue and start chewing on it gently. He starts pushing my ass back and forth, silently encouraging me to ride him harder.

At one point, I'm on my knees, trying to hold steady as he thrusts up hard from underneath me. I grip the tree trunk and try to keep my screams from alerting the whole of California.

"Yes," I gasp as pleasure ripples through my body. "Yes, yes, *yes!*"

I cum hard and I have to bite down on my tongue to keep my screams in check. I'm expecting him to slow down but he just keeps thrusting, giving me no room for relief. He grabs hold of my waist and twists me around so that I'm lying in the grass, and he's hanging over me. Those beautiful blue eyes of his are boring into mine like they're trying to unlock all my secrets.

I cup his face with my hand the same way he had touched my face a few minutes ago. He fucks me slow but deep, his jaw clenching powerfully.

There's something in his eyes that makes me shiver. And it has nothing to do with the chill in the air.

Please don't let him regret this. Please don't let him regret this.

Just when I think he's going to bend down and kiss my lips, he goes even lower and pulls off my bra with his teeth. Then he circles my right nipple with his tongue before he starts sucking on it desperately.

I've clearly been sleeping with all the wrong guys all this time because *none* of them have made me feel like Tobias does.

I run my hands through the back of his hair while he sucks on me, wrenching another orgasm from my body. This time, I can't quite keep the scream at bay. It comes out in a strangled moan that has me unraveling.

He's what I've been missing my whole life.

He starts fucking me harder, his eyes fixed on a single point at my shoulder. It makes me wonder if he means to avoid my gaze or if that's innocent on his part. I have to ask myself, *do I even care at this point?*

His body tightens around mine and he makes three more fevered thrusts before he releases inside me. For a second, I wish that he was bare. I want to be able to feel his cum inside me. The animal part of my brain wants him to mark me but at this point, I'll take what I can get.

He mutters something into my shoulder but I miss it underneath the fervor of my own sharp breathes.

He rolls off me and I hear the *smack* of the condom rolling off his cock, followed by his zip as he covers himself up. His chest rises and falls heavily, his eyes trained on the midnight blue sky above us.

"Fuck," he mutters. "What did we do?"

I decide to take that as a rhetorical question. I just lie in the grass with him, staring up at the sky, basking in the quiet of the moment.

Hoping we're not sitting smack dab in the middle of the calm before the storm.

CHAPTER 17

Tobias

Ping. Ping. Ping.
    I glance down and realize that both our phones are lighting up. "Shit," I snap, forcing myself upright. "That'll probably be Daniel."

Daniel: *Hey, just checking on an ETA. Thought you said you'd leave early today?*

Daniel: *No stress or anything. Just don't want the chicken pie to get cold. There. Now you've forced me to ruin the surprise. Bastard.*

"Fuck," I mutter as I type off a quick text in reply.

Tobias: *Sorry, something unexpected came up. We'll be there soon.*

"*Fuck*," I growl again.

"Will you stop saying that?"

I turn to Ashley, who's looking very much like a woman who's just been fucked in the grass. Even her hair's got little blades of grass running through it.

"I can't take you back to his place like that."

She frowns. "First of all, it's *my* place. And second of all, you can't take me back looking like *what* exactly?"

133

I sigh. "You just look a little disheveled."

"Well, I guess we're a matching pair then."

I force myself upright and start dusting the grass off my pants. How the fuck did I let this happen? The first time was bad but at least I could stand behind the fact that I didn't know who she was. But now?

What's my defense? What's my excuse?

Right. There is none.

"Stop it."

I glance towards her. She's looking right at me with those bright hazel eyes of hers. "Stop what?"

"Spiraling. I can see you going over to the deep end, but that's not helpful. Not right now anyway. We still have to sit through a whole dinner and pretend as though everything's alright."

She has a point. She's also wearing an expression that reminds me of exactly why I'd convinced myself she was older than she actually is.

She takes everything in her stride. She gathers herself up and dusts herself off. By the time she's done, she's got most of the grass blades out of her hair. All except one. "Um, you missed a spot," I tell her, pointing at the left side of her head.

She reaches up but doesn't quite manage to get the piece of grass. I step forward and tease it from the auburn strand of hair it's twisted into. She watches me with those glistening eyes of hers and for a moment, it looks like she's crying. But when I make eye contact, I realize that the stars are reflected in her irises.

Jesus.

"I'm sorry." I'm not quite sure what I mean by the apology but I feel the need to say it anyway.

"I'm not."

I drop my hand and swallow. "We need to get going. Daniel's waiting for us."

She just nods and follows me back to my car. The drive to her apartment is dead silent, but luckily, it takes us only ten minutes or so to get there. Apparently, our little detour through the park had allowed us to bypass the worst of the evening traffic.

As we walk up the stairs in her modest little apartment building, I keep glancing over at her, trying to determine where her head is at. Her expression is resigned, somewhat removed. I have no idea what she's thinking and it's driving me crazy.

Does she even realize that she smells of me right now? Which means I probably smell of her. How am I supposed to sit through an entire dinner with the taste of her still on my tongue?

Daniel throws the door open before we've even knocked. "There you guys are! I was getting worried."

Ashley throws on a smile and walks in. "Sorry, Dad. Had some work to finish up."

"Boss kept you late, huh?"

She nods smoothly. "Oh yeah, he's a real tyrant."

"So I've heard," Daniel smiles as he pulls me in for an embrace. "Good to see you, brother."

"Good to be here. Smells great."

I'll admit, I'm a little out of sorts as I walk into that small, cozy apartment. It's probably half the size of my master bedroom. And yet, it's filled with twice the amount of life. The furniture is cheap but sturdy, and there's a ton of color and lots of *stuff* that's lying everywhere.

"Wow, did you say you *just* moved in here?"

Ashley meets my gaze for a moment. "Ha-ha. I know. It

may look like I'm a hoarder but the apartment is just that small. That's all it is."

"Right," Dad nods, holding up a small pink bear with a worn-out smile. "And she insisted on bringing Pinky Bear with her."

"*Dad*," Ashley gasps, grabbing the teddy bear from her father and flinging it through the open door of her bedroom. "Jesus."

Daniel chuckles. "Oops, sorry. I shouldn't embarrass you in front of your boss."

"Outside of work, I'm not her boss. I'm just her…" *Just her what?*

"Uncle?"

"No!" Ashley and I say at the same time.

Daniel looks between us with wide eyes. "Okay. Jesus. It was just a suggestion. I get that you guys are entirely new to each other. How about a friend? We can all be friends, right? We're all adults here."

I'm really hoping he remembers he said that one day, on the off chance he finds out what happened between Ashley and I.

And I hope to God that day never comes.

"Friend works for me," Ashley says softly, glancing at me out of the corner of her eyes. "Um, I'm gonna go take a shower. Excuse me."

Yeah, probably because she needs to wash my scent off of her. I follow Daniel into the kitchen, where he's cutting up the pie he's just baked. "Jesus," I breathe. "That smells like Maynard Street."

Daniel raises an eyebrow. "That a good thing?"

I smirk. "Would you believe it if I said I missed that damn street?"

"Actually, I would. Life could be a shit show there, but

we had our moments." He grabs a beer from the fridge and slides it over to me.

"So… this is the best place she could find?" I ask, looking around.

"She searched for a while. It was the only place with rent control that she could afford."

"Come on, Dan. You could have chipped in a little. Helped her get a better place?"

It's a decent enough apartment with all the new furniture crammed in but it's too fucking small. And she's probably paying more than she should for a one-bedroom this size.

Daniel's lips come together in a tight line. "Yeah, she wouldn't have accepted my help. She wanted to do this on her own."

I raise my eyebrows. "She's stubborn, huh? Wonder where she gets that from."

Daniel flips me off and I smile. "Here," he says, pushing the salad bowl over to me. "Make yourself useful and mix that for me. What kept you guys?"

I tense up so fast that I'm sure he's gonna clock the change. Thankfully, he's still concentrating on getting equal pieces of his pie. "There was a fuck ton of traffic."

"And… how was it?"

"How was *what*?"

Daniel raises his eyebrows. "Hey buddy, don't bite my head off. I'm just asking a question. I was a little worried that the drive over might have been a little awkward for the two of you."

Fuck, I need to keep my shit together. I'm acting like a convict in a police station.

"The drive was fine."

"What did you guys talk about?"

"I don't know. Work. Scottsdale. California. Just stuff. It was fine."

Daniel actually looks relieved. "Good. Cause I really want the two of you to get along. You're both my family."

Urgh. I feel like the worst fucking friend right now. In more ways than one. Thankfully, I'm saved from having to respond when Ashley walks out of her room. She's changed into denim shorts and a black tank top that bears her sculpted shoulders. Her hair is wet and hangs off her shoulders.

Fuck, she looks good.

I avert my eyes and pretend to be engrossed in the salad I'm tossing. "Honey, would you mind setting the table? We can eat. I'm just gonna grab the condiments."

I carry the salad bowl to the table while Ashley starts setting plates around the table. Her hand brushes against my arm and it's like an electric bolt jolting through my body. I almost drop the fucking bowl. She meets my eyes for a second and it begs the question: *did she just do that on purpose?*

The three of us sit down together. Daniel and I are on one side of the table and Ashley is sitting directly opposite me. It's gonna be hard to avoid her gaze with this particular seating arrangement.

"I used to bake this pie most weekends when Toby was over," Daniel says, serving Ashley a big piece. "It was his favorite."

She raises her eyebrows. "*This* was your favorite. Really?"

Daniel frowns. "*Hey.*"

Ashley chuckles. "Sorry, Dad. I just mean that your repertoire includes way more elevated dishes. I'm surprised that a simple chicken pie beat all the rest."

"Well my repertoire wasn't as extensive at the time,"

Daniel points out. "And anyway, Toby has always been a man of simple tastes."

"Is that so?" Her star-bright eyes land on me and instantly, I feel a little hot under the collar.

"We didn't exactly have homemade food at my house. My brother and I lived off cereal and pop-tarts mostly. When that became too expensive, we had to steal what we ate."

Her eyes go wide and I realize what I've just said. "I-is that a joke? Or were you being serious?"

I cringe inwardly, aware that Daniel is looking at me with his *what-the-fuck* expression at the ready. "Um, I'm not proud of it," I admit. "But yeah, sometimes I stole. But once Daniel and I became friends, I didn't have to anymore."

"Was it really that bad?" Ashley asks softly. There's no judgment in her eyes. Just concern. Sympathy.

"My parents were young when they had us. They weren't really equipped to be parents," I say with a shrug. "Sometimes the best thing a parent can do—is leave."

Ashley's eyes go wide and Daniel's fork clatters to the plate. Had I just said that out loud? To *them*. "Fuck," I mutter. "I'm sorry. I didn't think—"

"You wanna know what my favorite Daniel dish is?" Ashley asks, seamlessly changing the subject.

I can still feel Daniel's eyes on me when I nod. "Tell me."

"He makes a mean roast chicken. Complete with honey-roasted vegetables and this red wine that just tastes amazing. It's always been our Thanksgiving meal."

"Wow, that does sound amazing." I glance toward Daniel. "Still no Turkey at Thanksgiving, huh?"

"Nobody's got the time to cook those birds. And chicken tastes better."

"Strongly disagree." I turn to Ashley and smile. "We have been having this argument most of our lives."

She smirks and everyone seems to relax a little bit. We get through the meal with pleasant conversation and I manage not to offend anyone else with my controversial opinions on parenthood. I have a feeling that Daniel won't forget that easily though.

"Okay, so I made apple pie for dessert but I forgot about ice cream," Daniel says while we're clearing away the plates.

"Oh, don't worry about it. I can live without ice cream."

Daniel and Ashley exchange a look. "Um, you simply *cannot* have apple pie without ice cream," she says, shaking her head at me.

Daniel looks at her. "I apologize about him. He doesn't know what he's saying sometimes."

I roll my eyes as Daniel heads for the door. "There's a 24-hour convenience store just around the corner. I should be back in fifteen."

My panic meter kicks up a couple of notches. The only thing I can think of is that *I can't be left alone with her.* "Hold on, I'll come with you."

"Don't be silly," Daniel says dismissively. "Stay in, keep Ashley company. I won't be long."

The door closes and it's just her and I. And an empty freaking apartment. I make sure to stay at the window so that the dining table is between us. She puts the plates down. "That went well."

"Ashley…"

She groans. "Don't say anything, Tobias. Please. It's been a nice night. I don't want to ruin it."

"What happened in the park—"

"And you're talking."

"—it can't happen again."

Her shoulders slump. "Why not? It's obvious you *want* to do it again."

I grit my teeth. "Daniel's my best friend."

"He was your best friend a few hours ago too. When you were fucking me in the middle of a public park."

I cringe. "I got caught up in the moment. But it was wrong. I can't betray Daniel like that. I don't want to hurt him."

She stares at me accusingly for a long moment. "But hurting me is just fine?" she asks softly.

"Ashley—"

I take a step towards her but she backs away immediately. "You know what? I'm tired and I don't really want dessert. You can tell Dad I went to bed."

"Ashley, please."

"Please what?" she demands. "You've already made the decision for both of us."

"You'll thank me for this one day."

Her eyes burst with fire as she spins around to face me. "Don't say that to me. You may be fifteen years older but that does not mean you know what's best for me. I may be young but I'm not an idiot. I know what's best for me."

She walks away and slams the door. I stare down at the empty plates in front of me. Quite apart from the Daniel of it all—it's about so much more than my relationship with her father.

Doesn't she get it? She can do so much better than me.

CHAPTER 18

Tobias

She's been quiet all day.

The only time she speaks is when I ask her a direct question. I notice that her silence extends past me too. She keeps to herself during the work hours, interacting with people only when she has to. She even eats her lunch alone at her desk.

I'm expecting her to run out of here the moment she's clocked in her eight hours for the day. But five-thirty comes and goes and she stays at her desk, pouring over paperwork and getting things organized for the week ahead. I dismiss her twice before I give up entirely. She's not gonna leave until she's good and ready.

However, when the clock hits eight and I'm still looking at a pile of work, I decide to head outside and check how she's doing.

"Ashley."

She gives me only a cursory glance. "Can I get you something?"

"No. I... um... I have a call with China in a bit. I'll be here another few hours. You're free to go home."

She shrugs. "I have a few things to finish up too. I'll leave when I'm finished with them."

She goes right back to her desk and I stand there, wondering how I can avoid her now without seeming like a total fucking asshole. "Hey, how do you feel about pizza? I was gonna order myself a pie."

She shrugs. "Anything's fine with me."

"Are you a pineapple on your pizza kinda gal?"

She raises her eyebrows. "I love pineapple on my pizza."

I shouldn't be surprised. Kristen loved that combo too. "I'll order one now. I'm also gonna take my call now, so if the pizza arrives, just bring it in."

Half an hour later and ten minutes after my call with China, Ashley walks in with a fresh pizza pie in hand. I get up to help her with everything but she kind of leans away, avoiding skin contact as much as possible. I can't say I blame her. Obviously, she knows I can't be trusted any more than I do.

I open up the pizza and place it on my desk. "Help yourself."

She looks hesitant for a moment. "I can take a slice out to my desk."

I frown. "If you'd prefer that, I won't stop you. But you're welcome to stay and eat with me." Now why did I go and make that offer? *Because you're a sucker for pain, that's why.*

A side effect of having a junkie for a father and an abuse victim for a mother, I suppose.

She doesn't talk through the first slice. Her eyes keep veering toward the view just behind me. Every time I'm on the verge of asking her what she's thinking, I stop myself. *You don't need to know.* Her thoughts are hers alone.

"How did it feel?" she asks suddenly, breaking the silence. "To move here after Scottsdale?"

I raise my eyebrows. "Terrifying," I admit. "At the time, I thought I was being brave. I thought I was taking control of my life and getting out of a bad situation. But… hindsight?" I look up at her. "I might have just been running."

"What's wrong with that?" she asks. "I mean, from what I've heard of your childhood, it was far from idyllic. You can't be blamed for wanting to head for the hills and leave all that dysfunction behind."

I shake my head. "I cut and run. I abandoned my family. That's a coward's move. You don't leave family behind."

She raises her eyebrows. "Says the man who said only last night that the best thing some parents can do is leave."

I cringe. "Caught that, did you?"

"It was hard to miss."

"Fuck," I mutter. "I regretted it the moment it came out of my mouth."

She shrugs. "You don't have to apologize for how you feel," she says with a tiny little smile that doesn't quite reach her eyes. "But an explanation would be nice."

I smirk. "I guess I define family differently. Family is who you *choose*, not who you're born to. If you're not willing to choose your kid, then maybe… you don't deserve that kid."

Her eyes soften a little but she looks away too fast for me to catch the expression in them. "Did you have any friends growing up, apart from my parents?"

I raise my eyebrows. "So much for light dinner conversation."

"Just answer the question."

Sighing, I take a piece of pizza. "No. Daniel and Kristen were it."

"How come?"

I shrug. "Because I didn't need anyone else. And honestly, I didn't have the time to invest in new friendships and there were very few kids who would've understood the shit show I came from."

"It can't have been that bad."

If she only knew…

"I was luckier than some," I say. "I got by. Your parents certainly helped."

"What were they like together?"

I suppose a part of me is expecting this. Clearly, Daniel doesn't spend a lot of time talking about Kristen and I was her only source of information. My ego definitely takes a hit but I convince myself to see this as a good thing. She's interested in finding out about her mother. Maybe when she knows enough, this weird *thing* between us will just kinda fade away. Maybe one day, we can forget it altogether?

"They were a pretty great couple, to be honest," I admit. "They kinda balanced each other out. Your Dad was the sensible voice of reason and Kristen was the free-spirited, adventurous one. There was one day when I woke up in the middle of the night because Dad was screaming at Mum. I went down there and he was beating her up. I was twelve and past the point of hiding under my bed until the storm passed. So I went down. I told him to get off her."

Her eyes go wide and she puts down her slice of pizza. "So he stopped hitting her. And he started hitting me. He didn't stop until I was unconscious."

"What?"

I probably shouldn't have told her that part. "It was fine. He hadn't broken anything that time—"

"Meaning he had broken things in the past?" she gasps.

"Well… there were two ribs when I was eight and a broken nose when I was fifteen."

"Jesus."

I shrug. "Honestly, the physical shit is the easiest to recover from. It's amazing how fast the human body can heal. Anyway, I went to the kitchen and I checked the time. It was almost time for school but when I went to get ready, I realized that my face was a mess. I had a split lip, a black eye and a ton of bruises. Your Dad, Kristen and I used to ride our bikes to school every day and when I didn't show, they came to the house to check on me."

"Daniel gets quiet when he gets upset. Kristen got proactive. She decided that we were all gonna play hooky from school. We were gonna grab a bus and head down to Fountain Hills. Hell, she was ready to ride our bikes there if we had to."

"And… did you?"

"Hell yeah, we did," I smile. "We stopped at every bakery along the way and ate our weight in sugar. It kept us going till we reached Fountain Hills. Then we sat by the water and talked about our future plans. Neither one of them ever asked me what happened or how I felt. They were just there for me."

"That's a nice story."

"If it were up to me or your Dad, we'd have been playing video games in Dan's room till the sun went down. When it came to Kristen though—she wanted to go out into the world. She wanted to *do* things."

Ashley nods. "I suppose that explains why she left."

I bite my tongue to keep from justifying her decision. I don't want to make excuses for Kristen. It's not my place to. But I do want Ashley to understand that Kristen was more than just that one decision.

"She volunteered at a soup kitchen every Thursday evening."

Ashley's eyes go wide. "She did?"

I nod. "And she baked cookies for the police department and the fire department every Christmas. Even roped Daniel and me into distributing them a couple of years in a row."

"I don't think of her as a villain, you know," Ashley says softly. "I assume that's why you're telling me about all her Good Samaritanism. But you don't have to. As I said, I don't think of her as a villain. You've got the wrong Payne."

"I just want you to know that she was a three-dimensional person. She was kind and funny and fearless. But she was equally insecure and frightened and stubborn. She definitely wasn't a villain but she was never the hero too."

"You talk about her as though she was."

I smile. "I suppose, because in some ways, she was a hero to me. So was your Dad."

"Did it hurt you too… when she left?"

I nod. "Yes, I suppose it did. But I can't say that it came as a complete shock."

She sits up a little straighter. "So… you saw it coming?"

I drop my gaze and focus on the pizza. "How about we eat this thing before it gets cold, huh?"

She doesn't press me for an answer. She bites into her pizza and I try not to watch her chew. "How's California treating you so far?" I ask, hoping for a nice innocent change of topic from here on out.

"It's been… fine."

"Wow, so much enthusiasm."

She smirks. "I wake up, I come to work, I go home. Then the cycle repeats itself all over again. That's pretty much my life in California so far."

"You need to get out more."

I look around. "My boss works me to the bone."

"I dismissed you three times today."

She shrugs. "I know."

"So why didn't you leave at five like the rest of them?"

She meets my eyes for only a second. "Because you're here."

I have no idea if I'm meant to take that at face value or if perhaps she means it in a different way—a romantic way. I'm too chicken shit to ask.

"Molly from the design team mentioned there was a rooftop somewhere in the building. She claims it has grass and everything."

"Fake grass. But yeah."

Her eyes go wide. "Are you serious?"

I raise my eyebrows. "Do you really think I'd lie about fake grass?"

She gets to her feet. "Can you show me?"

She looks like a kid on Christmas morning. How can I say no to her? I find myself getting to my feet and walking around my desk. "Just for a bit, okay?"

She nods emphatically. "Sure."

As we walk to the elevator together, I sneak a peek at her profile. I can see both Daniel and Kristen in her. But that's not why I'm drawn to her. Ironically, I'm drawn to all the parts of her that *don't* remind me of my best friends.

The dimple on her left cheek. The birthmark at the corner of her chin. The way her eyes wrinkle at the edges when she smiles. The way she plays with her nails when she's nervous.

Unlike her parents, Ashley is shy and cautious. She's pragmatic like Daniel and bold like Kristen but there's a vulnerability in her that's all her own. It has a way of drawing me in when I should be leaning out.

Which is probably why going up to the rooftop with her

right now is not a good idea. And still, I can't seem to press abort on this little escapade.

"Can you see the stars from the rooftop?" she asks, bouncing on the heels of her feet.

I smile; her small-town naiveté is endearing. "It's LA, Ashley. You don't get stars; you get smog. But if a plane flies low enough, we can pretend it's a star."

That gets a smile outta her and it burns brighter than any fucking star in the sky.

CHAPTER 19

Ashley

I t's amazing up here.

There's fake grass, as promised, and a couple of potted plants that line the railing's edge. The wind is pretty strong up here and it makes everything five degrees colder but it's worth it to see the city sprawled out at our feet.

Not to mention the stars hanging above us in the sky. The city lights are probably hiding billions more but I can imagine all of them up there, looking down at us and laughing at the problems people create for themselves.

"Wow… I know I see this view every day. But somehow, it feels different out here."

Tobias steps to my side. He's always careful not to stand too close. There's a respectable two feet of space between us.

"Different how?"

"I don't know. It just feels… bigger somehow. There's life in the air." I draw in a big gulp of air. "You can *hear* everything, smell everything, feel everything. Everything feels electric."

When he doesn't respond, I glance to the side to find him

staring at me with a smile on his face that I can't decipher. "Do I sound like a crazy person?"

He chuckles. "No. Just a person who's uprooted her entire life for another city. You just reminded me of how I felt when I first moved here."

I sigh. "Sometimes it doesn't matter how much you want it. It's still scary."

"That's true."

"Dad's here because of me," I admit quietly.

"Of course he is. He didn't come to California for me."

I shake my head. "No. I mean... the first few days after I moved here, I really struggled. Had a couple of panic attacks, called him in the middle of the night crying hysterically." I spare him a throwaway glance. Pretty sure my cheeks are burning up right now. "I'm not proud of it."

"It's not something you need to be ashamed of."

"I'm twenty years old, Tobias," I point out. "What twenty-year-old calls her Dad crying because she moved cities?"

"Uh, literally most twenty-year-olds," I insist. "Change is hard, Ashley, no matter how old you are. You're entirely too hard on yourself."

I close my eyes for a second and breathe in that crisp wintery air. "Why is it that the things we're scared of are the very things we need to do in order to be happy?"

He raises his eyebrows. "You weren't happy in Scottsdale?"

"I think I was for a while. But then I got restless. Dissatisfied. I had this feeling that if I didn't make a change now, I wouldn't ever make one. I'd just grow old in that town, surrounded by the same old people, working the same kind of job, settling for the life I was born into instead of chasing the life I wanted."

"And what kind of life do you want?"

I shake my head. "That's the thing—I don't know. I thought moving here would help me figure it out. But all it did was make things more confusing." I run my fingers through my hair. "The truth is—I'm not really good at this."

"At what?"

I shrug. "Life."

"I think everyone feels that way at twenty."

I shake my head. "You don't get it. You had Dad and Kristen when you were a teenager. Me? I had no one. I wasn't really good at making friends. I never really fit in at school and I guess the other kids could smell it on me."

"Smell what exactly?"

"The fact that I didn't belong."

"That's ridiculous."

"It's true."

"Is it though? Or is it just the excuse you make to yourself."

"Excuse?" I ask, doing a double take. "What am I excusing exactly?"

"The fact that you never let anyone get close enough to *be* your friend."

I frown. "And why would I do that?"

"Maybe because… you didn't want anyone else leaving you like Kristen did."

My eyes go wide. My jaw drops open. I can feel the heat flood my face. "You know what? Screw you!"

I whip around, ready to leave the rooftop and head back downstairs. I'm so pissed I decide to leave before he does. But he grabs my arm and pulls me back around. I stumble forward and almost smack my face against his chest.

Damn, that's a broad chest.

"I'm sorry. That was way out of line."

I try to pull out of his grip, but he's got a tight hold on me. "Damn straight it was. Just because you fucked me a couple of times, Tobias, doesn't mean you know me."

He drops my arm immediately. "Low blow, Ashley."

"Fuck," I mutter under my breath. "That… that just came out."

"Yeah…"

"I'm sorry."

"You don't have anything to apologize for," he says curtly. "You're right. I *don't* know you. And you don't know me."

My chest tightens at those words. Probably because, despite my angry words, I *do* feel like Tobias knows me. Or at least, it feels like he sees me. And that makes me believe that he has the potential to really understand me.

Not that he seems to want to anymore.

"You may actually be right," I admit softly. "Which is probably why I got so mad. I am constantly afraid that the people I care about will leave."

"So you do it first?"

"Not always." I lift my eyes to his. "I thought I was in love once. I don't know… maybe I was. It's hard to tell when you're sixteen."

His lips tighten into a flat line. "Who was the guy?"

"His name was Henry. He moved to Scottsdale from Seattle. The first time I saw him was in English Lit. He walked in with his feathery blonde hair and his easy smile and a jacket that was so cool I thought my head was gonna explode."

Tobias gives me a smile. "And you fell in love at first sight?"

I snort. "Hardly. But I did think he was the prettiest boy I'd ever seen."

"What happened?"

"We started dating, stole a few kisses between classes, called each other late at night and had long heartfelt conversations. It was the first time I felt like I had something that was truly mine."

Tobias shuffles in place. "Did he meet Daniel?"

"We were together for almost two years, so yeah, he met Dad."

"And? Did the old man approve of the boyfriend?"

Tobias's questions are coming a little too fast and a little too sharp to feel like a relaxed conversation but I decide not to read too much into it. That's probably just my own brain trying to trip me up. Trying to sabotage me into believing... or hoping that maybe he might be just a tiny bit jealous.

I laugh. "You know him. He's always been the cool Dad. He's only ever had one rule for me my entire life. Do not lie. About anything."

"It's a good rule."

"Yeah, and I'm breaking it for you."

He sighs. "We're not lying to him... we're just not telling him everything. There's a difference."

I shake my head. "I don't think there is, to be honest." I turn and start walking to the opposite side of the rooftop. The wind has picked up in the last couple of minutes. It's now howling so loud that I have to raise my voice if I want Tobias to hear me.

"Do you come up here often?"

"Never."

"Seriously? But it's so nice up here."

I shrug. "I don't really have the time."

"Not even when you work late and have the whole building to yourself?"

He smirks. "I'm not wired that way. I sit at my desk until everything's finished. Then I go home to my empty apartment. That's been the routine for the last several years."

"What about friends?"

"I don't have friends."

I raise my eyebrows. "We have that in common. But then again... you *do* have friends, don't you?" He looks mildly perplexed for a moment. "The woman you were having dinner with the night we met. The pretty one."

"Right."

"Does friends with benefits really work?"

"It has for me."

"You don't strike me as the type of guy who's afraid of commitment."

He looks at me questioningly. "It's not commitment I'm afraid of. I just haven't met a woman I want to have a full-blown relationship with. That hasn't changed."

I can't deny that it doesn't hurt. But I keep my expression neutral. "So when you asked to meet me again the night we met... that was just what? Cheap entertainment."

"I see a pretty girl. I talk to her. If we hit it off, we meet again. Maybe even a third time. But that's usually as far as it goes."

He looks slightly uncomfortable but he delivers the words without any apology. I turn my gaze to the city lights. "We have more in common than you think, Tobias."

"How's that?"

I shrug. "Remember what you told me earlier? I don't form friendships or relationships because I'm so scared that they'll leave me?"

"Yeah."

"You might have the same problem."

There's a little crease in his forehead that wasn't there

before. He clears his throat and takes a deep breath. "You never finished your story. What happened with Henry?"

"You already know what happened with Henry," I say, closing my eyes. "He left me."

When I open my eyes, he's looking right at me. "Why?"

I shrug. "He wanted more for his life. He wanted more than me."

Tobias shakes his head. "His leaving had nothing to do with you."

"How do you know? You don't know anything about Henry or about our relationship. You certainly don't know me. So how can you say that with so much confidence?"

"Because I know you enough to know that no man in his right mind would leave you unless he had shit he needed to deal with."

"Sounds like an excuse."

"Doesn't make it any less true."

I sigh. "You don't have to comfort me, Tobias. That's not why I'm telling you any of this."

"Why *are* you telling me this?"

I turn to him, my eyes going wide as I try to examine my own reasons. "You know what?" I say so softly that I'm not sure if he can even hear me. "I have no fucking idea."

He takes a step towards me and stares at me so intensely that I can't break away even if I try. His hand rises to my face and I feel his fingers graze across my cheek. It's cold out here but that simple touch warms me up instantly.

"You are so much more amazing than you give yourself credit for, Ashley. Truly."

"I bet you say that to all your women."

His jaw clenches and his eyes flash with anger. "You are *not* one of my women."

"Right. Forget. I'm just a distraction, huh?"

His teeth grind together and I wonder what's pissing him off so much. He doesn't stop touching me. He doesn't lean away either. "No. You're meant for more, Ashley Payne."

"More than what?"

"This city. This job. Me."

I frown. "Is this a new and innovative take on the whole *it's me, not you* spiel. Because I don't think I can—"

"Jesus Christ, Ashley!" He's so forceful that my mouth snaps shut. "Don't you see? Maybe Henry did you a favor by walking away. Maybe that's what I'm doing too."

"You're not walking away from me. You're hiding. There's a difference."

"You would know."

I scowl, aware of the fact that we're only a few inches apart. If he or I take another step closer our noses will be touching. I can catch his oaky scent. I can see the vibrant blue of his eyes. They put the city lights to shame.

"You know what I'm sick of? People deciding that they know what's best for me. I may be young but I'm no idiot, Tobias."

"I know that."

"Then stop giving me lame fucking excuses. None of this *I don't deserve you* bullshit. Stop pretending like this is about you or me."

"What—"

"This is about the fact that my father means more to you than I do."

He freezes, his eyes going wide as he stares down at me. "Ashley…"

I smile sadly. "See? You can't even deny it."

He swallows, his eyes tearing away from me to look out over the city. He takes a deep breath. "We should really get back inside."

I nod in defeat and turn my back on the view. It was silly of me to think I could be someone new in this city. As it turns out, you can't leave your baggage behind.

It just follows you wherever you go.

CHAPTER 20

Tobias

There was a moment up on that rooftop balcony when I'd leaned in.

She was telling me things that were hard for her. She was trusting me with secrets that she'd kept close to her heart. She looked so damn sad. And all I wanted to do was make her feel better. Make her smile.

I hadn't done either.

Instead, I'd almost made things a hundred times worse by kissing her. Thankfully, my sense of reason had kicked in just in time to stop myself. We'd gone back downstairs, finished the last of our work and headed off in our separate directions. I'd offered her a lift, of course, but she turned me down and I didn't insist.

Because I'm just *that* weak at the moment.

Now, I'm sitting alone in my four-bedroom penthouse, wondering why I felt like a stranger in my own home. I look around the blank walls and try to find something personal there that'll make me feel better. A memento from my childhood. Something that belonged to my mother. A keepsake from school.

But there's nothing.

Because I'd left everything behind when I moved to California, I'd abandoned all the things that I used to think were important. I heave myself off the couch and head to the bar in the kitchen. I pour myself an expensive glass of Vodka, the kind that would rack up an eighty-dollar bill for one tiny glass. I take a sip and walk it into my bedroom.

I head into the walk-in closet and sit down on the carpeted floor at the very back. There are three locked drawers at the bottom and the last one is where my shoebox is. It's a small black Nike box that remains one of my prized possessions. I'd worn out the shoes years ago but I'd kept the box to store the things that I didn't want to get rid of but couldn't bear to see every day.

I open up the box and look inside. When was the last time I did this? Probably a couple of years ago on Mum's death anniversary.

I cross my legs and look through the contents of the box. A couple of birthday cards—store-bought from Daniel. Handmade from Kristen. She went through a glitter phase at one point. There's still glitter at the bottom of the box from one of her cards.

There's a crumpled-up one-dollar note from the first paycheck I ever earned. A button off Nancy Pierson's blouse that I'd found under the bleachers right after we'd shared our first kiss. An essay I wrote in sixth grade that won me my first and only prize. A recommendation letter from my favorite teacher, Mrs. Svendsen, that I never ended up using. And then I pull it out.

The letter.

The one that I was always meant to show Daniel but never did.

The one that I've kept secret for so long that mentioning it now seems pointless.

Of course, if I even consider telling him about the letter now, I'll also have to tell him about everything that followed. I already know what Daniel will say to that. He'll feel as though I've betrayed him. And it's not like I can disagree.

"Fuck," I mutter, staring at the letter in my hand.

It's a double betrayal now. Now that Ashley is involved too. She's going to hate me if she finds out. Which is another reason I can't possibly be with her. Even if we were to push Daniel to the side and assume he'd come around eventually, how can I enter into any kind of involvement with Ashley when I'm keeping this huge secret from her?

It's impossible.

Which is why keeping my distance is the best-case scenario for all of us. The problem is in the execution.

I'm hoping that after six months to a year of experience, I can write her a recommendation letter that allows her to be hired by another big wig company. I'm on a semi-friendly basis with the CEOs of at least three different companies in the city. I could get her a great gig somewhere else and still feel like I'm being a good friend. But until a significant period of time has passed, it'll just strike Daniel as strange that I'm trying to send his daughter off elsewhere when I agreed to hire her in the first place.

I run a hand through my hair and try to figure out how I'm gonna manage the next year or so.

Ring. Ring. Ring.

I pick up my phone and answer without checking to see who it is. "Hello?"

"Hey, handsome."

Ah. Right.

"Hey, Jasmin."

"I got your text earlier today. I'll admit, it took me the better part of the evening to decide whether I was gonna call you back or just ignore it."

"You called."

She sighs. "I did. The last time we spoke was… what was it? A year ago? Two?"

"Something like that."

"I didn't really expect to hear from you again."

"Can I take you out for dinner sometime?" I chug on boldly.

"Seriously?"

"Yes."

There's a pause on the other side of the line. "Why?"

"Because… I want another chance."

"By that you mean you want to rekindle our whole no-strings-attached agreement? Because I gotta tell you, Toby, I'm past the point of meaningless sex and casual flings. It's the whole reason we ended things in the first place, remember? You wanted meaningless and casual. I wanted more."

I frown. "I never said that."

"You didn't have to. Any time I tried to have a real conversation with you, you shut me down. Anytime we did anything remotely relationship-y, you became distant. Any time I so much as tried to talk about my feelings, you ran the other way."

Shit.

"I did that, didn't I?"

"I got the message loud and clear. But this time, if you want to have dinner, I need to know where you stand. All cards on the table here, Toby."

"I'm tired of casual and meaningless too, Jas," I admit. "I want someone to come home to. I want someone to fall asleep to every night and wake up to every morning. I want more than just transitory relationships."

"That all sounds very confident."

"Because it's true."

"So... dinner?"

"I figure it's a start. Have one meal with me and if you decide you don't like me anymore, you can walk away. And I'll respect that."

She considers that for a second. "Okay, I suppose one date won't hurt me. You're paying."

"I wouldn't have it any other way."

"How about tomorrow at the Blue Ivy? I've always wanted to go. You can definitely pull some strings and get us in on short notice, right?"

"I can."

"Great, I'll meet you there at eight?"

"Uh, actually, would you mind stopping by the office first?" I ask, feeling like an A-grade schmuck when I make the request. "We can go to the restaurant together from there."

"Sure, I can do that. See you tomorrow, handsome."

"See you tomorrow, Jas."

I hang up and stare down at my phone for a second. I'd gone and done it now. As far as I was concerned, it was a cold way to go about it but it would get the message across. The moment Ashley sees Jasmin walking into my office tomorrow, she'd know that there is no hope for us.

I'm not planning on just using Jasmin either. I was serious about everything I'd said to her. I *do* want something serious, something real. And the closest I came to feeling a real connection with anyone—was her.

I used to tell myself that the timing was off when it came to Jasmin. She was beautiful and smart and definitely my type. But I couldn't commit to anything more than sex at the time. It had been the same for her in the beginning. But eight months in, things started to change for her. And I'd be lying if I said I didn't notice.

When she ended our arrangement, a part of me was relieved. I didn't want to have to pretend any longer. And the truth was—I was too stuck inside my own head to be a decent boyfriend. I didn't have the mental or emotional bandwidth to be there for another human being.

Not when I felt like I was drowning.

I finish my Vodka and put everything back in the Nike shoe box. Then I head out into the living room of my lifeless apartment and wonder who I did all this for. I end up putting my shoes on and getting out for a walk. I hadn't done that since I moved to California. Ever since the company started making money, I drove everywhere. Or I was driven. Late-night walks became a thing of the past.

The streets are still bustling despite the fact that it's approaching midnight. By the time I stop to think about where I'm going, I realize that I've walked myself right into Ashley's neighborhood.

How is it possible that even when I'm not thinking about her, I'm thinking about her?

And why her?

I've always had my pick of women. So why is *she* the one who's stuck in my head like a fever dream that won't let go?

I end up in an old school bar with a swing door and the kind of lighting that makes you feel like you're in the 1970s. The bartender is an older guy with a handlebar mustache and light watery eyes that make you want to bear your soul.

"Can I get a Whiskey… on the rocks?"

"You got it."

He's got a slightly Southern twang to his accent. "Alabama?" I ask.

"Tennessee," he smiles. "Left four decades ago though. Sometimes, I think I've lost the accent. Then some little prick walks in and calls me out."

I smirk. "Sorry."

He bows his head. "You a native?"

"Nah. I'm a transplant like you. Arizonian."

"No shit. My Mama was from Arizona. She met my Daddy when she was seventeen and moved to the south."

"Did she regret it?"

"Probably did. My Mama was never much of a talker. She was a doer. She worked hard. Pushed out seven babies and held down two jobs while she did it."

"Damn."

He chuckles. "Woman was made of stone."

"What was your Dad made out of?"

"Alcohol mostly."

I raise my glass. "Our dads had a lot in common. Although with mine, it was forty percent alcohol, sixty percent weed and crack."

The bartender raises his eyebrows. "You dress good for a crack addict's kid."

"Nicest compliment I've received in a while." I finish my drink and slam it back down on the counter. "Another, please."

He pours me another drink wordlessly and slides it across the counter towards me. "Parents, huh? Sometimes they make you. Sometimes, they break you. It's a toss of the coin on which kind you get stuck with."

"Was he a good Dad?"

The bartender raises his eyebrows. He must be in his seventies, late sixties at least. "My Daddy? I think he tried to be. But in the end, he chose alcohol over us kids. Over our Mama too and he loved her something silly."

"Did he really?" I ask. "If he couldn't stop drinking for her?"

The bartender shrugs. "It ain't that simple, boy. You can be two things at the same time. You can love a woman and hurt her. You can yell at your kids and still want the best for them. My Daddy was beat on by his own old man. He called us every cuss word in the book but he never once laid a hand on us. That's how we knew he loved us."

I've made quick work of that second drink. I'm wondering if the bartender is judging me. I know I'm judging myself right now. He eyes me curiously.

"Where's your Daddy now?"

I know I've just had two, no—three drinks but I'm already jonesing for another. Except if I ask for another then where does that leave me?

Just like him.

"My Dad?" I repeat. "He's in jail."

CHAPTER 21

Ashley

"You look like a girl who appreciates a good concert."

I give Ashton an awkward smile. "Doesn't everyone?"

He shrugs. "Actually, I had a girlfriend in high school who hated them. Then again, she turned into a raging agoraphobic, so maybe that's why."

I snort. "Does this conversation have a point?" I ask. "Because you're blocking my way into the lunchroom and I'm hungry."

He raises his eyebrows and looks down at his watch. "It's almost six o'clock."

"What's your point?"

"Um… you didn't eat lunch."

"I worked through lunch."

"Huh. Overachiever?"

"More like a harder worker."

"Same difference."

I have to try very hard not to roll my eyes. I thought Ashton was quite funny when I first met him last week. He was a PA for one of the other company execs. He wasn't bad looking either. There were definitely a few temps who had a crush on the guy.

I'm just not sure that Ashton and I have much in common. For one, it's clear that he comes from a rich family. That's evident enough from the suits he wears to work and the way he acts as though every single task he's assigned is beneath him. It had been funnier when I thought he was just hamming it up to make everyone laugh. Whole other thing is knowing that the dude's serious.

I push past him and head to the lunch room to rifle through the snack drawer. Ackerman Corp. lunchroom offerings are always on point. The sandwiches and salads are great, and every once in a while, there's a pasta cart that rolls around. Today, however, I have to contend with the leftovers from lunch. I settled for the last roast beef sandwich and a packet of barbeque chips.

"So anyway… like I said, concerts."

"Uh-huh, what about them?" I ask, sitting down at a table overlooking part of the city.

"There's one coming up next month. Coldplay. You interested?"

I raise my eyebrows. Sure, Ashton flirts with me from time to time. But then again, he flirts with everyone. I didn't think that would translate into a date.

"Um, are other people from the floor going?"

He frowns. "No. I was kinda hoping this would be a you-me kinda thing."

"Right. Coldplay, did you say?"

"Yup."

"I'm more of a Florence and the Machine kinda gal."

It's true that I love Florence and the Machine, but I also love Coldplay. I'd happily go to a concert if I could afford the price of a ticket. I'd have jumped at the chance to see them live if the man asking was someone I was actually interested in.

Like my broody boss.

I push the desire away. He's not asking.

"Oh, come on. You can't pass up the opportunity to see Coldplay perform. Hear they're great live."

"I'm sure they are."

"I've got on the rail tickets too."

My eyes go wide. "Jesus, that must have cost you a fortune."

He gives me a self-satisfied smirk. "My parents are kinda friends with one of Coldplay's managers. He scored us the best tickets in the house."

Definitely a rich kid.

"That's really cool, Ashton, but this is next month, right? I don't like to make plans too far in advance. Can I let you know?"

He looks kinda stunned. I'm kinda stunned myself. Why shouldn't I go on a date with this guy? Sure, he's a privileged rich kid with an ego. But that's no crime. He is polite, he can be funny and he seems pretty popular around the office.

With the long blonde hair and those blue eyes, he's got that whole pretty boy rock-star vibe going for him too. He's also twenty-four, which means he's age-appropriate.

The best part? He's not best friends with my father.

The decision should be easy. But I find myself sticking to my guns. Apparently, Ashton has the same idea. "Okay, no worries. How about dinner sometime then?"

Damn it.

"I work late most nights."

"You don't work weekends."

I've got to hand it to the guy—he's persistent. Then again,

he's also probably not used to rejection. Saying no to him will only make him dig deeper into his feelings.

"True, but my father's in town at the moment and my weekends are spent showing him around the city and stuff."

"Ha," he crosses his legs and settles into the chair. "That sounds nightmarish."

I raise my eyebrows. "Actually, it's not for me. My Dad and I are close."

"Then you're lucky. My Dad's an A-grade asshole and I think he's getting worse with age."

I laugh. "I'm sure he's not that bad."

Ashton nods. "You're right. Just typical father issues, you know. He wanted me to come to work for him at his hedge fund firm after I graduated from Princeton."

"Not your calling?"

"Nah, more like I didn't want to be at his beck and call 24/7. It's all about control with the old man. So I decided to stick it to him and join this company. It really riles him up knowing that I'd turned him down for this job."

"Worth it?"

"Definitely. The pay's shit compared with what I would have earned with him but at least here I know that I'm not getting a fat paycheck just cause I'm the boss's son."

Okay, that definitely earns him my respect. Not that I can afford to have much of an opinion, considering that the only reason I have a job at this company is because my father begged his friend to hire me.

Not that I'm rushing to divulge that information to anyone any time soon.

"I'd have done the same thing."

He smiles. "So… close with your Dad, huh? What's that like?"

I take a bite of my sandwich and shrug. "Pretty nice, actually. He's all I had growing up. It makes for a strong relationship."

"Ah. Makes sense." I'm grateful that he doesn't ask what happened to my mother. I'm really not interested in getting into the whole *my-mother-abandoned-me-at-birth* sob story.

"He was also super young when he had me. We kinda grew up together."

Ashton raises his eyebrows. "How young are we talking?"

"Sixteen."

"Fuck."

I nod. "Yeah. He dropped outta high school and started working full-time, all so that he could support me. He had help from his parents, of course, but they were on the older side, so they couldn't do all that much."

"What kinda jobs did your Dad work?"

"By day, he was a mechanic, and by night, he was a bartender."

"He sounds fucking cool."

I smile. "That's the general consensus."

"No wonder you're so cool."

I raise my eyebrows and try not to blush. I'm not gonna lie. It's nice getting compliments from pretty boys, even if you're not necessarily interested in them. It's still a nice ego boost. And my ego needs a boost what with all the rejection I've had to deal with lately.

Tobias had barely said two words to me all day. I'd basically just hung around my desk, trying to figure out how to get him to look at me, talk to me. It was getting to the point where I was just desperate enough to storm into his office and ask him what the hell his problem was.

Then I remind myself that he's still the boss and I'm the one he's doing a favor for.

"You're even prettier when you blush."

I hide my face behind my bottle of water. "Compliments make me uncomfortable."

"Clearly." He chuckles a little more and then thankfully changes the subject. "So... how's the new job treating you?"

"It's fine."

It feels like he's looking at me a little too closely when he asks the question. "Yeah? So Mr. Ackerman's a good boss?"

"I don't have much to compare him with but yeah, he's a good boss."

"Doesn't ride you too hard or anything?"

Actually, the last time, I was the one doing the riding. On the heels of that thought comes another blush that I'm fairly certain I manage to hide.

"No," I say, clearing my throat. "He doesn't."

Ashton rolls his eyes. "Everyone in this place thinks the sun shines outta his ass. But honestly, they only think that goes he's halfway decent looking."

I have to suppress a smile. The 'halfway decent looking' comment tells me that Ashton has noticed *just* how good-looking Tobias really is and it's making little Mr. Pretty Boy feel all kinds of insecure.

"He is extremely attractive." Oh, okay, so I'm riling him up a little. A girl's gotta have a little fun every now and again.

"You think so?" Ashton asks, wrinkling his nose up. "Really?"

"Only if you like chiseled jawlines, baby blues and the features of a Greek God."

"Jesus," I smirk at the sinking look on Ashton's face. "That's some description." I chuckle and reach for my water. "Whatever. You know he's a massive player, right? Has a revolving roster of women he fucks on the regular."

I wrinkle my nose. "With a face like that, I'm not surprised."

"Would you be interested in him?"

I tense up, instantly regretting my decision to tease Ashton. "He's a lot older than me."

"Thirty-five," Ashton shrugs. "My Dad's seventeen years older than my mother. It's worked for them so far."

"Right. Well um… no. He's my boss."

"Some would say that's the perfect position to have if you want a rich, white guy's attention."

I clear my throat. "Well, I don't want his attention." *Total lie but he doesn't have to know that.* "I just want to work hard, keep my head down and get that paycheck at the end of every work."

"Simple goals."

"Achievable goals," I correct. "Now, if you'll excuse me, I gotta get back to work."

"Seriously? The workday's almost over."

"Not for me."

I throw my sandwich wrapper in the trash and give Ashton a parting wave, completely aware of the fact that I've actively avoiding accepting two date invitations from him. Even if I wasn't totally hung up on my boss, I'm not sure Ashton would be my type. Embarrassing as it is to admit, I'd really only flirted with him for the validation his attention gave me.

When I get back to my desk, I look through the files on my desk. I'm just about to start organizing them when I hear the steady *click-clack* of heels against the glossy tile. I look up just in time to see the ethereal blonde wrapped in a skin-tight bandage dress look down at me.

She's got on smoky eye make-up, a red lip and the kind of smile that could convince a priest to forsake his vows.

"Hey there. You're new. Where's Julianne?"

"Um—retired."

She nods. "How long have you worked here?"

"Couple of weeks."

She smiles. "Right. Well I don't want to keep you. I have a dinner date with Mr. Ackerman."

I get to my feet. "I'll let him know that—"

She waves her hand in my face. "Don't bother. I'll go in and announce my presence myself. Thanks."

She disappears into his office but before giving me a full view of her ass, which is predictably perfect and expertly framed in that dress. A dress that has *seductress* written all over it. Not to mention the come-hither makeup that I'd never be able to achieve even if I watched all the makeup tutorials in the world.

My heart feels like it's gained a couple of pounds in the last few seconds. I feel sick. Angry. Annoyed. Confused. There are a few too many emotions rattling around in my head to keep track of.

Fuck.

Fuck.

That woman is definitely not here for business. No one wears a dress like that unless she's trying to catch someone's attention. Apparently, he'd dipped into his endless roster of women that Ashton had mentioned not five minutes ago.

He's dating other women right in front of me. Surely he's trying to get a message across? Maybe he just wants to rub it in my face?

Or worse. What if he hasn't even given me a second thought? Maybe he's just getting on with his life?

My eyes are clouding up a little when I pull up his schedule and look through his appointment booklet. There it is, right in front of me.

Friday 8.00 pm. Dinner with Jasmin at the Blue Ivy.

I wipe the moisture from my eyes and start moving fast

down the hall. I'm very aware that I'm not thinking clearly. But instead of telling myself to slow down, calm down and *breathe*, I just move faster.

I veer down the corridor and make a left. Ashton is at his desk, gathering up his things. "Ashley?" he says when he sees me. "Everything okay?"

I nod, doing my best to look as though nothing is wrong. "Yup. I was just thinking… you free tonight?"

His eyebrows rise and I feel a twinge of guilt. "Dinner tonight?" he asks. "As in… a date?"

"Uh-huh," I nod. "You game?"

He smiles. "Fuck yeah, I'm game. What did you have in mind?"

Don't do it.

"I've heard the Blue Ivy is really great."

Damn it.

CHAPTER 22
Tobias

"**Y**our new receptionist is pretty."

It's the first thing she says to me when I sit down beside her at our primo table in the very center of the restaurant.

I pick up my menu and turn it over. "I hadn't really noticed. Would you like a white wine tonight or a red?"

"You haven't really noticed?" Jasmin asks, narrowing her eyes pointedly. "Bullshit."

Sighing, I put my menu down and look up at her. "Do you really wanna talk about my PA?"

"Calling her a PA doesn't make the position any more respectable."

"What's wrong with being a PA?" I demand, instantly on the defensive.

She shrugs. "Nothing, I suppose. If you can't find a real job."

I narrow my eyes. "Were you always this much of a snob or is that a new thing?" I go back to looking at my menu, wondering how this date had gone off the rails so fast.

And we haven't even ordered appetizers yet.

"Shit," Jasmin murmurs under her breath. "I'm sorry. I'm being a bitch."

I look up at her. "What's going on?"

"I just… I suppose I'm not interested in playing second fiddle to anyone."

I take a deep breath. "I'm not a cheater, Jas. If I'm with you, I'm with you. If you don't want me to date other women while we're together, then I can do that."

She raises her eyebrows. "Seriously?"

"Yes."

"This is only our first date."

"Well I guess I know what I have to do if I want a second one."

She looks both pleasantly surprised and a little skeptical. "Can I ask what brought around this change?"

I shrug. "I guess I'm growing up. Having many different women has lost its appeal. I like the idea of coming home to one woman every single day."

Jasmin's eyes light up. "So… you're really ready for a real commitment?" she asks. "Marriage, kids—the whole nine yards?"

I tense. "Well… eventually yes. But right now, I can commit to exclusivity. I just don't know when I'll be ready for… the rest of it."

"But you do want kids, don't you?"

"Jasmin—"

She sighs. "Listen, my therapist told me that I needed to be upfront with my dates about what I want. It's about setting expectations, being upfront with my partners about my needs. If you're not interested in what I want—then maybe we shouldn't be wasting our time dating."

I nod. "That sounds… smart."

"Which is why I want to know—do you want children some day?"

Jesus.

"I guess. Maybe. One day."

She raises her eyebrows. Clearly, my answer has disappointed her. "Wow, that was enthusiastic."

"I'm sorry but right now I'm not sure that I want children. And honestly, I'm not sure I'll *ever* want children."

Her eyes go wide. "Ever?"

I nod. "I didn't exactly have the best parents growing up. I didn't have any good examples to follow. I'm not sure I'd be good at it."

She leans back in her chair but before she can lob her next question at me, the waitress appears to take our orders. I order the duck, Jasmin orders a salad, and once the wine is poured, the waitress retreats, leaving us to our awkward conversation, which at this rate feels more like I'm interviewing for a position.

The position of husband and baby daddy.

My palms have even started to sweat. "Listen, Jas, I get this is important to you, but maybe it's a little premature to be talking about marriage and babies."

"I have an end goal here, Toby," she says firmly. "I'm past the point of just dating and seeing where it goes. I want to know that the man I'm dating wants the same things I want."

"That's fair."

"It seems you still don't know what you want." The disappointment in her voice is glaring.

"I know that I want something real. Something long-term."

She shakes her head. "Unfortunately, I want a little more than that. I know that's asking a lot from a first date, but I'm not willing to waste my time. Even for a face as pretty as yours."

I smirk. "Okay. Truth?"

"Yes, please."

"I've never thought about marriage as particularly important. In fact, sometimes I feel it's kinda antiquated. It's something I could get on board with for the right person, but as for kids—I'm really not sure about that one."

"I see," Jasmin says with a drawn-out sigh.

"Sorry to disappoint you before the food's even hit the table."

"Thank you. For being honest with me."

I nod. "We're not gonna have a second date, are we?"

She smiles. "I don't see the point." She leans in and puts her hand on mine. "I want to be married in two years, Toby. I want to have a baby in three. I don't have time to waste on men who're still lost."

"Ouch."

"I didn't mean it like that."

"Sure you did."

She gives me a little wink. From my peripheral vision, I catch a couple walking past. The bright burst of auburn is what gets my attention first. With Jasmin's hand still on mine, I glance to the side.

Ashley?

And she's not alone. She's on the arm of that uptight little trust fund kid who works in accounting.

What...

The...

... Fuck?

They're seated three tables down from us, giving me a perfect straight-line view of them. Ashton still hasn't noticed me, but Ashley looks up just in time to catch me gawking at her. Her cheeks flush with color, then her eyes move down to the spot where Jasmin's still touching me. She looks away quickly and gives Ashton a smile.

"Hey... are you upset?" Jasmin asks. "Because I'm just trying to be honest. I'm not trying to upset you or anything."

I force myself to look at Jasmin. "I'm not upset. You're entitled to want what you want, Jasmin."

She smiles. "Thanks for understanding. We can still enjoy our dinner, right? Old friends catching up."

I'm not sure I can enjoy anything at this point. My heart rate is rising rapidly, and my fingers are clenching slowly. I hadn't liked that Ashton kid from the moment I laid eyes on him. Now I know why.

Our food hits the table, and three tables down, Ashley and Lord Entitled order their meals. How is it possible that she's having a date at the same restaurant I'm at? Then it hits me. She has access to my private date book.

Which means that she's here *because* I am. She's here to make me jealous. And annoyingly, it's working.

"Hmm, the food here is so good."

I nod distractedly. "Uh-huh."

She's wearing the same thing she wore to work, but she's removed a couple of buttons from the front of her blouse. I can see the black lace bra she's wearing peeking out from underneath. She also has let her hair down and added some make-up.

Stop looking over at them.

Isn't this what I wanted anyway? Going on a date was me committing to get on with my life. Make smarter decisions. Meet age-appropriate women. It was also a way to send a signal to Ashley that nothing could happen between us.

Apparently, she's gotten that message a little too well.

"What are you looking at?" Jasmin asks, clearly noticing

my preoccupation. She turns in her seat and follows my line of vision.

"Nothing," I say quickly, but it's too late. She's already caught sight of Ashley. Her shoulders tense, her eyes narrow. She turns to me with a scowl on her face. "Seriously?"

I shrug. "It's just weird to see my PA outside of work."

"Uh-huh. That's the reason you can't stop looking over there?"

"You're exaggerating."

She shakes her head and leans back. "Jesus, men are so damn predictable! Your secretary, Toby. Really? Is this the reason you can't commit?"

"No," I say earnestly. "Jasmin, this has nothing to do with her."

"She's too young for you."

"I agree."

"And it's such a freaking cliché. Have you thought about that?"

"She's the daughter of my closest friend, okay? I'm looking over there because I feel the need to look out for her. For Daniel's sake."

She frowns. "Are you just spewing bullshit now?"

"No. I wouldn't do that."

"You wouldn't lie to me?"

"I'm trying my best not to."

"Okay," she says, and I immediately regret that last answer. "Then answer me this. Are you at all attracted to her?"

Fuck.

"Well—"

"I *knew* it," she snaps. "A woman always knows. I clocked it the moment I saw her."

"What does that mean?"

"You've always had a thing for red heads with doe eyes."

"Not true."

She sighs heavily and crosses her arms over her chest. "I'm not even hungry anymore."

"Why should this make a difference?" I demand. "You've written me off already."

"Sure, but I was kinda hoping you'd be broken up about it. Not pining for a woman you can't have."

I smile. After a second, she does too. "I met her weeks ago before I knew who she really was. She was sitting at this bar looking lost and lonely and—"

"You decided to play the hero?"

"I was interested. We started talking and it was… easy. It felt natural, like we'd known each other for years. I figured she was younger but I didn't realize how much younger."

"Twelve years?"

"Fifteen."

Jasmin shrugs. "But that's not the real problem, is it? I mean, there are a ton of marriages with big age differences. That doesn't make or break a relationship."

"I wasn't lying earlier. She really is the daughter of my closest friend."

Jasmin raises her eyebrows. "Spicy."

"He called me up weeks ago and asked if I could hire her, give her a leg up as she moved here. He was counting on me to look out for her. And then I go and—"

"Fuck her?"

I give her a glare. "Jasmin." Out of the corner of my eye, I notice Ashley leave her table and head to the rest room.

"Did you?"

I clear my throat. "Um, excuse me. I need to use the bathroom."

Ignoring my better judgment, I head over to the

restrooms, which are half-covered by wooden room dividers with trellis work all down the front. I have no idea what I'm trying to achieve. All I know is that I need to speak to her. I wait outside the ladies' room, and two minutes later, she comes back out.

"Jesus," she gasps when she sees me. "You scared me."

"What are you doing here?"

She raises her eyebrows. "I'm… having dinner."

"Don't give me that bullshit. You saw the dinner on my calendar."

Her jaw clenches tight and her expression grows defensive. "What does it matter? Ashton asked me out and I've always been curious about this place. Why shouldn't we eat here? If you can bring your dates here, then why can't I?"

I take a step towards her. "I'm not playing games, Ashley."

She takes a step towards me. "I'm not playing games either, *Tobias*. I just wanted to enjoy a nice dinner with Ashton."

"Oh, cut the shit. You have no interest in that douche-bag."

"Au contraire. I am *very* interested. We have a lot in common."

"*Do* you? Please. Enlighten me."

She snorts. "I don't have to explain my attraction to Ashton to you. You're not my boyfriend or my father. You're not even my friend at this point." She's so damn close now that I can smell her perfume, if she's even wearing any. She smells of citrus and lime today. "And how dare you come down on me about who I choose to have dinner with when *you* are on a date of your own. Is this a classic double standard, huh? You can fuck whoever you want, but I can't?"

She is *so* fucking right about that. It is a double standard

—the worse fucking kind. The kind that I would typically be disgusted by. And yet, I'm having a hard time reigning in my worst impulses, even in the light of that realization. I guess the difference is that this double standard suits *me*. Also, she's too fucking good for that asshole. "You really want to sleep with that oofy little shit?"

"Maybe I do. At least with him, I don't have to beg him to pay attention to me."

"I've got news for you. He's not interested in what's in your head."

"Oh, and *you* are."

"This is not about me. I'm just trying to protect you."

Her eyes flare wildly. Those gorgeous full lips of hers look so damn juicy. All I want to do is bite them off. "Well, *don't*. I don't need you to protect me. I can take care of myself just fine on my—"

"*Ah-hem.*" Ashley and I jerk apart to find Jasmin standing a few feet away from us. "Sorry to interrupt but I needed the ladies' room."

Ashley swallows, her cheeks flooding with color. "Sorry," she mumbles before running back to her table.

"*Fuck*," I mutter under my breath.

Jasmin takes a step towards me, her eyebrows raised. "Damn," she says without taking her eyes off me. "I wasn't expecting that kinda chemistry. It was off the charts, even from where I'm standing."

"That's not—"

She just pats me on the arm. "Toby."

I sigh. "Yes?"

"You are in *big* trouble."

Then she gives me a wink and heads into the ladies' room.

CHAPTER 23

Ashley

What the hell am I doing?

First of all—he's my boss.

Second of all—he's my father's best friend.

Third of all—he's fifteen years older than I am.

And fourth of all—he's *clearly* moved on. I'm just the distant little car in his rearview mirror.

Somehow, point number four is the only one that seems to matter to me at the moment. Of course, she's *gorgeous*. And, of course, I'd made the poor decision of stalking her a little on my phone on the cab ride over here.

When Ashton had asked me what I was doing, I just told him that I was texting my aunt in Scottsdale. Yeah, I know. Pathetic.

Basically, Jasmin Kaminsky not only graduated magna cum laude from Yale seven years ago. She also models part-time. Gone are the days when you could see a pretty woman and just assume she was as dumb as a bag of rocks. Most women are beautiful *and* smart.

Goddammit.

Of course, Toby had seen right through me. Called me out

and everything. If that weren't bad enough, Jasmin had run into us fighting outside the restrooms. I wonder if he's having an awkward conversation with her right now. Kinda like the one I see myself having with Ashton in a couple of seconds. From the look on his face, he's definitely noticed something too.

"Jesus, did you know that Ackerman's at this restaurant too?"

I clear my throat. "Is he?"

"Yup, right over at that table. I saw him head to the restroom a little while after you left."

I try my hardest not to cringe. "What a coincidence. I guess if he'd be here, we know the place is gonna be good."

"Yeah… if it's uncomfortable for you, we can leave."

Instead of being smart and taking the opportunity to leave, I find myself shaking my head. "No, I'm good to stay."

"Okay," Ashton says with a shrug. "Guess Jasmin's back then."

My eyes go wide but I try not to look too interested. "Jasmin?"

"The woman he's with. He dated her for a few months a while back."

"How long is a while?"

He shrugs. "Dunno… over a year ago definitely. Then she disappeared and he replaced her with another blonde. But I guess she's back in the game."

"Do you know why they broke up?"

"Nah. I can't even say that they broke up. You have to be together first in order to break up with someone."

"Right," I mumble. "Tobias doesn't do relationships. He has dates."

"What was that?"

"Nothing," I say quickly before noticing Tobias and

Jasmin walking towards their table. I try my best not to make eye contact. My only option is to throw myself into this dinner with Ashton.

"So, what brought you to Cali?"

"A chance for a fresh start, I guess. I was getting restless in Scottsdale. I've lived there my entire life. It was time for a change."

"And college?"

"I dropped out."

"No way! Really?"

He looks like he thinks a little less of me now. "Do I detect some judgment?" I ask, calling him out on it.

"No. I'm just surprised. You seem like the kinda girl who follows through."

Not gonna lie. That one stings. I brush it aside. "Usually, I am. But—"

"College is not for you?"

"Not exactly."

"You didn't want to waste your life studying when you could be out there, living it up?"

I frown. "Do you always answer for your dates?"

He smirks. "Sorry. Go ahead."

"I couldn't afford college," I admit bluntly, as though it's a badge of honor. "My father was breaking his back, working overtime to put me through, and in the end, it just didn't feel worth it to me. I didn't want to be the reason he was in debt."

"Shit."

He's got that awkward look that people get when money is discussed. "Yeah," I nod. "I was smart enough to get into college. Just not smart enough to get a full ride. So I decided to postpone it for the moment, get out into the world, earn some money."

"That's… cool." He doesn't really sound sure.

I clear my throat. "So… you're a Californian native, aren't you?"

"Born and bred," he nods. "I live down Brinkley Street. Eden Tower."

"Eden Tower," I repeat. "Wow, that's a nice building."

"I have a two-bedroom. It's small but it's pretty good for a first apartment."

I have a feeling that he's not footing the bill for this apartment himself but I'm too polite to ask. I've got to give it to Tobias. What he's achieved, he achieved on his own, without trust funds or handouts or any kind of sympathy.

"Where do you live?"

"Oh, um, Eastwick Street."

"Damn, the south side?"

"Yeah."

"That's the dodgy area, isn't it?"

I give him a tight smile. "Well, we don't all have rich daddies who can bankroll us towards fancy apartments in town."

He raises his eyebrows. "Ouch. You're assuming a lot there."

Immediately, I feel guilty for taking my bad mood out on Ashton. Especially because it seems like Jasmin and Tobias are continuing their date quite pleasantly. Apparently, she wasn't at all threatened by me. Not that I blame her. I wouldn't be threatened by me either.

"Sorry. That was below the belt."

"Actually, it wasn't. It's my mother who's bankrolling me."

I raise my eyebrows and we both start laughing. I notice Tobias turn around at the sound of our laughter. His eyes land on me, wide and curious, for a moment before he turns away.

What is he thinking?

I wish I knew. He'd seemed pretty pissed back there. I've never seen him that riled up before. It was enough to make me think. Correction. It was enough to make me *hope* that perhaps he might have been jealous.

But a jealous man doesn't just go back to his table and enjoy dinner with the smoking hot blonde on his arm, right? Maybe I should just face the fact that this connection between us is all in my head. I've dreamed it up out of thin air because maybe, just maybe, I'm looking for some sort of savior. A hero who can whisk me up and sort out all my problems for me.

Yeah, I know. Not very feminist of me.

But honestly. There are some days when it takes work to be a feminist. There are some days when I just... want to be taken care of.

Jasmin says something and Tobias chuckles. He looks even more handsome when he smiles. Even his eyes get brighter. How can you not be distracted by that smile?

"I really like you, Ashley." My neck snaps back to my own table as Ashton puts his hand on mine. I'm really not expecting that. It feels strangely invasive despite the fact that it really isn't a very controversial gesture.

"Um, thanks."

He smiles. "Thanks?"

"Sorry. I wasn't expecting that."

"You know, I noticed you the moment you walked into the office."

I lean away slightly. "Yeah?"

He holds onto my hand a little tighter. "You have no idea how beautiful you are."

The words are sweet but there's something about this expression that makes me slightly uncomfortable. Maybe it's the expectation on his face.

"Compliments make me uncomfortable."

"Well, you better get used to them. Because I'm all about telling you exactly how sexy you are to me."

I try and pull my hand out of his but he keeps a tight grip on me. "I know this great place we can go to after dinner. It's this cocktail bar right next to The Eden."

"Next to… your apartment?"

He nods and I realize what that expectation is. He didn't just ask me out for dinner. He's asked me out for sex too. How had I not seen that before now?

"Um, Ashton, that's a nice offer. But tomorrow's a busy day for me and I need to wake up early. I think dinner might have to be it for the night."

"Then we'll skip drinks," he says. "You can just come up to my place for a nightcap."

I smile. "I don't go back to the guy's home on the first date."

He raises his eyebrows. "That's kinda old-fashioned, don't you think?"

"I think it's a pretty good rule. Worked for me so far."

"Yes, but this is the big city. Time to do what big city girls do."

Is he serious? I'm willing to excuse his behavior only because he's knocked back three glasses of wine at this point. But I'm losing patience fast.

"So—do you have any siblings?" I ask, making a blunt topic change.

He chuckles a little and snaps his fingers at the waitress. "Another bottle of wine, please."

"Ashton, don't you think you should take it easy? You've pretty much finished one bottle all by yourself?"

He looks annoyed. "What are you? The alcohol police?" I have to try very hard not to roll my eyes. *Witty.* "Just loosen up a little. You're young and hot. You should be enjoying your life."

That's the thing with men like Ashton. They think only in terms of enjoyment. They've never really had to hustle for much in life. Which is why they like to numb any negative emotions with emotional band-aids—drugs, alcohol, sex.

The more this night goes on, the less I like him.

"I'm too busy trying to survive it."

He rolls his eyes. "Aw, don't play the victim. It's so lame."

"As opposed to what? Overindulging on over-priced wine and acting like a complete asshole?"

He raises his eyebrows. "Jesus. You're tightly wound."

"No," I say, getting to my feet. "What I am—is done. Excuse me, I'm leaving." I open my purse and pull out a fifty-dollar note. Which is pretty much *all* my cash. "There, that should cover my half. Goodnight, Ashton."

I don't dare glance in Tobias's direction. I know he's probably watching the whole thing and thinking it *serves her right*. I don't blame him; I'm kinda thinking the same thing too. What the hell was I thinking accepting a date with a guy, *any* guy, just because I thought it would make the guy I was interested in jealous?

That was so high school. The irony? I didn't even pull this shit when I was in high school.

"Hey! Ashley. Wait."

Oh God, please don't follow me.

Except that's exactly what he does. I pivot fast and try the back exit out of the restaurant. It winds through the starlit parking lot, but I need some space at the moment. I need a place that's free of people.

Unfortunately, however, Ashton doesn't seem keen to just let me go. "Jesus, Ashley, will you just *stop* already!?"

He's breathing pretty heavily for a young guy and I'm guessing that has something to do with all the alcohol he's been drinking. But since we do work in the same office and I'll have to see him again tomorrow, I stop and turn.

"Can we please not do this?"

"Do what?"

"We went on a date. We didn't click. It's fine. Let's just go back to being friends."

He frowns. "Well… I'm okay with being friends. Just as long as there are a few… benefits."

He raises his eyebrows pointedly and my eyes go wide. "Are you serious?"

"Come on. We're young and hot. We might as well live a little while we can." He grabs my hand without warning and pulls me into him.

I rip my hand from his grip. "*Don't* touch me. That's not what I'm after."

He glowers at me. "What *are* you after? Because it doesn't seem like you know either."

"I'm leaving now. Don't talk to me again."

The moment I turn my back on him, I'm yanked back around. This time, it doesn't just shock me. It sends a shiver down my spine. "Hey, I'm trying to be nice here."

"If that were true, you'd let me go."

"We were having a nice time."

"Were you at the same table?"

"There was some laughter."

"Nervous laughter doesn't count."

The smile slides off his face. All those pretty boy good looks disappear behind a scowl so dark that it has panic running through me. How did I not notice the fact that his eyes have tiny red veins running through them?

How did I not notice how much he was drinking?

Probably because I was too focused on Tobias and his date. I was so wrapped up in other problems that I didn't even realize that I was creating another subconsciously.

"You're a fucking cock tease, aren't you?"

His grip on my arm tightens and I strain against the sharp sting that tears down my arm. "Please, Ashton. Stop it. This isn't funny. You're scaring me."

"No. Don't do that. Don't make out as if I'm the villain."

"You're drunk."

He glowers at me. "I'm horny. There's a difference."

I try to push him off me, but that ends up being a mistake. He just gets more pissed off. He throws me onto the hood of a sleek black Benz and before I've got my balance, he twists me around, his groin pushing against mine.

He's hard.

The panic takes over and I act on instinct. I swing my hand back and slap him across the face. He stumbles and I try to run, but he grabs my arm and yanks me back towards him.

"You fucking BITCH!"

I cringe back when his hand rises. Oh my God. I move to the city and get hit by a man. This isn't the way it's supposed to be.

Then I hear a strangled gasp, and suddenly, the pressure of his hand on my arm vanishes. I look up and see him standing there, looking like thunder under the moonlight.

And he's got Ashton by the collar of his shirt.

"Tobias," I whisper.

CHAPTER 24

Tobias

I'm not sure what exactly happened. But something definitely happened. Because not long after Jasmin and I return to our table, Ashley gets up and walks out on her date.

It's definitely a walkout. She looks pissed and he looks disbelieving. He calls out after her but she doesn't stop. She's heading for the main entrance, and he's following her. Maybe that's why she pivots suddenly and tries to avoid him by using the back entrance outta here.

"Isn't this a plot twist?" Jasmin says, eyeing me carefully.

I clear my throat as I keep one eye on the douche from accounting. He had some sort of douche-jock name. Clayton. Aaron. Ashton.

That was it.

He walks back to the table and pulls out his wallet, looking frustrated as hell and borderline pissed. Judging from the number of glasses of wine he had tonight, it seems he's pissed in more ways than one.

"It's not my business."

"Really? Because you're certainly making it your business."

I'm expecting Ashton to take the main entrance out of the restaurant. But he follows Ashley out the back door. Somehow, that doesn't sit well with me.

"Jesus!" Jasmin exclaims, throwing her hands up in the air.

"What?"

She rolls her eyes. "Just go."

"Jasmin—"

"Save it, Toby. I know where you stand, and honestly, I don't blame you. If I had that kinda chemistry with a man, I'd be married and knocked up by now. Just go. I'll expect flowers and a box of Godiva in the coming days."

I get to my feet, press a kiss to her cheek and nod. "Forget Godiva. You'll get fucking Gucci."

"Yeah, yeah."

I turn and rush towards the back entrance that leads directly into the parking lot. It's eerily quiet as I enter the street outside. The lot is big enough to get lost in. But it's also quiet enough that picking up stray sounds is easy.

Like the sound of a couple in the midst of a heated fight.

I start walking fast, trying to figure out where they are. But it's not so easy in the huge, poorly lit lot. And the wind seems to be carrying their voices in every direction. Then I hear Ashley's voice raised in a scream.

Something roars through me in a burst of adrenaline that has me moving faster. *If he's hurt a single fucking hair on her head…*

I rush past a bunch of fancy convertibles and spot them near a black Benz. He's actually got her pushed up against the car. Rage boils through me and my head switches off. I throw myself into the situation, grab him by the collar and yank him off her.

Ashley blinks up at me, her eyes glazed over with fear

and shock. I turn the bastard around so that he can see me and then I bash my forehead into his. His eyes cross for a moment before he stumbles back. I swing my fist into the side of his face and he lands on his ass on the ground.

"Fuck," he hisses as blood starts pouring from his nostrils. "I think you broke my nose."

"You're lucky I don't break more than that. You fucking bastard!"

I walk over and he crawls backward on his hands and knees. "I-I... I can sue you."

"For what?" I hiss. "Defending an innocent woman whom *you* were assaulting?"

His eyes veer to her for a moment and his mouth turns up in a sneer. "She isn't so innocent. She fucking *wanted*—"

I reach down, grab him by the front of his shirt and pull him back up to his feet. "*What* was that?"

He starts trembling violently. "Nothing."

"Tobias." Her voice comes through soft and self-conscious. She's standing off to the side, looking between us with wide eyes. "Let him go. He's not worth it."

My fingers are coiled tight around his shirt. Letting him go doesn't feel like an option at the moment. All I want to do is make the little shit pay.

"Please," she says again. This time, there's a noticeable quiver in her voice.

I turn back to the smarmy bastard who's staring at me with obvious trepidation. I desperately want to beat the shit out of him and leave him lying in this parking like the trash he is. But I'd promised myself that I was going to leave this part of me behind. This isn't who I am anymore.

"If I ever see your fucking face again—you can bet your ass I'm dragging you into court for assault and attempted rape," I growl. "You understand me?"

"I-it wasn't like that," he stutters. "She—"

"If you say she wanted it one more fucking time, I *will* rearrange your entire face. Not even your fucking mother will recognize you anymore." He gulps and nods. "You are officially fired. Don't bother asking me for a recommendation letter." I push him back down hard. Pretty sure he smacks his head on the ground. "Now get out of my sight."

He scrambles slowly to his feet and starts stumbling in the direction of his car. I turn quickly to Ashley, who's standing there with her arms wrapped around her body. It's as though she's trying to hold herself together.

"Ashley, are you okay?"

She blinks at me, her mouth opening slightly before it closes again. "Um—" And then she bursts into tears.

I don't even think about it. I pull her into my arms and hold her close. She clings to me as though I'm her last lifeline. She sobs until my shirt is soaked through in the front. All I can do is hold her and whisper that everything is going to be alright. That she's fine. That I'm here for her. It doesn't seem to make a difference.

When she finally pulls away, she doesn't look close to being okay. "God, I'm sorry. This is so embarrassing."

"Don't be embarrassed. This is not your fault."

She nods. "It is my fault. I should never have said yes to that loser in the first place."

"You said yes to a date, Ashley. You didn't deserve the way he treated you."

She tries to hold back a sob. "I wasn't even interested in him." Then she covers her face with her hands. "I feel like such an idiot."

"You may be a lot of things, Ashley Payne, but an idiot is not one of them."

She gives me a teary smile. "I can't thank you enough, Tobias."

"Don't thank me, please. I'm just glad I got here in time."

Her bottom lip trembles and she looks around as though she doesn't know what to do with herself. There's no way I can let her go home in this state.

"Come with me."

She raises her eyebrows. "Where are we going?"

"Back inside. We're going to sit down and take a breath. We're going to order you something strong to drink."

She looks slightly uncertain. "Um, I'm not twenty-one yet," she points out.

I shrug. "Right, like that's stopped you before."

She gives me a small smile and takes my hand. We walk back into the restaurant together and I ask for a private room. We're shown into one of the little private pods that overlook the Koi pond in the gardens.

"Wow," she breathes as she looks around at the golden scones and the textured wallpaper. "I didn't even know these rooms existed."

"You have to request them," I tell her as I help her into a chair. I order two whiskeys and then sit down opposite Ashley. The tables are small enough that we're not that far apart. In fact, I can feel her leg against mine.

Focus Tobias. This is not about you.

"I'm sorry you had to go through that."

She shakes her head. "Nothing happened."

"But it could have. Sometimes that's just as traumatic."

She glances at me out of the corner of her eye. "I… I didn't think I was the kind of girl who would just… take that kind of thing lying down," she admits. "I always thought of myself as the kind of girl who would fight back. Scream. *Do* something. But… it was like my body was shutting down on me. I was freezing up."

"Fear can do that to you."

"I guess I'm much less of a badass than I thought I was."

"You *are* a badass, Ashley. You're just human too. You weren't expecting him to be such a humongous asshole."

"No…"

The waitress enters a few moments later with the whiskey. She sets it on the table for us and bows out with a smile. Ashley picks up her glass and stares at the golden liquid. "This is the second time I've ruined your date."

For a second, I genuinely have no idea what she's talking about. "What do you mean?"

"Your date," she says, raising her eyebrows. "The blonde you were having dinner with."

Oh.

"Right. Jasmin."

"Where is she?"

"Left."

She cringes a little. "I hope it's not because of me?"

How do I answer this question? "It's not *just* because of you."

"Oh God."

I chuckle. "Seriously. That isn't on you, Ashley. Why don't you try a sip?"

She brings the whiskey to her lips and takes a sip. "*Mmm*," she sighs. "That tastes amazing. So rich yet bitter." She takes another sip and sets it back down on the table. "You fight like you're on the streets," she says softly.

I raise my eyebrows. "Do I?"

She nods. "That headbutt was… quite something. And that punch—it wasn't the kind of punch that an educated CEO throws."

I snort. "When you grow up with a drunk and an addict for a father, punches and headbutts come in handy."

Her eyes go wide. "You used to get into physical fights with your father?"

"Only when I had to," I say reluctantly. "And sometimes… when I was angry."

She looks at me pointedly, probably waiting for more of an explanation. I just don't have the energy for one right now. So I drink the rest of my whiskey and try not to get stuck in the past like I used to.

"Can I ask what happened to your father?"

I really want another glass of whiskey, but I'm craving it right now, and I promised myself a long time ago that I'd never have anything I was craving. It was the gateway to a lifetime of addiction, debauchery and regret. I'd watched my father waste his potential, but I wasn't about to do the same.

"He's in jail."

She raises her eyebrows. "Dad never mentioned that."

"Not surprised," I say, my hands twitching towards her glass. I take a deep breath. "He got into a brawl outside a local pub. The cops were called. They tried to break up the fight when Dad punched the officer in the face. He was charged with aggravated assault on a police officer and he was sentenced to four years. That was six years ago."

"What happened?"

I shrug. "*He* happened. He was released two years ago. He walked himself to the nearest bar, got piss drunk. Stayed that way for a few months, as far as I can tell. He called me a couple of times. Even came down to the office to try and talk to me."

"About what?"

"Money," I say dryly. "He'd heard I was doing well for myself, and he wanted to milk me for all I was worth. I told him the only thing I would pay for was rehab." Her eyes never leave my face. I wonder if that's the reason I can't seem to stop talking. "He tried to throw a punch at me. I had to kick him out of the building."

"Tobias…"

Her hand lands on mine and warmth spreads through me. No one has ever been able to make me feel this good talking about my father.

"He went back to the hole he crawled out of. A few months later, I heard he was back in jail. A woman accused him of rape. The rape charge wasn't proven but the assault charge was. He's looking at ten years. They don't go easy on repeat offenders."

"Do you ever see him?"

"I went down to see him only once while he was in there…" I can't bring myself to tell her the rest of the story though. Not because I don't trust her. Not even because I don't want to. It's mostly because I don't want her to know just how bad a shit show my family was. "It was a long time ago."

She squeezes my hand. "I'm sorry."

"It is what it is, Ashley. There's no point crying about shit you can't change."

She smiles sadly. "Dad says that a lot."

"Where do you think I learned it from?"

She sighs deeply. Then she pushes her glass of whiskey towards me. "Take it."

I shake my head. *Fight it. Fucking fight it.* "No thanks. I'm good."

"Thank you… for everything."

I'm not quite sure what the 'everything' refers to. But I take it anyway. She gives me a small smile that's laced with tears. "I don't want to be alone tonight."

"You won't be. Your Dad will be waiting for you at home."

She removes her hand from mine. "I can't go back there, Tobias. Not tonight." *Oh boy.* "Can I spend the night at your place?"

Those beautiful, bright eyes stare at me helplessly. And for the life of me—I can't say no despite the fact that there are a million reasons why I *should* say no.

I've spent my entire life saying no to the things I crave.

"Of course," I say softly. "I'll take you back to mine."

So, what makes her the exception?

CHAPTER 25

Ashley

"Whoa," I gasp, looking up at the architectural wonder of the building that Tobias lives in.

It's a traditional skyrise design, but it has a second sloping building that's being held up by thin metal claws that wrap around the whole structure.

"I live up there."

"In the sloping tower?"

"That's the one. But don't worry, it doesn't slope on the inside."

It's the kind of building with security, a doorman and 24-hour surveillance. The doorman definitely gives me an eyebrow raise when we pass by. I have no idea what that means. Maybe he's not used to seeing Tobias with a woman? But that makes no sense, considering he has a reputation as a serial dater.

I decide not to think about it. The fact that he even conceded to bring me back here speaks volumes. He cares.

We take the elevator up fifty-seven floors up to the penthouse. It opens directly into Tobias's apartment, and for a second, I don't even want to step out onto the plush beige carpet that covers the entrance hallway.

"I think my shoes are dirty."

Laughing, he takes my arm and pulls me into the entrance hall. Except for a few tasteful pieces of art hanging off the walls and a sleek console table where Tobias drops his keys, there's nothing here. At the bottom of the entrance hall, there are two high-arched doorways without doors.

"This one leads to the main living room," Tobias says, pointing to the right. "And that one leads to the kitchen. Come on."

He takes me straight to the living room. Its high ceiling makes the space look twice as large. My eyes go wide as I take in the amazing views. One that includes the Golden Gate Bridge.

"Jesus," I breathe as I walk towards the floor-to-ceiling glass windows that seem to look down over the entire city. "This is really… something."

"Yeah. It was my first real home."

I turn my back on the view and take a look at his place. Beautiful, classy, sleek. But there are no personal touches. The only thing that comes close is the paintings on the walls.

"I know what you're thinking."

I raise my eyebrows. "What am I thinking?"

"It's impersonal. Cold."

I smile. "I wasn't thinking cold. But impersonal… maybe."

He sits down on the sofa and looks up at me. "Yeah… I guess I haven't really spent that much time in this place."

"How is that possible?"

He shrugs. "Building a business is hard work. I've slept at the office more often than I've slept here. Especially in the first couple of years."

"How did you manage to start Ackerman Corp.?" I ask.

"Blood, sweat and tears," he says. Then he gives me a self-conscious smile. "No, it wasn't nearly as dramatic. After my Dad left and Mum passed away, the house was written in my name. I sold it and put it towards building something of my own. That's where the investment for Ackerman came from."

"And Ackerman was... your Mom's maiden name? That's what Dad told me."

He nods. "It felt right to use her name for the company. That house was hers before it was mine. And I was never a fan of having to carry my father's name anyway."

"Do you enjoy it? Being a CEO, being your own boss?"

He smiles. "Hell yeah. For me, it was everything. It was the whole reason I wanted to be my own boss. I didn't have a whole lot of autonomy in my life, and I guess running my own company felt a little bit like I was taking my power back."

I nod. "I suppose that's what it felt like for me too. Making the move to California in the first place."

"So college was just... not for you?"

I sigh. "Has Dad talked to you about it?"

"About what exactly?"

"Me dropping out of college."

"Oh. Honestly, he hasn't. I mean, he did tell me you had dropped out, and it was obvious he was disappointed about it, but he didn't mention anything specific."

I take a deep breath. "We had a huge fight about it before I made the decision to move. He told me I was throwing my life away just like she had."

He raises his eyebrows. "That wasn't fair."

"I accused him of being emotionally manipulative. Told him that whenever he wanted me to make a certain kind of decision, he used her name to try and push me in whatever direction he wanted."

He's looking uncomfortable now. "That's… harsh."

"It's kinda true though," I admit. "Even now. I don't think he even realizes when he's doing it, but sometimes it feels like he uses her as a weapon."

"I'm sorry, Ashley. That must be hard for you."

I shrug. "I don't know if it's hard. It certainly makes things so much more confusing. Especially after speaking to you about her."

He tenses up immediately. "What do you mean?"

"Well… Dad's always acted like Kristen was some sort of villain. Like we were a part of some diabolical plan that she started and then abandoned half way through. But talking to you has made me realize that maybe… she was more than that."

She purses his lips up for a moment. Then she sighs. "She was."

I nod. "It's nice to know that."

"I bet you already did."

I shrug. "I hoped. But I didn't *know*. And to be honest, sometimes it was easier to believe she was the villain. That meant that she left because of *her*. Not because of me."

His eyes go wide. "Ashley. She *did* leave because of her."

I shake my head. "You don't have to do that."

"Do what?"

"Lie to me. She wasn't expecting to get pregnant. She wouldn't have skipped town if it hadn't been for me." He looks conflicted for a moment as if he's not sure if he should leave me to my assumptions or correct them. "What was your mother like?" I ask before he can say anything.

"My mother," he repeats softly. "She was… soft spoken,

introverted. She liked to knit and sew sometimes. She even cooked. But that was when she could function."

I frown. "What do you mean by... function?" I walk over to the sofa and sit down beside him.

He sighs. "She was diagnosed with clinical depression when she was a teenager. It was kinda like living with someone with bipolar disorder. Who knows, maybe she did have bipolar disorder. She could go from happy to sad in seconds. And you had no idea what set it off."

"I thought your father set it off?"

"Usually. But there were days when he would disappear suddenly. No explanation. He'd just disappear on us, and life went on as if nothing had changed. Mum would seem fine, and then suddenly, she would hear something or see something, and it was like a switch had been flipped. She'd take to her bed and stay there for hours. Days sometimes. She didn't eat, barely drank. Just kinda... laid there."

"Shit..."

"Sometimes having parents isn't all it's cracked up to be, Ashley. I'm not saying that it was a good thing your mother left. I'm just saying that maybe she knew what she was capable of."

"You're trying to say she left because she loved me. She was doing me a favor... is that right?"

His expression is wary. "Is that so far-fetched?"

"It feels like a convenient excuse."

He lies back on the sofa. "Okay. I'll give you that. That doesn't mean it's any less true though."

I lean back too. It's so tempting to just close my eyes and drift off. I am tired but it's the kind of tired that sets into your bones and makes you feel heavy. My mind is wide awake, darting from place to place like a runner on steroids.

"Did you ever hear from Henry again?"

My eyes dart open as I turn to Tobias. Of all the questions I was expecting him to ask, that was not one of them.

"No."

He nods. "Sorry," he mumbles. "I probably shouldn't have asked at all."

"Probably not. But now that you did, I'll tell you the worst part about Henry." I run my hands over my face. "He knew my story. He knew the way that Kristen had left. And he basically did the same thing. I went over to his house one day and his mother told me that he had left early for college."

"Fuck."

A lump starts to form in my throat as I'm pulled back to that day. We hadn't really discussed what our plan was once Henry was accepted into college. I just knew that I wasn't willing to give up on us. It was only until later that I realized that getting that acceptance letter signaled a new start for Henry. One that didn't include me.

"He came back the next summer to see his folks but I didn't see him. I actively avoided seeing him, in fact. Not that I didn't want closure. I most definitely did. I just didn't want him to know that. I wanted him to believe that I had moved on too."

"I'm sorry…"

I shrug. "Sometimes, I think I should have walked up to his door and demanded an explanation. We spent two years together. That's not a small thing when you're both teenagers."

Tobias nods. "It's not. All it shows is that he didn't deserve you."

I snort darkly. "That's what Dad said too. That sentiment always felt kinda hollow. He may not have deserved me but he didn't want me enough in the end, so really—what does it matter if he deserved me or not?"

"Didn't you meet anyone afterward?"

I glance at him. "Are we reviewing dating histories now?"

"You don't have to tell me if you don't want to."

I shrug. "Fuck, what do I have to hide?" He flinches a little and that takes me by surprise. Why would *that* comment make him flinch? "I dated a few different guys after Henry. None of them lasted more than a few months. I guess I always cut and run before it got too serious."

"Self-preservation?"

I smile sadly. "Exactly that." He stares out the window and I take the opportunity to admire his perfect profile. He really is one of the most handsome men I've seen up close. "Were you ever in love?" I ask softly.

He turns to me, those deep blue eyes shimmering underneath the subtle lights. "I don't know about love," he admits. "But I do remember the first time I saw a girl and thought *wow, I want to know*. I was thirteen."

I smile. "Thirteen, huh? What was her name?"

He raises his eyebrows. "You already know her name."

It takes me a moment. But then my eyes go wide as the realization hits. "Kristen," I whisper, feeling a strange pressure in my chest.

Tobias just nods. "Yes. Kristen."

CHAPTER 26

Tobias

I t was probably a stupid thing to admit to her *daughter*. Much less the daughter she abandoned. But there's just something about this girl that makes me want to crack my chest open and let it all spill out. It's devastatingly dangerous too, and yet, somehow, I can't seem to pay heed to the warning signs. Of all the women in the world, why did *she* have to be *his* daughter?

I clear my throat and fix her with a careful expression. "I just wanna make one thing clear. I was never in love with Kristen. I just… I *could* have fallen in love with her."

"What stopped you?"

I smile. "Your Dad did. We were up in Daniel's room when the small blue Chevy drove up and parked in front of the house that the Crispin family sold earlier that month. Her Mum got out first. Then Kristen. It was clear that she didn't really want to be there. She looked down the street as though she wanted to be anywhere else."

I remember the way she'd looked. That dark auburn hair falling down to her lower back. Her face covered in freckles that could be seen from across the street, two stories up. She was chewing on her fat bottom lip, her hands shoved into the pockets of her baggy jeans.

She was probably the prettiest girl I'd ever seen up until that point. I'd turned towards Daniel to say exactly that and I'd stopped short. His eyes were trained on her, his jaw hanging open. He looked like he'd just seen an angel.

"*That* was love at first sight. All it took was that one look."

"Really?"

I nod. "He was pretty much hooked on her from that moment on. I knew that there was no way I was gonna get in between that."

"So you stepped aside?"

I scoff. "I can't even say that I did. It wasn't ever a competition. Daniel and Kristen were meant for each other."

This time, *she's* the one who scoffs. "Meant for each other?" she repeats disdainfully. "They were meant for tragedy, you mean?"

"The relationship worked for a long time before it didn't," I point out. "And ultimately, it had a purpose."

"Which was what?"

I raise my eyebrows. "You."

Her jaw unclenches and she sighs deeply. "I wish I could see it the way you do."

"Maybe one day."

"Don't hold your breath."

"How did they… start dating?" she asks hesitantly. It's like she's fighting her own curiosity and losing the battle right in front of my eyes.

"Her bike broke. Daniel fixed it for her. They got to talking and that was that. They didn't start dating right away or anything, but I don't think either one of them looked at anyone else after that."

She sighs. "I wish it had a happy ending. And don't you dare say that *I* was the happy ending."

I chuckle and hold up my hands. "Scout's honor."

She stretches out and puts her legs on the coffee table. "Bet this place is a real chick magnet."

I snort. "It's not."

She rolls her eyes. "I find that hard to believe."

"Well, it might be if I ever brought girls back here."

She sits up a little straighter and fixes me with a puzzled expression. "Why wouldn't you?"

"I guess I don't want women in my space."

"Why not?"

I frown. "Um… am I under interrogation here?"

She smiles. "I'm just curious."

"The word you're looking for is nosy."

She laughs. "Sounds like you're avoiding the question."

"Noticed that, did ya?"

"It all comes down to the same thing, huh?" she says softly. "Commitment issues. You don't like anyone getting too close."

I would love to be able to correct her, but I'm really not so sure she's wrong. "Do you like ice cream?"

She raises her eyebrows. "Ice cream? Who doesn't."

Smiling, I gesture for her to follow me. I lead her into the kitchen and open the freezer. "Whoa," she breathes when she takes in my freezer stuffed with Ben and Jerry's and Häagen Dazs.

"That's some haul you've got there."

"Insurance for a rainy day." The moment I say it, I picture her on my living room couch with her bare feet kicked up over the arm of the sofa, her hair falling over the edge.

You've always got to have insurance for a rainy day, Toby. How do you think I got over my parents' divorce?

Since then, it didn't matter where I went. My freezer was always stuffed with ice cream. "Pick your poison."

"Belgium Dark chocolate, please."

I pull out the whole tub, take off the lid, and slide it across the table towards her. Then I pull out two spoons. I take the seat next to her, and we dig in together.

"Oh wow," she sighs. "That's good ice cream."

"Nothing makes you feel better as fast," I say, stealing Kristen's words. Not that I'm about to tell Ashley where I learned to self-soothe with ice cream.

"A good song can do it too," Ashley says. "A little Elton John. Sting. Guns and Roses."

I nod. "Fair enough. I used to have a pretty epic record collection once upon a time."

Her eyes go wide. "Yeah?"

"Well… it wasn't mine," I admit reluctantly. "It belonged to my brother."

She looks down at the tub of ice cream. "You don't really talk about your brother very much," she points out.

"No…"

"Is there a reason or are you gonna make me guess?"

The strange part is… I kinda *want* to tell her about Benjamin. When was the last time I felt that way? Oh, right, I remember—*never*.

"He died… right after my mother."

Her jaw drops. "Oh my God. Tobias. I'm so sorry. I didn't realize…" She frowns, looking confused for a moment. "I can't believe Dad never mentioned that to me."

"That's probably because of the circumstances of his death," I say softly.

"What do you mean… the circumstances of his death?"

"It was suicide." I'm amazed at the fact that my voice doesn't shake. "He took his own life."

"Oh my God," she gasps. "No…"

I nod, and somehow, saying it out loud feels… liberating. Almost like the act of keeping it close to my chest has been weighing on me all these years. It's the whole reason I'd been avoiding therapy. I didn't want to have to talk about Benjamin.

"He was only a year older than me. Thirteen months older, to be exact. When we were younger, most people assumed we were twins."

"You must have been close."

"We were when we were younger, but as we grew up, we kinda drifted apart. Benjamin was a really quiet, introspective kid. He was a lot like Mom that way. He hated confrontation, hated any kind of aggression. Whenever Dad came home either drunk or high, he would rush up to his room and lock himself in there until Dad was either passed out or gone again."

I put my spoon down. "Sometimes, I resented him for it. It just sometimes felt like he was leaving me to deal with the train wreck that was our parents. He couldn't seem to find the strength to fight our father or be there to look after our mother. He just kinda retreated into himself. It wasn't until much later that I realized that he was just trying to survive our home, our childhood. He couldn't deal with anything else because he was falling apart himself."

She puts her hand on my arm. "You couldn't have known that at the time, Tobias."

"I didn't really bother to try. I left whenever I could. I made a family with Daniel and Kristen, and Benjamin fell by the wayside."

"You were a kid—"

"We were *all* kids. It's not an excuse."

I can feel the pressure of each one of her fingers digging

into my skin. Her eyes never leave my face, and I realize that I can't look away either. I can't break the eye contact.

How is it that this woman can make me talk? How is it that I actually want to talk when I'm with her? Why does everything hurt less when she's with me?

"I'm sorry… I probably shouldn't have gone there…"

She shakes her head. "I'm glad you did. I feel like I know you better now."

I swallow and my throat hurts. "I should have done more for him. I was making money at that point. I could have gotten him the help he needed."

"Tobias—"

"But our relationship had been reduced down to a call once or twice a month. That was the extent of things and I never tried to get closer to him. He represented a part of my life that I'd left behind. And selfishly, I wanted to keep it that way."

"You can't blame yourself for what happened to him."

I look at those compassionate hazel eyes of hers. They're so damn beautiful that they brighten the entire room.

"Yes, I can. I should have been there for him. I should have protected him."

"No one can protect you from yourself."

"I could have tried. But I was too focused on myself. On getting out, making money, being far away from all that pain. I didn't even stop to consider that Benjamin might be in more pain than me."

I stare at her, waiting for her expression to change. Waiting for her to look at me with judgment or distaste or loathing. The compassion never leaves her soft features. "Do you know how alone he must have felt to believe that suicide was the only way out for him?"

"I always thought that maybe because of what we went

through in that house, we'd be closer as adults. But it was the opposite. And maybe that was mostly my fault. I picked my friends over him."

"Don't say that—"

"It's true."

"Hey." Suddenly, she's standing. Her hands come down on either side of my face. She cups my jaw, forcing me to look at her. "You're not the kind of person who turns his back on anyone who needs help. Least of all your family."

My eyes go wide. "How do you know what kind of person I am?"

She shrugs. "I just do. I can feel it… Right…" She takes my hand and places it on her chest, "…here."

My heart is beating so fast that I can barely keep up with it. There are alarm bells going off in my head, telling me to get the fuck out before it's too late.

May day. May day. May day.

"It's not your fault, Tobias. Everyone else's pain is not your fault. It's not your responsibility either."

"I was his brother."

She gives me a small smile and hugs me. "You're still his brother, Tobias. His death doesn't change that."

I wrap my arms around her and breathe in her citrus scent. It's intoxicating, it's overwhelming. It feels like she's peeling back the layers I'd put in place after each new tragedy, each new life-changing event. It's like she's wading through all the bullshit and looking at me, the *real* me.

When I open my eyes, I notice that the ice cream is melting slowly, sweating out onto the counter. I should probably break this hug and give her a lift back home. There's still time to stop it before it's too late.

But there's a nagging voice in the back of my head that's saying *it's already too late. Forgive me,* I think to myself, even though I have no idea who I'm talking to. *Please. Forgive me.*

"Can I see a picture of him?" Ashley asks, pulling me out of my reverie.

At this point, why the fuck not? "I have a few pictures stashed away in my bedroom," I tell her, gesturing for her to stay put while I go get them.

I pull out the old, worn album from the bottom cabinet drawer opposite my bed. When I turn around to walk it back to her, I realize she's standing on the threshold of my door, looking right at me.

"The view's even better from here."

She walks past me towards the windows, admiring the view with a little smile playing on her face. I stand where I am, wondering what the hell I'm supposed to do now. It's bad enough she's in my apartment. But now she's in my *bedroom*?

This can't be happening.

I distract myself by pulling out an old picture of Benjamin. I'm in it too, but my back's to the camera, and I can mostly just see a tiny profile with a bunch of dark curls. Benjamin's looking right at the camera though. He's probably about five in the picture. All smiles and laughter, something sweet and sticky, smeared at the edges of his mouth.

Underneath that picture is another one that features both of us when we were older. I was probably fourteen and Benjamin was fifteen. We're standing side by side, our shoulders touching. I was already three inches taller than he was at that point. Neither one of us is smiling anymore. We're just staring blankly at the camera as though we'd been ordered to. In fact, now that I think about it, we probably had been ordered to.

Ashley walks up to me and I hand her both pictures. She

stares at the first one for a long time. The one of us when we were teenagers.

"Wow," she breathes. "He looks a little like you."

"You think? People used to say that all the time but I never saw it."

She shrugs. "I think that's normal. But look at the shape of his face, his eyes... the two of you could pass for twins."

"We often were."

"See?"

She moves on to the second picture of us as little boys. "Oh," she sighs, a smile playing across her lips. "This is a beautiful photo."

"Pretty sure Mum took it on one of our birthdays. Can't remember whose it was though."

"He looks so happy. So do you."

She traces her finger over the ring of curls that's covering my face from view. "You're beautiful." She hands the pictures back to me and I put them away. "You haven't changed much, you know."

I raise my eyebrows. "Really? Because sometimes when I look back, I can't even recognize myself."

"Do you miss him?"

"Sometimes," I admit. "But the thing is, we drifted so far apart as we got older that I didn't know him well enough in the end to miss him. That's a horrible thing to admit, isn't it?"

She shakes her head. "No. It's just honest."

"I wish I knew just how much he was suffering. I wish I'd been around more. I could have helped him."

"Don't do that to yourself. You can't change anything now."

I sigh. "No... I can't..."

She puts her hand on my arm. "I'm so sorry, Tobias. You really don't deserve the hand you've been dealt."

I raise my eyebrows.

I smile. "As far as the hand I've been dealt, I think I got a pretty good one."

She shakes her head. "You've earned all this," she says, looking around. "And that's amazing. But a fancy apartment and expensive clothes and all the luxuries in the world can't buy happiness or peace of mind or security. Those things can only come from yourself, from other people."

I raise my eyebrows. "How'd you get to be so smart?"

She smiles sadly. "I've spent a lot of time feeling sorry for myself, hating myself, blaming myself and trying to figure myself out. And at the end of the day, I'd like to think I know what's really important in life."

"Which is what?"

She runs her hand over my arm. "This," she whispers. "Connection. Isn't that what we all want at the end of the day?"

She takes a step towards me and I know I need to stop her. But then her lips land on mine and I know there's no way I can stop this. It just feels too damn good. Too damn natural. And then my body starts taking control.

And I know—there's just no stopping this.

CHAPTER 27

Ashley

W e've been talking for a long time.

So long, in fact, that this feels inevitable. The more I spoke to him, the more I wanted to share. The more he seemed to be willing to open up to me, the more he shared, the more I realized—I *know* this man.

I may not know everything there is to know about him. But I understand his deepest instincts, his darkest fears. I understand who he is at his core and that's not something I've ever been able to say about any other man in my life.

With my father, I've known and understood parts of him. But I've never been able to disassociate the man from the father.

With Henry, it was a lot of emotion. It was the thrill of first love and the obsessive nature of a first relationship. But looking at it with fresh eyes, I can see that what I felt for Henry didn't even come close to what I feel for Tobias right now.

Henry was a boy and Tobias is a man.

Henry fulfilled all my girlish fantasies, the idealistic

nature of my personality that rarely got fed. But Tobias was the incarnation of what I wanted as a woman. As an adult. He was the stability that I'd craved all my life but never received. It was a stability, a security that came from knowing who you really are and accepting it.

Every time I kiss Tobias, it feels like I'm right where I'm meant to be. It feels like I'm coming home.

And yes, there are butterflies and fireworks going off at the back of my head. But I don't lose myself in him like I used to with Henry. It's more like I *find* myself with Tobias. Whenever I'm with him, I feel like I know myself a little better.

It's the kind of connection that makes you *better.* And up until recently, I thought that kind of relationship was a myth that lived on the pages of great romance novels.

So even though he'd told me a dozen times that nothing could ever happen between us, I guess the simple answer is—I don't believe him.

Because who stumbles across a connection like this one and turns their back on it? Who comes face to face with the kind of romance that great love stories are made of and says no, not today?

If I know one thing about Tobias Mason Ackerman, it's that he's stubborn as hell. And he thinks that because he's got fifteen years on me, that he knows best. Well, I've got news for him. He *doesn't* know best. And I'm gonna prove it to him —one kiss at a time.

Not that we've come up for air in the last two minutes. His lips are fused to mine and when his lips finally part, my tongue entwines with his, trying to take as much as I can before he pulls the rug out from underneath me.

"Ashley," he murmurs as my lips slide down his neck. "Fuck… we can't…"

"We already have," I remind him. "Twice."

His hands land on my hips but the way he touches me is tentative. Like he's worried that he's going to break me if he pushes too hard. Maybe that's why I rip his shirt apart and push him onto his massive king-size bed.

He bounces on the mattress and I steady him by climbing aboard, letting my hands roam down his sculpted chest, the perfect lines of his abs. He's got eight of them. That's another thing I assumed was just a myth.

"Ashley," he keeps saying my name as though that'll compel me to stop. But I can feel his erection pushing through his crotch and I know that he wants this as much as I do. He's just ashamed that he does.

"I see you, Tobias. I understand you. I know that scares the hell out of you but *this*—" I pull at the waistband of his trousers and start to unzip him, "—is what I want."

He mutters a muted curse as I pull his cock free and slide down his torso until I'm on my knees. He sits up and tries to grab me. "Don't…"

"Give me one good reason why not?"

He opens his mouth but nothing comes out. I bend my head down and slide his cock inside my mouth. "*Fuck,*" he moans. "Ashley…"

And this time, when he says my name, I know he's not trying to stop me. That's encouragement if ever I've heard it.

I run my tongue over his tip, taking his head into my mouth and sucking on him like a lollipop. I realize as I take him deeper into my mouth that he might just be the first man I've ever enjoyed oral sex with. It's the only time I've ever *wanted* to suck a man off. The only time I've felt like I can get off on the idea of making *him* get off. It doesn't feel transactional at all. It feels like this is for the both of us. Together.

"Jesus," he gasps as I take him deeper. "Ashley…"

I love how easily my name slides off his tongue. I love the way his hands reach for me, grappling to touch some part of me. I wait until his body is spasming out of control before I finally pull back, desperate to quench the heat between my legs. It's never felt like this before—this urgent, this intense.

I feel as though my body just might explode if I don't give it what it's craving. I pull off the remainder of my clothes as I climb on top of him, straddling him hard. His erection sits between my thighs, slick with my saliva. His eyes are trained on me, and there's a burn in those irises that makes me feel like I'm the one on fire.

I raise my hips and with my eyes on him, I sit down on his cock. He slides inside me seamlessly, filling me up until my jaw drops and my eyelashes flutter.

"Ohh," I gasp.

Is it possible to cum with just one thrust? It certainly feels that way from where I'm sitting. I place my hands on his chest and use it to lift myself off him. I raise my hips and slam them back down on his cock while his hands glide over my body with reverence.

"God," he whispers. "You're so damn beautiful…"

As his hands slip over my breasts, I start riding him harder. My hair flies wildly around my head and my legs start cramping slightly but I still keep going, chasing the high that I can feel coming up slowly.

"Ahh," I moan. "Yes, yes… *fuck*…"

Just when I think I'm going to explode. He sits up a little and grabs me by the hips. Then he twists around, taking me with him. He rolls around so that he's the one on top and he starts slamming his hips against me, fucking me so hard that I can't control my screams any longer.

I gasp and moan and cry out without any sense of inhibition. I don't even care that the neighbors will hear me. I don't care if the whole damn city hears me. I want this. And I want it with this man.

The first orgasm feels like freefalling. The second one makes me feel like I'm flying. The only thing I can hear is the sound of flesh on flesh. The only thing I can feel is my own heartbeat thundering wildly against my chest. The only thing I can smell is him—that deep, woodsy musk that I wish I could imprint onto my skin.

"*Fuck*," he moans as he comes inside me, his teeth gritted so hard that I can feel their metallic grind.

He rolls off me almost immediately, his breathing coming in fast and harsh. Just when I'm about to reach for him, he sits up and my hands fall to the bed.

"Tobias," I say gently.

He flinches as if I've shouted. Before I can say another word, he gets up and retreats to the bathroom. It's amazing how quickly the high wears off. I sit up uncertainly and look around. Our clothes are strewn all over the bedroom floor. I sit there long enough to understand that something is not right with him.

So by the time he walks back out of the bathroom again, I'm fully clothed and staring out at the view, my shoulders tense with expectation.

"Ashley."

I turn around slowly, steeling myself against the same old roadblock we seem to face off against every single time.

Apparently, even amazing, mind-blowing, transformative sex isn't enough to break down the roadblocks.

His face is somber. He definitely doesn't look like a man who just had an orgasm. He looks alert and wary. He looks like a man who wishes he had thought a little harder before jumping into the ice-cold lake.

"Listen—"

"Are you on the pill?"

I stop short. "What?"

"Are you on the pill?" He glances at the bed. "It all happened so fast that I didn't have time to put on a condom."

My eyes go wide. *That's* what he's thinking about right now? "Yes," I say curtly. "I'm on the pill."

"Do you need the morning after—"

"You don't believe me?" I demand.

He takes a deep breath. "Of course, I believe you. I'm sorry. It's just… that was the first time I've ever… got so carried away in the moment. I should have thought about protection."

"We weren't really thinking."

"Clearly."

I flinch. "What's that supposed to mean?"

He runs a hand through his hair and avoids my eyes. "The sun's coming up," he says without answering my question. "Won't your Dad be worried?"

I frown. "I'm an adult. He knows he doesn't have to worry about me."

"Then he's a liar. Every parent worries about their kids."

"Except for the ones that do drugs or abandon their kids while they're still babies."

This time, he's the one that flinches. I immediately regret saying it though. I don't want to fall into a space where I use the things he's told me in confidence against him. I don't want to turn all those intimate conversations we've had into something ugly.

"I'm sorry," I say. "That was outta line."

He nods. "Let me drive you home."

I raise my eyebrows. "You want me to leave?"

"Fuck," he mutters under his breath. "You can't stay here,

Ashley! This… *fuck*… this should never have happened. It was a mistake. *You* are a mistake."

I draw in a sharp breath. The shock of hearing those words hits first. Then comes the hurt. It just feels so damn *personal*.

I swallow back the words that are threatening to roll off my tongue and push past him. "*Shit*," I hear him mutter from behind me. But I don't bother glancing around or stopping. I make straight for the elevator.

I hit the button only to discover that I need a freaking code to open the elevator doors. "Can you open them for me, please?" I ask heatedly.

"Ashley, wait!"

"You wanted me to go. I'm going!"

His expression is pained. "You don't even have your shoes on."

I glance down at my feet and realize that he's right. I'm so desperate to get out that I've completely forgotten my shoes. I grab them quickly but I don't bother putting them on. "I'll wear them in the elevator. Can you just *please* get the doors open for me."

He moves towards the access code. "Ashley… I'm sorry."

"Don't."

He sighs and punches in the code. His finger lingers over the last digit. "Please understand. Daniel would never forgive me."

"What about me?" I demand. "Does my forgiveness count for nothing?"

His eyes slide away from me and he punches in the last digit. I rush into the elevator and click the ground floor button three times in quick succession before it closes. He's standing there in the center as the doors come together.

"I'm sorry," he mouths one last time before the doors shut on his face.

CHAPTER 28

Tobias

I half expect her to call in sick that Monday.

A part of me actually hopes that she does. But in the end, she's at her desk by eight-thirty with a fresh cup of coffee in hand. I wonder if it's just my imagination or if she looks extra special today.

She's wearing her hair loose, which is out of the ordinary. She usually keeps it in a sleek bun or at least a ponytail when she's working. She's also wearing a tight black pencil skirt and a blood red silk blouse that's just translucent enough that I can make out the faint outline of what is a very sexy black bra. Even her heels have an extra inch on them and the heel is the thin, sharp kind. Not the thick, short, flat heel that I'm used to seeing her in.

When she walks into my office with my updated schedule for the week, I notice that she's even got a little make-up on. It's subtle, just a little eyeshadow, blush and lipstick but it's eye catching enough to get my attention.

Then again, *anything* she does at this point is bound to catch my attention.

I'd spent most of the weekend obsessing about the last

Friday night, going through every little detail. Cursing myself out and then turning myself on in a hamster wheel that I couldn't seem to get off of.

The one moment that I just couldn't seem to get out of my head no matter how hard I tried.

Those blissful three seconds of complete and utter, pure unadulterated pleasure when she'd lowered herself down on top of me bare. It had genuinely felt as though my heart was going to jump right outta my chest.

I had never been inside a woman bare before.

There was always, *always* a condom. The last two times I'd been with her, I'd remembered to put one on. But this time?

I'd completely lost the plot. I was so desperate to be inside her that I'd forgotten about protection. It wasn't like I was scared of pregnancy or anything. I believed her when she said she was on the pill. I was just worried about what being inside her bare was gonna do to my already flailing will power.

How am I supposed to resist her now? How am I supposed to be a good guy, a good friend and walk away when I know what it's like to be inside her, with nothing between us?

Because *fuck*, does it feel good. The kind of good that's life changing, transformative—all-consuming.

The kind of good that means I just. Can't. Stop. Thinking. About. It.

"Beijing called and asked if the nine-thirty Zoom meeting scheduled on Wednesday could be moved to ten-thirty."

The shade of lipstick she's wearing matches the subtle bloom of her cheeks. Her lips look fuller today too. "That's fine."

"I printed out the schedule already but I can make an amendment."

"Don't bother. Just write it in. Actually, I can do it myself."

She nods but she doesn't leave. She just stands there looking like every fantasy I've had in the last forty-eight hours come to life.

"Is there anything else?"

She sighs, letting the PA persona drop for a moment. "Dad wants me to invite you over for dinner again tomorrow night."

Shit.

"I don't think that's a good idea, Ashley."

"Well then, tell him that. And if he asks you can tell him why too." She turns towards the door. "I'm sure as hell not about to make your excuses for you. My job description doesn't stretch that far."

"Ashley!"

She stops short and turns reluctantly. "Yes, sir?"

"Come on… don't do that."

"Don't do what?"

"Act like I get some sort of sick pleasure out of hurting you. I don't. It kills me but—"

"You know my Grandma used to say that saying 'but' disqualifies everything you say before it. I'm inclined to agree."

"*However—*"

"That's just a fancy but."

I sigh. "I'm sorry."

She shakes her head. "Don't you ever get tired of apologizing?"

"All the time," I admit. "But apparently, I'm not smart

enough to keep myself from doing the stupid thing that requires an apology."

Her eyes go wide. "So… I'm the stupid thing you did that you need to apologize for, huh?"

Jesus. How do I always manage to say the wrong thing where Ashley's concerned. It's like I've constantly got my foot in my mouth. Or my cock in her… well you know.

Basically, I've always got my body parts in places they have no right to be.

"That's not what I meant. At all."

She nods. "Whatever, boss. I've got to get back to my desk. I've got reports that need filing and documents that need organizing." She gets as far as the door before she turns around and fixes me with that direct gaze of hers. "Not for nothing—Dad's gonna get suspicious if you keep avoiding him. The more you act like there's something to hide, the more he's going to know you're hiding something. Just saying."

She snaps the door shut and leaves me to stew.

"Fuck," I mutter to my empty office.

I'm trying to think of an excuse to call her back in here when my phone starts to ring. The number is unidentified but I pick up anyway.

"Hello?"

"*An inmate from California State Prison is trying to contact you. Do you accept this call?*"

It's amazing how easily I can fall back into the angry young man I was a few years ago. It's been a while since I got one of these calls. Then again, it's been a while since I last visited him.

"*Sir, do you accept this call?*"

There's clearly another person on the other side of this phone but it sounds strangely automated. As life in a prison sucks the life right out of you and leaves behind only robots. My palms are sweating already and my entire body feels tight —tense.

"Yes, I accept."

There's a weird clicking sound and then I hear his breathing. He still breathes the same way. Heavy and menacing. As though he has to fight for every breath. I try and imagine him in his prison uniform, holding the phone with his wiry hands, the same ones he had used to beat on Mum; to beat on me.

"Trent."

I stopped calling him Dad a long time ago. But strangely, it's easier when I'm face to face with him. It feels strange using his first name over the phone.

"Toby." His voice is raspy. Deeper than I remember too. I'm guessing he's still finding ways to smoke whenever he can.

"I'm here." What do you ask your incarcerated father? How the hell do you make conversation? "Is there… a reason you're calling?"

I can hear the clicking of his tongue. He used to do that when he was annoyed at something but he knew that losing his temper would be counter-productive. He didn't call to talk to me. He didn't call to ask how I was doing. He was calling because he needs something and I'm his last resort.

"You haven't come to see me for a while now."

I raise my eyebrows. "I didn't think you wanted to see me."

"That's bullshit. You stopped coming because *you* didn't want to."

I take a deep breath. There was no slow build with Trent. It was no holds barred right from the get go. "Yeah, okay. Fine. I wasn't interested in seeing you. It's not like you made those visits particularly pleasant."

"You want me to roll out the red carpet for you, boy?" he snarls. "Get a fucking welcome party all ready? I'm in prison. It's not a fucking sorority house."

"You called for a reason. What do you want?"

There's a few moments of silence on the other side. "I need money. I need to buy shit from commissary and I never have enough."

"Last I heard, you have a job."

"My *job* pays fifty fucking cents an hour," he growls. "I don't even make a hundred dollars a month."

"Well the state is taking care of all your other expenses, so I don't see why you would need any more."

It's not that I actually believe that. I just want to piss him off. Whenever I hear my father's voice, all I want to do is punch his lights out. It's the complete lack of humility or apology in his tone. It makes me fucking wild.

"Are you fucking serious? You're a fucking tycoon and your old man is forced to share a bunk with three other fuckers every night with a shiv under his pillow."

"Kinda makes up for the time Benjamin and I had to sleep with shivs under our pillows, huh?"

The moment I go there, I regret it. The best way to create chaos is to bring up the past, especially with the people who refuse to face it.

"We are talking about that shit again. Lemme tell you, you boys had it fucking *easy*."

"Are you serious?"

"My old man used to burn me with his fucking cigarettes just for fun. He used to beat me until I was unconscious. He used to take a cane to my back any time I pissed him off. And trust me, everything I did pissed him off."

"So you're excuse is, I had a worse father so stop complaining?"

"That's exactly what you need to do. Stop complaining. I may have been harsh when you were a boy, but I made you the man you are today. Do you think you'd have that big successful company or that fancy ass life if it weren't for *me*!"

I freeze as he so casually claims credit for everything I've accomplished.

"You should be fucking thanking me. Not punishing me. My father would have strangled me in my sleep if I ever spoke to him the way you fucking speak to me."

"You *did* try to strangle me once," I hiss, getting to my feet. "I took a beer out of your six-pack one night, remember? You stormed into my room, told my friend to get out and when I told you to get the fuck away from me, you punched me in the face and tried to strangle me. You might have actually killed me if my friend didn't smash her skateboard over your head."

There's silence for a moment on the other line. "That didn't happen."

"Of course it fucking happened."

"I didn't do that."

"Well you were high on a cocktail of drugs and alcohol, so you probably don't remember. But you were stone cold sober the day you decided to 'teach Benjamin a lesson' by waterboarding him in the bathtub."

A small part of me is aware that I'm shouting. But I can't bring myself to calm down or quiet down. I pace up and down my office, trying to get this fucker to take responsibility for one single thing that he'd done.

"You remember Benjamin, don't you, Trent?" I demand. "He was the kid you beat into depression until he turned out just like Mum. He killed himself with a fucking rope. Put in a fucking hook and tied the rope to it so it was clear he'd been planning it for a while. Remember how you used to tell him that you wanted to string him up like a piece of meat. He did it to himself, no doubt with *your* fucking voice in his ears."

"Where were you?"

I stop short, freezing in place. All the light streaming in through the windows is confusing somehow. Especially because in my mind, I'm standing in Benjamin's dank little apartment where light went to die.

Where was I?

"You're going to blame *me* for his death."

"I was in fucking prison. Didn't have anything to do with me."

"Jesus Christ, you're a fucking monster. Your oldest son fucking *killed* himself."

The tongue clicking is getting faster and faster. "It's nature's way of weeding out the weak, boy. Benjamin was too fucking weak for life. Least he had the sense to take himself out before someone else did."

"You mother*fucker*—"

"I need a couple of hundred," he snaps harshly. "You owe me that."

"I owe you *nothing*."

"I may be a monster but I'm the monster who gave you life. And I'm the only family you have left."

Somewhere in the midst of all my hate, I'm able to recognize the same thing. Mum's gone. Benjamin's gone. Kristen's gone. The only person I have left, I've already fucked over by fucking his only daughter.

I knew it was wrong and I did it anyway. I've been trying to convince myself all this time that I'm nothing like my father. He was addicted to chaos and I wanted the opposite. I wanted a small, secure, boring life.

I might have been able to stick to that narrative even after sleeping with Ashley the first time. But the second time? The third?

"I'll put some money in commissary for you," I growl. "But just so you know, I am the man I am today *despite* you. Not because of you."

I hang up, feeling as though I'm floating up out of my body. How is it that after all these fucking years, he still has some sick power over me? Even from prison, his hold is strong, his words still have the ability to cut me down and make me question who I am.

When I put my phone down, I notice my hand is shaking.

"Tobias."

I whip around and find her standing inside my office. The door is closed. I have no idea how long she's been standing there; how much she heard.

She walks over to me silently, her eyes fixed on mine. Just when I think she's about to say something, she takes another step forward.

She hugs me.

And just like that, I'm back in my body. I'm back in my life.

And somehow, I can breathe again.

CHAPTER 29

Ashley

I t's the first time I've felt this way.

The need to be strong *for* someone else. The need to get my shit together just so that I can put someone else back together. I've always felt like I was on the brink of self-destruction. Like whenever I got to a place where I might be happy, I'd self-sabotage. That instinct had become familiar, even comfortable.

But right now, it felt like a stumbling block. One that I needed to kick to the curb if I was ever going to be able to be there for Tobias the way he needed me to be.

He doesn't exactly hug me back but I don't care. After hearing his side of the conversation, I couldn't unsee the images rattling around in my brain. His father didn't just abuse them. He had *tortured* them.

The fact that Tobias has turned out to be a good man and an upstanding citizen despite his childhood is beyond me. Especially considering his childhood scars were so much worse than mine.

So my mother had abandoned me? What was that

compared to a father who had almost killed him with his bare hands. And for what? Taking a beer out of his six pack?

Jesus Christ.

I'm not usually in the habit of comparing pain. But in this case, I can't help myself. It puts everything into perspective. I understand now why he keeps telling me that sometimes the best thing a parent can do for their child is leave. I'll bet he had that often enough growing up in that house.

He clears his throat and pushes me away gently. "You don't have to do this," he says gruffly.

"Do what?"

"Be here. Comfort me." He turns his back to me. "It's not your job."

"I'm not here as your PA right now. I'm here because…" What is the right way to finish that sentence? *I'm here because I may be in love with you? Because you're the most amazing man I've ever known. Because I care more about you than I do about myself?* "… because we're friends."

"Friends," he mutters under his breath. "Is that what we are."

"For the purposes of this conversation, I'm gonna say yes." He almost smiles. I join him at the window and we watch the skyline together. "I wasn't aware you were in communication with your father."

"I'm not. Not for a while at least. But he called and… I didn't have the fucking guts to turn down the call."

I raise my eyebrows. "It's not about your guts. You didn't have the heart to turn down the call."

"Why do you assume I'm so much better than I actually am?" He actually sounds annoyed.

I shrug. "It's because you *are* so much better than you think."

"You're biased."

"No. I really don't think I am."

"Based on what evidence?"

"Based on the way you treat the waitstaff at restaurants. The fact that you make eye contact whenever you ask them for something. The fact that you tip well. The fact that you look after your employees. You know their names, their kids' names. You *care*. Most rich men don't." That stumps him for a moment. "You're a good man, Tobias Mason Ackerman. Time to accept that."

He smirks. "Thanks."

"For what exactly?"

He glances at me. "For everything."

I have no idea what he means by 'everything' but I decide not to press him. His body is still tense, probably still reeling from the shock of that call. I know it's still in *my* system and I had nothing to do with his father or his childhood.

"He's in jail," Tobias says softly. I raise my eyebrows and he nods. "He's had a few fights in prison so he's serving longer than he was sentenced."

"Jesus."

I nod. "I don't know why I can't just cut the bastard off. Lord knows I don't owe him shit."

"You're looking for closure," I say immediately. The answer seems pretty obvious to me, but Tobias's head swivels in my direction as though I've introduced a whole new concept to him.

"Closure?"

I nod. "I mean… it's the whole reason I can't stop thinking about my mother. It's not that I want a magical fix to our relationship. I don't think I even want a relationship at all. I just want… answers. Some clarity. Perspective."

"I'm not sure we can expect to get any of that from the people who hurt us."

I smile. "Are you always this optimistic?"

One corner of his mouth turns up but it goes back down again just as quickly. "Sometimes it's hard to believe that you're only twenty. You've got all this wisdom that makes you seem so much older."

I smirk. "You're only as old as you feel, right? Well I've pretty much felt like I was fifty since I was fifteen."

"I always did have a thing for older women."

I glance at him and we both laugh together. "Shit," he sighs, running a hand over his face. "I shouldn't have said that."

"It was funny."

"I think the word you're looking for is ironic."

"Same difference."

He snorts. "Right." He turns to me slowly, his eyes scanning my face as though he's searching for something. "Why is it so fucking easy to talk to you?"

"Because you like me. And because you trust me."

He nods. "I *never* talk about my childhood. And I certainly never talk about my father… to anyone."

"Well—I was kinda eavesdropping."

"That's true."

I bite my bottom lip. "I just… I couldn't ignore it, Tobias. I heard you shouting; I heard the pain in your voice and I just couldn't leave you to deal with it on your own."

He frowns. "Like I said, friends or not, it's not your job to take care of me, Ashley."

"What if I want to?"

He grits his teeth and scowls. "Then you're a damn fool."

I flinch back from the venom is his voice. "I'm a lot of things," I hiss. "But a fool is not one of them. You pretend like you can't cross this imaginary line you've invented in your head because of Dad. But it's not about him at all, is it? He's just the *excuse* you're using to keep me at bay."

His eyes flash. "And why would I do that?"

"Because deep down, you *know* that this thing between us is real. And you're terrified of letting me get too close because you're terrified of the possibility that you might lose me someday." His eyes go wide. "I get that you're worried about what Dad will think and honestly? I am too. He might get upset but he'll get over it. He'll get over it the moment he sees that what we have is real." He flinches and I know I've hit a nerve. "You act as though we're so damn different from one another. Well, I've got news for you, buddy. We're two sides of the same damn coin."

He stares at me wordlessly for a long time. The silence stretches on and I wonder who's going to break first.

Fuck that. It's not gonna be me.

"You need to leave, Ashley." His voice is cold and formal. "You've crossed a line."

"Tobias—"

"The next time you overstep again—I'm gonna have to find myself a new assistant."

My eyes go wide with shock. *Is he serious?* He's gonna turn around and turn all the no-nonsense boss on me *now*? After all those heartfelt conversations? After all that insanely mind-blowing sex? He's going to treat me like I'm a fucking stranger?

The intellectual part of my brain tells me that this is typical behavior for someone with walls as high as Tobias's. I've cracked through his iron-clad surface, so he's pushing me away, trying to create enough distance between us so he can build his walls back up.

But the emotional part of my brain is wracked with hurt and needy with longing. Is it possible that I've met the love of my life and he thinks it's his duty to reject me? And for my *father*?

He's right about one thing though. The whole situation is cruelly ironic.

Well fine. If he wants to play it that way—I'm game.

"Apologies, *sir*. It won't happen again."

Then I twist around and walk out of his office.

CHAPTER 30

Ashley

The lunchroom is stuffed to the gills as more people file through in honor of Louisa's surprise farewell/retirement party. It's six o'clock and Louisa's due at any moment.

People are keeping the chatter to a minimum as they wait to hear footsteps from down the hall. I glance towards Helene, another PA on my floor. "Why does she think she's coming here?"

"Oh, don't worry, Mr. Ackerman's got it covered."

I raise my eyebrows. "Wait. Tob—um, Mr. Ackerman's coming to the party too?"

"Of course. He's always at every retirement party for his employees. From the directors right down to the janitorial staff."

Of course he is. That checks out. The man is a great boss and a good man, which is why it's so difficult to be mad at him. Not that I'm not trying damn hard right now.

"He foots the bill for these parties too," Helene says, giving me a wink. "Honestly, if I weren't worried about being fired for sexual harassment, I'd harass the hell outta that man."

"*Helene*!"

She grins unapologetically at me. "Can you blame me? He's fucking *delicious*. And I'm only human."

"You also have a live-in boyfriend," I remind her.

She rolls her eyebrows. "Honestly, I think Malcolm would give me a free pass for Mr. Ackerman. Just like I'd give him a free pass if he ever ran into Angelina Jolie."

I smirk. "How charitable of you both."

She laughs. "It's what keeps the relationship hot." She glances towards the door and then back at me. "Is this your first retirement party for the company?"

"Yup."

She grins wider. "Sweet. They're always tons of fun. Mr. Ackerman really doesn't scrimp. We get the good food and the good booze. And there's *always* a cake. Come on, let's go see what we have got today."

I follow her to the long, narrow table that's been set up by the window. It's loaded with food and Helene's right. Everything looks delicious. Like we're at an upscale cocktail party instead of an after-work party for a retiring employee.

"How long has Louisa worked for Ackerman Corp.?"

"Pretty much since it started. She actually started as Mr. Ackerman's assistant. But apparently, he promoted her after the first couple of years. Even gave her shares in the company."

I raise my eyebrows. "No way."

Helene nods. "He's the only man I know that can look at someone and see a business woman with the potential to start a second career instead of a grandmother pushing sixty. Pretty sure Louisa was around that when she started working here."

I suppress a sigh. I really need to stop talking to Tobias's employees about him. Every single person in this room is either madly in love with him or deeply envious of what he's achieved. The men tend to fall in the latter category.

"*Shh,*" someone hisses. "They're coming."

The room goes silent and Louisa and Tobias's voices come through loud and clear. "Mr. Ackerman really… I don't even need retirement benefits. You've taken care of me well over the years…"

"It's what you're owed, Louisa. I'm not doing you any favors."

"Now that's just—"

They turn the corner and everyone jumps out right on cue. *"SURPRISE!"*

Louisa jerks back with her hand on her heart. "Oh… my…"

Tobias steadies her with a hand to the shoulder and she turns to him in shock. "You. You did this."

"Actually, *everyone* pitched in. That's how much you're loved, Louisa."

She turns around and takes in the mass of people crowded into the lunch room. Her eyes get all foggy and she sniffs loudly. "Oh boy, here come the water works."

Tobias politely gets out of the way while everyone moves forward to speak to Louisa. Across the sea of heads, his eyes meet mine. I look away instantly and turn to the first person on my right, who just happens to be sneaking himself a little treat from the food table.

"Shit," he gasps, the cream bun in his mouth preventing him from saying anything else. I giggle as he hides his face behind one hand. I pass him a napkin and he swallows. "Sorry."

"Don't be sorry. I do the same thing all the time."

"I can't even pretend that I'm hungry. It's just greed. I love me a cream bun."

"That makes two of us."

"Yeah?" he says, grabbing one of the tiered trays and handing it to me. "Then join me. Let's celebrate Louisa together."

Smiling, I take the bun I'm offered. But unlike him, I don't put the whole thing in my mouth. I just take a small bite. "I'm Ashley by the way."

"Sam," he says. He has a nice smile. A dependable face. The kind of quiet attractiveness that would have caught my attention well before now if I hadn't been so preoccupied with everything else going on in my life.

"Hmm, you're right. These are great."

"They're done by this family bakery on the South side. Everything's made in-house. Fresh ingredients. Can you taste the slight tang in the…"

He trails off when he sees the look on my face. Then he starts blushing. "I'm a foodie."

"I'm shocked."

He laughs. "It's weird that we've never really talked before now. We do work on the same floor and we're both new employees."

"Which is why we're always busy, trying to prove we deserve to work here."

He bows his head in agreement. "Truer words have never been spoken. I felt like such a fraud my first week here. Almost quit a bunch of times."

I frown. "You did get the job fair and square though."

He looks instantly uncomfortable. "Umm… to be honest, my brother helped me get this job. He works in the sales department and he recommended me for the job when it opened up." He gives me a cautious glance. "Do you hate me now?"

I smirk. "I can't afford to. My father got me this job."

His eyes go wide. "No *way*."

"Oh yeah. In my defense, I didn't know that my Dad had pulled strings to get me in here. I found out after."

Sam cringes. "How'd you find out?"

"When I realized the man I was working for is also my father's best friend."

"Tobias Ackerman?"

"He went by Mason back home. Took his mother's maiden name when he moved to Cali."

"Damn, that must have been awkward."

"It was. But I couldn't even stay mad at my Dad for long. He just wants what's best for me and this move was a lot for him to wrap his head around."

"Protective Dad, huh?"

"Well, he's never really been overly protective. I think he just felt guilty."

"About what?"

I shrug. "The fact that I dropped out of college and moved here." I realize that my explanation is wanting. "Um, turns out, college can be quite expensive. And I didn't get the scholarship I was hoping for and Dad was busting his ass trying to put me through college. In the end I decided it wasn't worth it."

"Shit, that's heavy."

I shrug. "I made the right decision in coming here. He just needs to know that I'm alright."

"Hence the job."

I nod. "Exactly."

"Well—" Sam's gaze flickers past me and his eyes flare slightly. "Oh um, hi Mr. Ackerman."

I tense up instantly but I try and keep my expression neutral as I turn on the spot. Sure enough, he's standing just opposite us on the other side of the table. But his gaze is trained on Sam.

"Sam, am I right?"

"Uh yes, that's right. I can't believe you remember me."

"I hired you. Of course I remember you." Tobias smiles but the smile doesn't quite reach his eyes. "Having fun?"

"Oh yeah," Sam nods. "The food is amazing."

"I ordered food from all Louisa's favorite places in the city," he says, his gaze flitting to me for only a moment.

Sam smiles nervously, probably wondering why in the hell the CEO of the company is talking to him right now. "I hear Louisa was one of your first employees?"

"She was. I probably wouldn't have gotten through that first year without her."

The two of them keep talking and I kinda stand there in limbo, not knowing what to do. In the end, I grab another cream bun and retreat into the crowd, hoping to get lost in the party. I succeed for all of two minutes before I notice Tobias a few feet away from me, talking to the accounts team.

No matter where I go, my eyes keep going back to him. He really does have a great rapport with his employees. Everyone seems to love him. There's a real sense of familial harmony within the group.

As the music kicks up a notch, Sam finds me in the corner of the room by the windows. "Hey you, I was wondering where you'd disappeared to."

"Just observing," I say.

"It's a pretty rad working environment, huh? Never worked anywhere where the people seem to like each other so much. *Definitely* never worked anywhere where they've liked their boss so much."

I look to the side and catch Tobias again. It's not exactly hard to do, considering he stands about a foot taller than everyone else. He's chatting with one of the higher-ups; a fellow director with long blonde hair and a tight navy blue dress that accentuates her figure. The two of them together are the very definition of a power couple.

He says something and she laughs, her hand landing on his arm. I wait for her to remove it but she doesn't. And he certainly doesn't seem to mind.

"People do seem to be smitten by him," I say, unable to keep the bitterness from my tone.

Sam catches it instantly. "You're not a fan?"

I roll my eyes. "He's a good boss. I just... it's complicated."

"The whole my best friend's father thing?"

I smile. "I guess..."

"Say no more."

I turn to Sam and decide that I do really like him. He's cute, sweet and he definitely doesn't give off asshole vibes. Maybe he's just the distraction I need. Someone age-appropriate who has no connection whatsoever to my father.

"You wanna get outta here?"

Sam looks slightly taken aback by the question. "Now?"

I nod. "Why not? We can grab a bottle of wine and find a quiet room to... talk." I *say* talk but I'm pretty sure he knows that I don't really mean *talk*. "Whaddaya say?"

There's a slight blush creeping up his cheeks. "Um, sure. I'd like that."

I grab a bottle of wine and gesture for him to follow me. We maneuver through the crowd, past the middle of the lunch room where everyone's created a sort of make-shift dance floor. We've just gotten out of the lunch room when—

"Ashley."

I stop short. We both do. I turn around and Tobias appears at the door. Sam's looking exceptionally guilty and he kinda shuffles away from me like we're teenagers caught by our parents.

"Yes, sir?"

Tobias's eyes narrow slightly. It's so subtle that I almost miss it. "I have to talk to you about the brief you left on my desk this evening."

My eyes go wide. *Is he serious right now*? "You want to discuss that *now*?"

"Yes, Sam—" Tobias says with that unyielding confidence of his. "Would you mind giving us a few minutes?"

What!?

Sam clears his throat. "Um, of course." Sam glances at me apologetically. "I'll just... get back to the party."

He hurries back inside the lunch room, where the music is practically blaring now and I'm left in the corridor with Tobias.

I take a fighting step towards him. "What the hell was that? We both know you have nothing to discuss with me about that brief. It was flawless."

His eyebrows. "I beg to differ."

"I'm off the clock."

"You're *my* assistant. You're never off the clock."

I shake my head. "You are unbelievable, you know that?"

"Ashley—"

"No! Screw you. I'm outta here."

Then I twist around and start storming off down the hallway. And yet, as angry as I am, as frustrated as I feel, there's a tiny little part of me that's hoping—he'll follow me.

CHAPTER 31
Tobias

"Ashley," I growl, following her down the hallway.

I know I shouldn't be following her at all. She's emotional and I've had a few too many drinks. I usually limit myself to one, especially at office parties. But seeing her flirt with that boy scout who works under Bertie, I couldn't stop myself from reaching for another drink.

I know I'm being an unfair asshole but the alcohol isn't helping my sense of reason.

"Ashley."

She doesn't turn around as she flips me off over her head. Is it weird that it turns me on? Probably.

In two long strides, I grab her arm and pull her into one of the empty meeting rooms. The doors are glass but the lights are off, so the city lights jump into the space, filling it with dazzling shadows.

None as dazzling as she is right now though.

That red lipstick she's wearing really makes her skin glow. And that white office dress she's in… I've been imagining myself peeling it off her body since the moment she walked into my office this morning.

"This is highly unprofessional, *sir*."

Those bright eyes of hers are alive with fire. All I want to do is touch her, but at the moment, there's three feet of space between us and I have to remember to maintain it.

She's managed to keep up the formality for days now. She only refers to me as 'sir' anymore and she keeps our interactions short and limited to business. It's been fucking torture.

"He's not good enough for you."

Her eyes go wide. "Are you serious?"

I forget my own rule and take a step towards her. "Yes, I'm fucking serious. He's not good enough for you."

"You have no right to make that call. It's my decision who to date and it's my decision who to fuck."

I flinch back at the venom in her voice as she steps towards me. Now we're only a foot apart. I can catch her lavender and honey scent.

"I'm just looking out for you."

"Bullshit!" she exclaims. "You're not looking out for me. You're looking out for *yourself.* You claim you don't want to have anything to do with me but the moment another guy shows any interest, you're right there, ready to cock-block me."

"Jesus, Ashley—"

"If you don't want me, there are plenty of guys out there who do!"

"You *know* this is not about me wanting you, for fuck's sake!"

"I don't care what it's about anymore. What I do know is that I'm getting laid tonight. So if you'll excuse me, I'm gonna go find Sam."

She turns towards the door. I know I have to let her go. If I'm serious about the whole 'keeping my distance' thing, I know I'm gonna have to live with the fact that she's going to go out into the world, meet new men, sleep with new men, fall in love one day.

Just—not today.

Before I can stop myself, I grab her arm and twist her around towards me. She slams into my body, her eyes landing on mine. I push her against the wall, my hand sliding to the side of her face. I trap her against the wall with my body.

"You want sex?" I growl. "Is that it? That's all you want?"

My hand trails up her skirt and I feel goosebumps ripple over her body. Her eyelashes flutter and her lips part.

"Tell me. Fucking tell me what you want."

She gasps and bites down on her bottom lip. I don't even have to nudge her legs apart. She spreads them the moment my hand lands on her thigh.

"I want sex."

"You want me to fuck you, is that it?"

"That's all you can offer me," she snarls right back. "So why the fuck not?"

She's wearing the thinnest lace panties I've ever felt before. They're held together by nothing more than a piece of string. I hook a finger into the strap and rip it right off her. Discarding the fabric onto the floor, I glide my finger down her pussy. She's already wet. *Really* wet.

"This is just sex," I growl at her. But even to my ear, I sound like I'm trying to convince myself.

"That's just great because that's all I want from you anymore. Just sex." Her eyes close as I push one finger inside her. "*Mmm...*"

"This is what you want, isn't it?" I ask, pushing another finger inside her. Her folds wrap around my fingers, coating them in her warm juices.

"Mm-hm," she groans. "Give it to me... *fuck...*"

The music drifts down the hall towards us. If anyone walks down this way, we're definitely going to be seen. Those glass doors don't hide much. But I'm too fucking hard to care and clearly so is she.

I lower my lips to her neck and start sucking on her as I finger fuck her to her first orgasm. Her back hits the wall over and over again the rougher I get. But she just clings to my back and holds me tighter.

"*Mmm...* yes, again. Again. More... harder, harder... *ahh...*"

I wait till she cums before I rip my hand out of her and pull her skirt up around her hips. She starts clawing at my shirt, ripping at least two buttons off in the process. I suppose that's payback for her panties. She's definitely not gonna be able to wear those again.

I pull my cock out. There's already a few drops of pre-cum at the tip and align it with her pussy. "Fuck," I mutter. "Condom..."

Her eyes find mine. She looks fucking gorgeous. She also looks *feral*. Like a wild animal who's finally been let loose. "Fuck the condom. You've been inside me bare before."

"Yes but—"

She grabs ahold of my shoulders and pushes her hips right into me. My cock slides inside her and I completely lose my mind. There's nothing like the feeling of sinking into a woman with nothing on. Her tight little pussy stretches to fit me and my balls slap the back of her ass.

"*Fuck*," I moan desperately. "You're gonna be the fucking death of me, woman."

She gives me a wicked smile. "Well then—let's make this count."

I grab her by the ass and hike her up. Her legs wrap around my waist and I start fucking her hard against the wall.

"Yes," she screams every time her back hits the wall. "Yes, yes, yes, *yes!*"

I hike her up and hold her tight as I turn and walk her over to the long table that's usually reserved for important board meetings. I place her down on the cold surface, grab ahold of her hips and start ramming into her hard.

Then I undo the buttons running down her dress so that I can take a peek at those gorgeous breasts of hers. Her tits bounce freely as I thrust hard. I grab a hold of them, massaging them with my hands while I try desperately to delay my orgasm. I need to make this last as long as I possibly can.

That's when I hear the sound of laughter coming down the hall. *Fuck.* Someone's leaving the party and that means they're gonna walk right past this room.

Two people appear on my right just outside the glass doors. I place my hand over Ashley's mouth and freeze. She does the same. All I can see are the whites of her eyes. Slowly, I glance over to the side.

A man and a woman. Both interns. Both appear to be highly intoxicated. They're hanging over one another, making out and laughing and tripping as they stumble down the hall, probably trying to find an empty room to themselves too.

The girl's gaze slides over the board room but she looks right past Ashley and I. In fact, I don't think she's really seeing anything but the lights and the reflections it throws. They head off down the hall, laughing to themselves and I turn my attention back to Ashley.

"Fuck," I laugh as I pull my hand from her mouth. She joins in the laughter, pushing her hips against mine as if to remind me that the job's not done yet.

As if nothing had interrupted us, I continue fucking her, thrusting harder now to build the momentum back up again.

"Harder, Tobias," she gasps.

I smirk. "What happened to sir?"

She bites her bottom lip. "I'm sorry, *sir*. I forgot. Am I in trouble," she moans loudly. "Are you gonna... *mmm*... punish me..."

If it's possible, I get even harder. I pull out of her and twist her around so that her breasts are on the table and my cock is perched right between her ass cheeks.

"Fuck yes. I'm gonna punish you," I growl. I slap her ass and she lets out a strangled scream. "That punishment enough for you?"

"No," she moans. "More... I need more to really learn my lesson..."

I thrust inside her again, watching as her perfect ass ripples from the force of my entry. Then I keep slapping her juicy ass, leaving my hand prints on both her cheeks. She just whimpers helplessly as I fuck her, her moans and screams getting more and more uninhibited.

Unable to contain myself any longer, I explode inside her. Pretty sure she cums at the same time but I'm so lost in my own pleasure that I can't quite keep track of hers. I collapse on top of her, my lips hitting her back left shoulder. She smells of sex and sweat.

She smells of me.

We straighten up quietly; get dressed in silence. She doesn't make eye contact with me as she picks her torn panties from the floor.

With the wild passion of our combined desire satiated, the truth of our relationship settles in. We can both pretend that this was just sex.

But I know it's not.

And she knows it's not.

And since I'm not prepared to admit that—there's nothing left to do but leave.

CHAPTER 32

Ashley

"Good morning, sir," I greet pleasantly as I walk into his office.

Tobias looks at me from between his eyelashes warily. I can understand his reservations. He has no idea where my head is at after last night. Hell, even I'm not sure myself.

All I know is that last night was freaking amazing. And as much as I knew it would complicate things further between us, I wanted it anyway. I'd woken up this morning feeling satisfied and confident. And as for regret?

I had none.

I'd dressed for myself today, picking my favorite black pencil skirt. The one that I'd caught Tobias checking me out in countless times. And a new sleeveless blue silk blouse with a bow tie up in the front.

His eyes traverse my body reluctantly before he clears his throat and closes the file he'd been looking at when I walked in.

"You're here early."

"I, um, couldn't really sleep last night, so I decided to get a head start today."

I nod. "Can I get you a coffee?"

He lifts his mug and I can see fresh steam swirling off the top. "I'm way ahead of you." I take a few steps forward and the smell of coffee hits me right in the face.

"Wow… strong."

"I needed it," he mumbles.

I hand him the files in my hand as well as his updated schedule for the week. "Your two o'clock appointment has been canceled. Apparently, Ms. Hargrove is sick today so she wants to reschedule for next week."

He's looking at me with a strange expression on his face. Probably wondering if he should address what happened between us last night. Well, if he wants to discuss it, then he's the one who's gonna have to bring it up because I'm certainly not jumping down that rabbit hole again. That conversation always has us going around in circles until we land back in the same place.

Which is usually—sex.

Considering the kind of sex we have, I'm not complaining. I'm just going to surrender myself to the process, no matter how unhealthy it might be.

"Also, Shiro Takeda called this morning. He wants—"

"Why didn't you tell me you dropped out of college because of money problems?"

My jaw snaps shut. "Excuse me?"

"Last night, at Louisa's retirement party. You were talking to that intern—"

"PA."

"Whatever. You told him that you had to drop out of college because you didn't have the money to complete your degree."

I purse my lips up. "It's not a big deal."

"Of course, it's a fucking big deal. Why the fuck wouldn't Daniel tell me about that?"

"Probably because he knew you'd offer to pick up the cost of my tuition and he was too proud to accept."

Tobias's forehead ripples. "That's ridiculous."

"College isn't cheap, Tobias. He probably didn't want to impose on you and honestly, I can understand why. I wouldn't have been comfortable taking money from you either. It's bad enough I got this job because of nepotism."

Tobias scoffs. "You got this job because you're smart and capable."

"You didn't know that before you hired me. All you knew is that I was your friend's daughter."

He sighs. "Why didn't *you* tell me?"

I frown. "Because it's none of your business."

His eyes go wide for a moment as though he's just realized something. I wonder if I'm being too harsh but then he sighs. "You're right... we all have secrets."

He says that last part so softly that I almost miss it. Tobias has secrets? *More* secrets?

"Are you saying I don't know all of yours?"

It's meant to be a joke, half teasing, half serious, but his expression ripples with unease. He doesn't exactly answer my question though. "Do you want to go back to college?"

I square my shoulders. "Maybe one day. But I'll do it without your money, Tobias, so don't bother offering."

"Jesus. You're just as proud and stubborn as he is."

"Just some of my best qualities."

He scoffs with frustration. "You deserve the chance to finish your degree, Ashley."

"And maybe I *will* one day," I insist. "But I'm not accepting charity from you, Tobias. You've done enough by giving me this job. I can't let anyone else pay for my tuition."

"Your father was paying your tuition."

"Yeah, he's my Dad. He's *family.* It's different."

He rears back as though I've hurt his feelings. *Have I hurt his feelings?* Why? Because I basically implied he wasn't family?

"Tobias," I say gently, moving forward.

"Thanks for the schedule. You can go now."

His tone isn't cold exactly, but it's certainly bordering frigid territory. I sigh frustratedly. "Honestly, I don't *get* you. One moment you're warm. The next moment you're cold. What *is* that?"

He whips around. "It's me trying to keep my distance from you and failing miserably," he snaps. "Last night was—"

"Was *great*," I interrupt immediately. "And you and I both know it. It wasn't a mistake either but you want to call it one because that makes it easier to stay in denial."

His eyebrows rise. "Denial of what?"

"About the fact that this might be more than just casual sex. That we might actually be in a relationship."

His eyes go wide. "That's not what this is, Ashley."

I smile and walk around his desk slowly. He actually takes a step back before getting trapped between me and his massive black wingback. I reach out and trail my hands down his shirt. "Okay then. It's just sex. Does that make you feel better about it?"

"Not really."

I laugh. "This thing between us is *real*, Tobias. If it weren't, you'd have put a stop to it a long time ago."

"I'm trying."

"No you're not," I say confidently. "And I'm gonna prove it to you." I turn and head for the door.

"Ashley—"

I glance back over my shoulder without stopping. "You have a meeting in five with Italy. I don't think you wanna miss that."

～

BY THE TIME EVENING ROLLS AROUND, MOST OF THE STAFF have cleared out for the day. But of course, Tobias is still in his office, fielding calls from all over the world. He's currently on a call with Spain that's been twenty minutes long so far.

"Hey, you."

I glance to the side as Sam comes up around the corner. "Hey," I smile. "Sorry I snuck out last night without saying goodbye. I was beat."

"Right." He gives me an awkward smile. "I just wanted to check to see how you were doing. You seemed kinda pissed actually... not that I blame you. I can't believe he tried to stick you with work at the party."

"Oh. That. It wasn't so bad. He apologized about it today."

"Really?"

I nod. "He's not an asshole boss, really. He just—"

"Didn't like that you were with me last night?" I stop short as Sam fixes me with an awkward grimace. "I've seen the way he looks at you, Ashley. It's pretty obvious."

I clamp up immediately. Which is probably not the best way to feign ignorance. "Listen—"

"I've seen the way you look at him too."

I stop short. My jaw drops. I try and deny it but I'm pretty sure whatever I say is gonna come out sounding like a lie. So instead, I look down. "I'm sorry."

"Do you have feelings for him?"

I nod silently and Sam sighs. "I was kinda hoping for a different answer."

I raise my head slightly and look at him through my eyelashes. "For what it's worth, I really wish I didn't have feelings for him."

Sam smiles sadly. "Weirdly, that doesn't make me feel better." He exhales sharply. "Can I ask you one question?"

"Sure."

"He hasn't… treated you unfairly, right? I mean, you are his PA and he is your boss. This isn't like a sexual harassment type situation, is it?"

I shake my head. "Definitely not. If it is, it's probably the other way around."

Sam cringes and I immediately regret admitting that. "Sorry. TMI, huh?"

He smiles awkwardly. "You don't have to apologize to me, you know. It's not like you and I were… well, you know. No hard feelings."

"I really do like you, Sam."

He smirks. "Yeah. But compared to him…" he glances towards Tobias's closed office door. "I can't compete with that."

"You shouldn't have to."

"Oh I agree," he says. "Which is why I'm not throwing my hat in the ring. I only fight battles that I have a decent chance of winning."

"Smart."

"I just wanted to come over here and say hi. I don't want things getting weird between us."

"They're not going to."

He nods. "See you around, Ashley."

I smile. "Thanks for saying hi, Sam."

He waves and heads off down the hall. I turn my attention

to Tobias's door, feeling all the pent-up frustration I've been carrying around with me the whole week, boil over a little. Apparently, anyone with eyes in their head can see that there's something between us. The only person who seems intent on denying it, is him.

Emboldened and perhaps just a little bit misguided, I get up and enter Tobias's office. His swivel chair is facing the view so his back is to me. He's talking fast and it's obvious that he has no idea I've just entered the room. I don't exactly announce myself as I walk forward.

"… Of course. I'll have Harold handle the purchase order himself. We can discuss that in detail during the conference meeting next week…"

He twists around and catches sight of me. He freezes just a little but he doesn't break off the conversation. His eyebrows are arched curiously but he doesn't seem mad to see me.

Curious, maybe. This is the first time I've entered his office during one of his Skype meetings.

"Uh-huh," he continues. "Tell Gina to go ahead. Everything's in order on this side."

I'm not sure what I'm thinking as I sink down to my knees in front of him. He tenses up instantly, his eyes going wide with disbelief. But when I reach out and unzip his pants, he doesn't stop me.

He glances at the screen but thankfully, it's an audio call only. No one can see him. His headphones are on too, which means no one's likely to hear anything other than his voice. I take that as a sign.

I push down his boxer briefs to discover that he's hard. Not just hard either—*rock* hard. His eyes are fixed on me and it seems as though he's holding his breath.

"Uh… s-sorry, what was that…?"

273

He's distracted. There's a catch in his voice that makes me tremble. He's nervous. *I'm* making him nervous. Among other things…

I start running a finger around the head of his penis. He shudders violently but he doesn't push me away. Apart from the startled look in his eye, he gives me no indication that he wants this to stop.

He bites down on his bottom lip as I fist his cock in my hand and start rubbing him up and down. His eyes flutter a little as I start to massage his balls too.

"Sorry…" he mutters distractedly. "I missed that last… *Jesus*…" He breaks off abruptly and swallows. "Sorry, Gary, just… uh, dropped something… go on…"

I decide to kick things into high gear. I lower my head and slip his cock into my mouth. I lap up the bead of pre-cum coating the top of his penis. His entire body jerks violently. His hand jerks out and grips the edge of the table. I take his cock deeper into my mouth until it's hitting the back of my throat.

His body goes ram rod straight, he stops talking altogether. I keep sucking on him desperately. I have never enjoyed giving head so much. Honestly, I could do this all day. All night if I have to. Then his hand comes down on my head and he slips deeper into my throat. I'm practically choking on his cock and I actually *like* it.

Only when I start gagging does he release me. I come up for air and he pulls his headphones off. I have no idea if he's finished his call or not—but I certainly intend to finish what I just started. I don't give him time to push me away. I grab his cock and push it back into my mouth.

"*Fuck*," he mutters, his hands going back to gripping his desk.

I run my tongue up and down his shaft until I feel his

body spasm uncontrollably. When I'm sure he's about to cum, I take him down my throat again. I suck hard.

"Jesus *Christ*," he gasps. "Ashley… *fuck… fuck!*"

He explodes inside my mouth and I suck him dry. My pussy is tingling for attention but I ignore her as I pull out and wipe my mouth delicately. I barely glance at him as I get to my feet and straighten my skirt.

He's panting furiously, his hand still gripping the edges of his desk. His knuckles are stark white.

"You see?" I say, lifting my eyes to his. "If you'd asked me to stop, I would have. Consider my point, proven."

Then I walk out of his office without another word.

CHAPTER 33

Tobias

Long story short—I'm fucked.

I've got to give it to her—the woman certainly knows how to prove a point. I've spent the whole weekend reliving her very graphic point in my head. Over and over again. Until my balls had turned blue and my attitude had become resigned.

Daniel had called twice yesterday. I'd ignored both calls and texted back that I was sick. It was a lame fucking excuse but I didn't have the energy to come up with anything else. Maybe a part of me wanted him to come around and demand to know what I was hiding.

Then I could tell him the truth.

I had sex with your daughter. And what's more—I might just be in love with her.

God. Even thinking it made me shudder. It was so wrong on so many levels. But even that acknowledgment wasn't enough to make me stop.

Ping.

I glance down at my phone and my heart beats a little faster when I see Ashley's name on the lock screen.

When was the last time seeing a woman's name on my phone caused me to feel butterflies? I could say with some confidence—never.

I pick up my phone and open the text thread.

Ashley: *Are you really sick?*

Tobias: *In the head. Sure.*

Ashley: *I'll try not to take that personally.*

Cringing, I take a deep breath and try to stop acting like a petulant teenager. Jesus Christ, I'm supposed to be the older one in this weird, twisted *thing* we're involved in.

Tobias: *I'm sorry. That's not what I meant.*

Ashley: *I've been obsessing over what happened on Friday and… I wanted to say, I'm sorry.*

Jesus. *Was she* apologizing to *me*?

Tobias: *Why are you apologizing?*

Ashley: *Because I sexually harassed you in your own office.*

That actually makes me smile. Like ear to ear. *Pathetic.*

Tobias: *It was kinda one of the best moments of my life.*

Ashley: *Seriously?*

Tobias: *Seriously.*

Ashley: *Tobias—we need to talk.*

I take a deep breath and stare at my view for a moment. Of course my immediate view includes the coffee table I'm resting my feet on at the moment. It's littered with tissues and empty beer bottles.

Tobias: *I know.*

Ashley: *What are you doing now?*

Tobias: *Mostly just reliving what happened in my office the other day.*

What was the point in pretending anymore? I wanted her. She knew it; I knew it. I may as well be a man and own up to it.

Ashley: *I'm at Firestone down Jackson Avenue. It's only a short walk from your building. Will you come meet me?*

I've had dinner at Firestone a few times. It's a nice restaurant. Bluesy vibes, trendy without being a try hard; the perfect place to have a nice private conversation without feeling overly exposed.

Tobias: *I'll be there in ten.*

I hop into the bathroom for a quick shower to try and wash off the stench of confusion and masturbation. Then I put on jeans and a white shirt. I'm reaching for my keys when my phone starts ringing. I'm so sure it's Ashley that I almost pick up without checking to see who's calling. I stop short when I see the name flashing across my lock screen.

Fuck...

It's a stark reminder that I have a lot of shit to get in order before I can even contemplate getting into anything with Ashley. I decline the call and stuff my phone back into my pocket.

Forget a relationship. I'm gonna have to have an honest conversation with her first.

Yes that's good. Let's start with that.

Five minutes later, I walk into Firestone and I'm shown to the back of the restaurant, where Ashley is waiting for me. She's dressed in a high-waisted skirt and a crop top that highlights her flat stomach. She looks so damn sexy and so damn *young*.

But her expression is somber and slightly wary as I sit down opposite her without leaning in for a hug. I glance at the Negroni in front of her and she blushes slightly.

"Sorry, I needed a little liquid courage."

I glance at the waitress. "I'll have one too, please." The

waitress gives me a lingering smile and heads off to get my drink. "Fake ID again, huh?"

She smiles slightly. "I'm gonna be twenty-one in a couple of months."

"Still."

"Numbers really matter to you, don't they?"

I raise my eyebrows. "They don't mean anything to you?"

"I think in many cases they're arbitrary," she admits, leaning back in her seat. The table is broader than most. So it feels like she's sitting far from me. It's weird how that's making me squirm in place, desperate to be closer to her.

This is not what this night is about.

"Where does your Dad think you are right now?"

She raises her eyebrows. "I'm an adult and Dad's never been in the habit of checking up on me. I told him I was going out and he told me to have fun. Honestly, I think he kinda likes having the apartment to himself. It's not like he had much of a bachelor experience with me around."

"He really did manage to pull off the whole cool Dad thing, huh?"

She smiles. "You didn't believe he would?"

"Honestly? No. I remember the week after you were born, he was terrified of everything. He used to wake up every other hour to make sure you were still breathing. He'd drive you to the doctor every time you had hiccups. He jumped every time you cried. The man was a helicopter parent for sure."

She stares at me with wide eyes. "Wow, *really*?"

I nod. "Fatherhood took him by storm."

"And… Kristen? I happen to know that she stuck out the first week. Must have been a terrible one for her since she decided to leave right after."

I tense up. "She was overwhelmed, Ashley. I think she

was probably going through postpartum depression too. She was around but your Dad was the one who was hands-on. He picked up the load right off the bat, right from the moment you slipped out of your mother."

She cringes slightly. "It's weird to think that you saw me as a baby."

"Honestly, I try not to think about it anymore."

A burst of laughter escapes through her teeth. "Sorry," she says, holding up a hand. "I don't mean to be laughing. This situation is just so *weird*."

I sigh. "You don't have to tell me."

She nods and starts fidgeting with the cutlery on the table. Thankfully, the waitress shows up at that moment with my Negroni. Before she's even cleared the table, I've finished half the drink. Ashley looks at me with a knowing smile on her face. "Nervous, huh?"

"A little," I admit.

"Me too." She takes a deep breath and places her elbows on the table. "I'm gonna tell you something and I'm gonna need you to listen to me first. I've made a decision and I want you to know that I've made this decision not to hurt you or be spiteful but because I can't live with it anymore."

Jesus. That certainly doesn't make me any less nervous, but all I say is, "Go on."

"I may be only twenty, and in your estimation, that's clearly not old enough but that doesn't mean I'm stupid or immature or unaware." When I open my mouth to interrupt, she stops me. "I *am* young but that doesn't mean I don't know myself. I have abandonment issues that started with my mother and continued with my first boyfriend. I'm a deeply insecure person and for a long time... actually, *still* sometimes I blame myself for why *they* left."

She sighs. "I'm not sure that will ever go away and I

suppose I have more work to do on myself until it does, but the point is, I'm aware of my issues. I'm aware that I'm a work in progress. I think most people are, regardless of their age."

I can't help marveling at her as she speaks. There's a grace and maturity about her at twenty that I'm not sure I possess even now. And it made me think—who the hell was I to tell her she was too young?

She clears her throat awkwardly. "I guess what I'm trying to say is… because I've always been scared of people leaving me, I've never really allowed myself to form deep attachments. I've kept people at arm's length. So when I do form a connection with someone, it's completely out of my control. It's more chemical than anything else."

Those smoldering eyes of hers meet mine and I feel my skin heat up. This is the kinda thing you're supposed to feel as a teenager. All that excitement and anticipation of a first crush, a first love.

How had I gotten to the ripe old age of thirty-five without ever coming close to this feeling? Why is it happening *now* with this girl?

No. Not girl. She's a woman. That much is clear.

Maybe I've just tried to keep her a girl in my head so that I can keep her at arm's length myself.

She takes another breath and sips on her Negroni. She doesn't quite look at me when she continues. "I have feelings for you, Tobias," she breathes.

My eyes go wide. It takes a lot to admit how you really feel to someone who has spent the majority of their time trying to reject you. Not that my rejections took very well; but still.

"I think you already know that. I wish sometimes that I didn't; it would make life a whole lot easier but I can't stop how I feel. It's completely out of my control." She sighs, still avoiding my eyes. "I know where you stand and I know how you feel. And I'm going to have to learn to respect that. Which is why I've come here to tell you two things."

I tense up immediately. *Two things?*

"Tell me," I encourage calmly, even though I feel anything but calm inside.

"I'm handing in my resignation."

I raise my eyebrows. Isn't this what I'd been hoping for from pretty much the first moment she started working for me? So why does it feel so fucking awful to hear her say that she's leaving?

"Ashley—"

"I've made my decision, Tobias. According to my contract, I'm supposed to hand in three months' notice so that's what I'm doing right now. Consider this my three months' notice. Of course if you would prefer to wave that time and let me go immediately, I'd understand too."

Jesus.

My brain feels like it's short-circuiting. How am I *this* blindsided by her decision?

"Ashley, you don't have to leave."

She shakes her head. "Actually I *do.* I'm your PA, Tobias. I should be focused on the job. But instead, I'm distracted. All I do most days is daydream about you." She sighs. "The point of coming to California was so that I could prove myself; make it on my own two feet. I can't claim to be doing that if I'm riding your coat tails."

"That's not what—"

"I should have quit the moment I knew who you really were. The only reason I didn't is because I was so—" She stops short, her cheeks firing red. "I was so... smitten with you. And I suppose I was hoping that if I gave you enough time, you'd realize that you wanted to be with me too."

That one throws me for a loop. *Does she really think that I don't want to be with her for any other reason than her father is my best friend?*

"You told me time and time again that you didn't want to cross that line with me and I kept pushing you. Which was not fair." She bites her plump bottom lip. "So my resignation takes care of that part of the equation."

"Your father will want to know why you quit only a few months into the job."

She nods with resignation. "Which brings me to the second thing I wanted to tell you." She lifts her eyes to mine and the wariness is back.

And I thought the resignation was the worst news I'd hear tonight.

"Tell me," I say gently.

She closes her eyes for a moment. When she opens them again, they're kinda hazy, nervous, uncertain—begging for understanding.

"When Dad asks me why I'm quitting, I'm going to tell him the truth."

CHAPTER 34

Ashley

My skin prickles with tension. His expression hasn't really changed apart from a slight glare in his eyes.

He nods a couple of times. Sits backs. Taps his hand against the table. Nods again.

"Are you gonna say anything?"

He clears his throat. "Just to be clear… you're going to tell Daniel that you're quitting because—"

"I have feelings for you." I swallow hard and continue. "And that we slept together before either one of us realized who the other one was." His mouth turns down and his brow creases with worry lines. "If it makes you feel better, I'll leave out the part where we slept together *after* we knew who the other one was."

He runs a hand through his crisp brown hair. "Fuck…"

"I'm sorry, Tobias. I'm really not trying to get you in trouble here. I know it probably looks like I'm being a spiteful bitch—"

"Hey," he says quickly. "That's not what I think."

I smile gratefully at him. "It's just that, like I said, I don't have many wholesome, healthy, close relationships in my life.

I'm pretty much down to my Dad now and I promised him I'd always be honest with him. I don't want to fuck that up by starting a new life in California by lying to him. Any more than I already have, that is."

"You're a better person than I am, Ashley Payne."

I shake my head. "I don't feel like a better person right now. I feel... confused. Lost. A little broken."

He winces as though hearing me say that is physically painful for him. "I hate that I contributed to that feeling."

"No, this is on me. Not you."

He reaches out suddenly and puts his hand over mine. I'm so shocked by the gesture that I just stare at our hands. When I finally raise my eyes to his, he's staring at me thoughtfully. "Thank you."

I frown. "Thank you?"

"For giving me a heads up. I know you didn't have to."

My eyes go wide. "You're not going to try and talk me out of it?"

He shakes his head. "No. In fact, I actually think you *should*."

My jaw drops. Had I just heard him, right? "You're actually supportive of this decision?"

"I am."

"Jesus. Not that I'm complaining or anything but you've spent months trying to hide what happened between us from Dad. What changed?"

"The realization that you're right. Lying never solved anything. My friendship with Daniel is one of the most important things in the world to me. But can I call it a true friendship if I'm lying to him?"

I give him a little smile. "He's probably gonna wanna kick your ass."

He laughs. "Oh, he's *definitely* gonna kick my ass. And you know what? I'm gonna let him. I deserve it."

I frown. "I don't think that's fair. You don't deserve it. We were both consenting adults, and we had a real connection."

My skin prickles with the need to touch her. "I'm not sure he's gonna see it that way."

"Then I'll explain it to him," I say confidently. "It'll take some time for him to process but he's gonna come around eventually. Trust me. You're not going to lose him over this, Tobias. I'll make sure of that."

"You don't have to make me any promises."

"Yes, I do. The whole reason you didn't want to start anything with me is because of *him.* I don't want you to lose him over this. *Especially* after you chose him over me." The moment the words come out of my mouth, I regret them. "Shit. That came out wrong."

"Ashley—"

"What I meant is—"

"I was lying to myself!"

I stop short, taken aback by the fierceness in his voice. "W-what?"

"If it comes down to a choice. You or Daniel…" he swallows hard, looking a little lost for words. "I think I might have to choose you."

My eyes go wide. "You're kidding…"

"Trust me. I'm not."

"*You're* the one who's been pushing me away all this time."

"Because I've been *trying* to do the right thing. And I thought that meant keeping my distance. But you turning in your resignation just now made me realize something. I can't *not* see you anymore, Ashley. I can't have you walking around this city and not be a part of your life. I mean, *Jesus,* my favorite part of the day is walking into the office and seeing you at your desk each morning for the first time."

His hands move erratically across the table until I finally reach out and grab them. "Hey," I whisper softly. "Hey… take a breath."

He exhales gently. "*Shit*. That wasn't very smooth, was it?"

A giggle bursts through my lips. "This feels surreal. Like I'm dreaming and I might wake up at any—"

Ring. Ring. Ring.

I nearly jump out of my seat at the sound of Tobias's loud ringtone. "Sorry," he mumbles, glancing down at his phone.

His expression changes instantly. He pulls his hands from mine and declines the call before I can see who's calling. His face actually pales a little as he puts the phone away. "Sorry," he mumbles again.

"Um, did you need to take that?"

"No," he says. "It's all good."

I notice that he makes no attempt to tell me who was calling just then. Not that he needs to but his reaction has made me curious. And maybe just a little bit worried.

"You look a little… pale."

He definitely doesn't look like himself. He leans back in his chair, puts his elbows on the table and clasps his hands together. "I'm just… trying to figure out a couple of things."

Okay, so maybe I misread that? Maybe he's just processing everything I've just dumped on him?

"D-do you have anything you wanna tell me?"

His eyes connect with mine. "It's fucking cruel, is what it is." I raise my eyebrows in alarm but he continues without a pause. "Of all the women who've come into my life, you're the only one who's left a mark. It's fucking cruel."

I shrug. "We can't help how we feel."

"That's the thing—I've never believed that. I've always thought it was a choice."

"Was it though?" I ask. "Look at my parents. They were probably terrible together, but they couldn't stay apart. They fell in love, and for better or for worse, they had me. You can argue about choice and autonomy, but the truth is that they couldn't help it. It was chemical. Just like you and me."

He nods. "It's easier to stay on your high horse when you don't have skin in the game."

I smirk. "I feel like you're trying to tell me something, Tobias."

He runs a hand over his face. "I'm trying to tell you that I fucking *want* you, Ashley. I know I shouldn't. You're too young for me. Too beautiful. Too good. But I want you anyway."

I nod. "So… it's not just sex, is it?"

He laughs ironically. "Fuck no. It never was. I walked over to you that night because I wanted to *talk* to you. Not because I wanted to fuck you."

My heart feels like it's about to burst but I stop myself from celebrating. I'm still not sure where his head is at. The frown lines on his forehead are still holding strong.

"What do you want to do now, Tobias?"

"I want you to let *me* talk to your father."

My eyes go wide with shock. "W-what?"

"I'm serious. I should be the one to tell him what happened, Ashley. I need to sack up, look him in the eye and tell him myself."

I have no idea what to say to that. Is it a good idea? A bad one? I have no barometer to measure against. Just my instincts, and at the moment, my instincts are confused as hell.

"Maybe we should tell him together?" I suggest.

"No. That's gonna feel like an ambush. He's not going to be able to deal with seeing us together as a couple."

Excitement shoots up my spine the moment he says the word. *Couple.* It feels insane. And wonderful and crazy all at the same time. It also sounds like he's trying to create a foundation that will allow us to build a future together.

"A couple, huh?" I ask gently.

He smiles. "I'm doing this all wrong, aren't I?"

I chuckle. "I just want to make sure we're really on the same page. I don't want to get my hopes up and—"

"I'm done fighting this, Ashley." He takes my hand and brings it to his lips. "It seems like we both want the same thing and it would be a shame to let this pass us by because we were afraid to tell Daniel the truth."

"*You* were afraid."

He smirks. "Okay. Fair point."

"I'm willing to forgive that now."

He kisses my hand again. "I appreciate that."

I can't stop the grin from spreading across my face. Is this really happening? Because it definitely *feels* real. Or at least it's starting to.

I'm leaning in to try and kiss him when he stops me. "Um, I just have one caveat."

My ass drops back into the seat and I groan noisily. "I *knew* it."

He chuckles. "Hold on now. It's not that bad. I just want to do this right."

"Okay?"

He gives my hand a little squeeze. "I don't think we should um... *do* anything until after we've told your father."

I raise my eyebrows. "Are you saying we can't kiss or have sex until after we've told him?"

He nods. "Like you said, a fresh start can't start with a lie."

"We're not lying to each other."

"No, but we are hiding this from Daniel and he is still my closest friend. Which means I am lying to him. And I don't want to anymore."

I sigh. "This really means something to you, doesn't it?"

"We went through a lot together, Ashley. I owe him this."

Despite my disappointment, I find myself nodding. "So... when do you want to do this? Tell him I mean?"

He considers it for a moment. "I'm gonna give him a call tomorrow. Ask him out to dinner this coming weekend. I'll tell him then."

I raise my eyebrows. "A week? You wanna stretch this out a whole week?"

He gives me a smirk. "Impatient, are we?"

My pussy tingles in agreement but I cross my legs tight. "I can wait a week if that's what you need."

He actually looks a little relieved. "Thank you, I appreciate—"

Ring. Ring. Ring.

He freezes at the sound of his phone but he doesn't rush to pull it out of his pocket. It's almost like he knows who's calling and he doesn't want to answer.

"Fuck," he mutters when it doesn't stop ringing. He pulls out the phone and stares at the screen. I desperately want to know who's calling but I bite my tongue and sit back.

It's none of your business. If he wants to tell you, he will. Until then—trust him.

He ends up cutting the line without answering. "You sure everything is alright?" I ask reluctantly.

"Just don't feel like dealing with it tonight, that's all. I'll handle it tomorrow."

He makes it sound like it's a problem that needs solving. "Can I help in any way?"

He surprises me by raising his eyebrows. "You just may be able to," he admits. "But not just yet. I think I just need a little time to figure things out."

I have no idea what he's talking about anymore. "Um, are you talking about us and Dad... or the call?"

"Both," he sighs. "Everything."

Ping.

This time, it's my phone that's vibrating on the table beside my Negroni glass. I glance at the lock screen to see a text from Dad.

"Speak of the devil," I say, picking up my phone and opening the message. "Excuse me a sec."

Dad: *Hey honey, you still out?*

Ashley: *Yup. Everything okay?*

Dad: *Just dandy. I have a huge fucking favor to ask.*

Jesus, when was the last time my father asked *me* for a favor?

Ashley: *I'm intrigued. What's the favor?*

Dad: *I'm on a date. Don't make a big deal about it, I just figured since you're getting on with your life, I may as well too.*

Ashley: *It's about freaking time.*

Dad: *:p thing is, she's got young kids at home and she's not keen on bringing me around in case they see us together. It's going well between us and I don't really want the night to end. And it's been a while since I felt that way about a date.*

Ashley: *Say no more. You can have the apartment for the night.*

Dad: *Only if you have a place to crash. Otherwise, we can figure something else out.*

Ashley: *Nope, I'm already making alternate plans for the night. Enjoy the rest of your night. Use protection!*

Dad: *You don't want a baby brother or sister? ;)*

Ashley: *I'm good, thanks.*

Dad: *Thanks, kid, you're the best.*

Laughing, I put my phone away and glance up at Tobias, who's watching me carefully. "Judging by the smile on your face, I'm guessing everything's okay?"

"Dad's on a date."

Tobias looks as stunned as I feel. "No way!"

"Yup, he's finally getting out there. This is the first time he's openly admitted to going out on a date. Or just *like* the woman he's dating."

"Jesus."

"Apparently, the date's going well. He asked if he could have the apartment tonight."

"Oh." Is it my imagination or does Tobias's face actually drop? Between that and the call he won't tell me about, I'm starting to feel just a little bit self-conscious.

"Um, listen, don't worry about it. I can find someone at work to crash with. Gina and I have gotten pretty close and—"

"I *want* you to spend the night with me, Ashley," he says abruptly. "Which is precisely why I'm so damn nervous right now. I mean Jesus, how am I gonna keep my hands off you all night?"

I try not to smile too widely. "Well… I guess tonight will be a testament to your willpower."

"Shit," he mutters. "I'm so fucking screwed."

CHAPTER 35

Tobias

She does *not* try to make it easy on me.

After I've given her a pair of my drawstring sweats and an oversized t-shirt, she decides to ditch the sweats altogether and just walk around in my t-shirt. And I mean *only* my t-shirt. Yeah, that's right, she's not wearing a stitch underneath it. Not a bra or panties. Her nipples pop through the thin fabric and every time the t-shirt rises, I can see the perfect apples of her tight little ass.

Every time she bends over, I have to physically grab hold of something to stop myself from grabbing her, ripping the t-shirt off and fucking her against whatever surface is closest.

I'm so damn hard that I can actually *feel* my balls turning blue.

"Something wrong?" she asks coyly, sitting down on the sofa next to me. A little too close for my liking. "You look a little hot under the collar."

I narrow my eyes at her. "You know exactly what you're doing, aren't you?"

She giggles. "Just trying to have a conversation with you."

"Can you have a conversation with me from that chair over there?"

She leans in a little and shakes her head. "I prefer the sofa."

"Maybe I should move then."

I actually try and get up but she grabs my arm and pulls me back down on the sofa. "I promise I'll behave," she says in an innocent voice that I don't trust in the slightest. Then she raises both her hands in surrender. "I'll keep my hands to myself too."

I clear my throat and try and focus on anything but the fact that her t-shirt has ridden up over her thighs. Her pussy is right there for the taking, but for tonight, it's entirely off limits too.

"It's a big deal that he's on this date tonight, huh?" I ask, hoping that talking about Daniel might calm my erection a little.

She nods. "He's never really dated anyone seriously. I've never seen him in a relationship ever unless, of course, he hid it from me and I doubt he would have."

"I'm glad he's finally moving on."

"Yeah. Only took him twenty years."

I smile sadly. "Some relationships take a long time to recover from."

"Yeah, I get that. I swore off men after Henry. I've pretty much been single since then." I eye her curiously and she clears her throat. "I told you that I went over to his place one day and his Mum told me he had left early for college." I nod. "What I didn't tell you is that we had a plan. He was going to defer his acceptance for a semester and we were going to go off to college together."

I raise my eyebrows. "Jesus."

She smiles sadly. "Yeah. We had an off-campus apartment

picked out and everything. He just decided he'd rather do it alone."

"He sounds like a fucking asshole."

She shakes her head. "I used to think so too. But he wasn't really. A coward, maybe. But not an asshole." She takes a deep breath and looks out towards the view. I can't help but wonder what man in his right mind would walk away from someone like her. She was fucking magnificent.

"And he didn't leave without a word," she continues softly. Her eyes dart to me and then back to the view. "He left a note. His mother gave it to me."

I so desperately want to reach out and touch her. But I'm afraid that if I do, I won't be able to stop touching her.

"What did it say?"

She plays with the hem of her t-shirt. "It was short and to the point. *I'm sorry, Ash. I have to do this alone. I need to figure out who I am. And you need to figure out who you are. Doesn't mean I don't love you.*"

"How did that make you feel?"

"Worthless," she admits. "But he was right. I did need to figure out who I was… I'm still figuring it out."

"That's what your twenties are for."

She smirks. "Does that mean you're all figured out?"

I snort. "Hardly."

"See? Sometimes, it's not about age at all. Some people need more fixing than others. It's only because they're more broken than everyone else. And you know what I think?"

"What?"

"There's nothing wrong with being broken. Sometimes, that's where your strength comes from." She reaches out suddenly and takes my hand. "You're one of the bravest men I know, Tobias Mason Ackerman."

I actually do a double-take. "Me?"

She smiles. "Yes, you. That's probably why I was so drawn to you right from the beginning. I could sense it in you. The same kind of brokenness hiding in plain sight, underneath all that strength."

My throat feels tight. "It's not true."

"It *is* true. You survived a drunk and abusive father. You defended your depressed and abused mother. You lived through the suicide of your brother. You have the grace to deal with your father even after everything he put you through. You built an amazing business from the ground up and somehow, you're not an asshole to the people who work for you."

For a moment, I can't speak. She's looking at me with wide, tear-filled eyes and I want so badly to deserve her admiration, her respect. But then again—she doesn't know the whole story. She doesn't know the truth I'm keeping from her.

She doesn't realize that I'm as big a coward as her ex-boyfriend.

"You're making me out to be a better man than I really am."

She shakes her head confidently. "Are you kidding? You're the best man I know."

Jesus.

For a moment, I'm actually on the verge of telling her. I so badly want to rip the band-aid off and be as honest as I can. She'll probably hate me for it but maybe if she hears it from me, she'll understand. Maybe I can make her understand.

But right as I'm about to tell her my secret, she leans forward and presses her lips to mine. First, the warmth engulfs me. Then the comfort. Then the adulterated desire. *This woman was made for me.* Maybe that's why I've lived through thirty-five years avoiding any real romantic commitment. Because deep down, I was waiting for her.

My hand slides down her side and suddenly, she's sitting on my lap, straddling me. Did I pull her onto me or did she climb aboard? I have no freaking clue and I'm not sure I can summon up the energy to care anymore.

Her tongue slides into my mouth and entwines with mine. My hands grab hold of her pert little ass as she bucks her hips against my erection. *Yup*, my balls are definitely full-on blue at this point. I can't even think straight—it's that painful.

"Shit," Ashley gasps as she breaks away from me suddenly. "I'm sorry… I can't believe I broke my promise already."

A burst of laughter escapes through my raw lips. "I can't say *I'm* sorry. If ever you were gonna break a promise, I'm glad it's this one."

She laughs too, her eyes twinkling brightly. "I am sorry…"

"Never apologize to me," I tell her firmly. "Never."

She leans in and places her forehead against mine. "I'm gonna stop now, okay?" I'm definitely disappointed but I don't stop her when she climbs off me. Her eyes trail down to my very obvious erection. "Can I get you an ice pack for that?"

"Please."

Smiling a little too gleefully, she heads off to the kitchen just as my phone *pings*. I read through the messages carefully, my heart beating hard against my chest. It isn't like me not to reply. Of course she's getting worried. Quickly, I open the text thread and type out a hasty message.

Tobias: *I'm sorry I've been MIA recently. There's a lot going on at the moment. I'll explain, I promise but first I have to sort out a couple of things here first.*

"Everything okay?"

I nearly drop the phone as Ashley walks back into the room stealthily. I turn off my phone and put it on the table, face down. "Yup, just… work."

I cringe inwardly at the blatant lie. Why the hell aren't I just being honest with her? I tell myself it's because I haven't spoken to Daniel yet; I have to explain everything to him first before I tell Ashley. But I know that while it's part of the truth, it's not the whole truth.

Because the truth is—I'm scared.

Scared of losing the one woman who's ever truly meant anything to me. Scared that I've fucked it all up before we've even got started.

Scared that my past is coming back to haunt me, just like I always feared it would.

～

When I wake up the next morning, I feel victorious. Not only did I manage to keep my hands off her, I feel a certain lightness in my chest.

By no means is this over. In fact, it's just begun. I have a lot to explain. A lot to apologize for. And it starts with Daniel. I pick up my phone, careful not to jostle the bed too much and wake up Ashley, who's sleeping soundly next to me.

I spend a few minutes crafting the next I'm gonna send my best friend. In the end, it's short and simple.

Tobias: *Daniel, I need to talk to you. Let's meet for lunch today at the Blue Bistro down Emerson Road. This is important.*

It's urgent enough that I know Daniel will take notice. I catch him online for a few seconds but he goes offline again without replying. I put my phone away and turn to Ashley.

She's so damn beautiful. Her eyelashes flutter softly in sleep and she's got a slight smile playing at the corners of her mouth. I could lie here and stare at her all day.

When have I ever felt this way about a woman?

Never.

I feel like a fool now for denying it for so long, but it's better late than never. Unable to resist, I lean in and press a soft kiss to her lips. She stirs slightly but she doesn't wake up. Quietly, I slip out of bed and head into the kitchen. I put a fresh pot of coffee on and raid the fridge for something I can turn into a gourmet breakfast for Ashley when she wakes up.

It's almost nine o'clock. I've slept three hours longer than I usually do. First time that has happened in a while. Maybe ever.

Apparently, what I was missing was the right person to sleep next to.

Knock, knock, knock.

Taken aback, I poke my head out of the kitchen and look down the hall towards the entrance foyer. Is someone outside my door? Feeling slightly unease, I abandon the coffee bean bag on my counter and head towards my door.

Knock, knock.

"Hey come on, Toby! Open up."

I freeze. *Fuck!* Daniel? What the hell is he doing here at this time? I look towards my bedroom door but it's shut tight and Ashley's still sleeping. Maybe I can get him outta here before she wakes up?

"Hurry up! I can hear you moving around in there."

"Shit," I mutter under my breath as I pull open the door and plaster a fake smile on my face. "Daniel, what the hell are you doing here?"

"I had a date last night."

"I take it from the grin on your face it went well?" I chance a glance over my shoulder.

"I mean, she's not my soul mate or anything but I actually enjoyed myself last night. She slept over."

"Wow, congrats."

"You okay?"

"Hm?"

His eyebrows arch. "You seem distracted."

"Oh uh… I just woke up is all."

"At this time?" Daniel teases. "Lazy bastard. Unless… you had an eventful night yourself last night?"

"God *no*," I hiss immediately.

Daniel does a double take, clearly alarmed by my reaction. "Are you sure you're okay? Cause you seem really jumpy. And honestly, that text message you sent me felt kinda serious."

"Well… it was. I mean, it is. I just… I'm okay. Really."

"You sure? Because you still haven't invited me in yet."

Fuck me.

I can feel the impending doom. This is gonna blow up in my face before I have a chance to do damage control. "Well, I was kinda hoping we could talk at lunch."

Daniel's eyebrows rise. "And I would have met you for lunch but Lisa and I woke up this morning and got breakfast together. I was in the neighborhood so I decided to just stop by a little earlier than planned."

"Which is fine. We can make lunch a breakfast date then?"

He definitely looks concerned now. "Toby, I just ate breakfast."

"Coffee then. You can never have too much coffee, right?"

"Uh…"

"Wait right here. I'm gonna go change and then we can head out, okay?"

"Okay sure."

I'm so worried about what he might see if I open the door to the master bedroom that I opt to head down the hall to one of the guest rooms. I dress at the speed of light and hurry back, hoping that he's still waiting in the foyer. But no, he's in the living room, staring out at the view.

"I'd never get tired of this view."

"It's a good one," I say hurriedly. "Ready to go?"

"Jesus," Daniel says, whipping around. "What's going on with you today? It feels like—"

The door to the master bedroom opens. I feel the blood drain outta my face. *It's over. I'm a fucking dead man.*

"Tobias… where are—"

Ashley stops short the moment she sees her father standing by the windows. A little gasp bursts through her lips. She grabs her t-shirt, technically my t-shirt and pulls it down as far as it will go. I don't think it matters though. It's pretty clear she's not wearing pants.

"D-Dad."

Daniel just stares at Ashley, his eyes wide, his nostrils flared, his jaw hanging off his face like it's in danger of breaking.

"Daniel," I start. "Listen—"

"Stop!" His voice is louder than I've ever heard it. "Have you been sleeping with my daughter?"

"Dad—"

"No," he growls. "I'm not talking to you right now." His gaze flickers at me. His eyes are cold and angry. I can see the betrayal hiding behind all that anger. "I'm talking to Toby. Answer me. Have you been sleeping with my daughter?"

My jaw clenches. There are so many things I want to say.

But I know they'll all sound like excuses; useless, hollow justifications.

"Yes."

There are three beats of silence in which I can hear all three of our breathing. Daniel's is heavy, Ashley's is fast and panicky and mine... well I don't think I'm breathing at all right now.

I take a step towards him. And that's when he lunges at me. "You bastard!" he roars. "I'm gonna fucking kill you!"

"NO! Dad!" Ashley screams. She jumps forward, putting herself in between me and Daniel. "Stop, this isn't like you!"

"Ashley, get outta my way."

I find myself agreeing. "It's okay, Ashley. I can handle this. Don't get in the middle."

"Don't you fucking talk to her!"

"Dad!" Ashley pleads. "This is not some casual fling. He's not taking advantage of me and I'm not using him. I love him, Dad!"

Those words... they take my breath away. *Love?* Did she just say that she loves me?

Daniel seems to be having a hard time processing that reveal too, same as me. "Love?" he repeats in a stunned voice.

"I'll explain everything to you. But *please,* you need to sit down and stay calm." She moves forward and takes her father's hand gingerly. "We've always been able to talk to each other, Dad. Let's not stop now."

His eyes flicker to me but I can see his anger starting to fade. "Jesus," he mutters, pulling his hand away from Ashley's so that he can run it through his hair. "How long has this been going on for?"

"Sit down, Dad," Ashley says softly.

He actually listens. He takes a seat on the ivory fainting couch that faces the sofa.

"Daniel, I'm so fucking sorry. I didn't want you to find out like this."

"Is that what your text was about this morning?" he asks bitterly, avoiding looking me in the eye.

"Yes." I didn't want to have to do this in front of Ashley. I kinda wanted to tell Daniel first before I told her. But I'm out of reasons for delaying this explanation any longer. "I—"

Click.

Ashley turns to me with a frown. "Was that your front door?"

"I think so. But no one else has a key except..." *Oh God.*

"Except who?" Ashley asks.

"Jesus Christ," Daniel gasps as his eyes slide to the open doorway that leads to the foyer. Ashley follows his gaze to the tall, auburn-haired woman standing on the threshold, looking at all three of us with a wary expression. "*Kristen!?*"

Yeah.

Kristen.

CHAPTER 36

Ashley

K risten, as in… my *mother?*

The woman who had abandoned me when I was just weeks old?

The woman who had ripped out my father's heart and stomped on it when she left?

The woman who had left me with an abandonment complex that would probably take years of therapy to resolve. If it ever resolved at all?

It feels very surreal to be standing in the same space as her. She certainly takes up room. Her presence has a strange, simmering kind of power that I can feel from here. She's beautiful and even I can see, with some level of objectivity, that she looks like me.

Or rather, I look like her.

She's standing in Tobias's living room as though she's been here before. Hell, she'd walked into his apartment without even knocking. The only way she could have gotten in is with a key. And the only way she could have a key is if *he* gave her one.

She's carrying a duffel bag over one shoulder that she

drops onto the floor and kicks to the side with her high-heeled ankle boots. "Hello Daniel," she says softly. "It's been a while."

Dad doesn't say a word. He looks almost catatonic. His face is pale white and there's a dangerous tick in his jaw that I've only seen once before when this old dude and smacked my ass at the public pool. Long story short; he'd kicked the shit out of him.

"Uh... I'm sorry. I shouldn't have just walked in..." her gaze flits around the room but it never actually lands on me. It's like she's *trying* to avoid looking my way. "Toby, you didn't really reply to any of my calls or texts. I guess I got worried."

"*Fuck*!" Dad explodes. But he's looking at Tobias now. "How much have you been keeping from me?"

"I can explain, Dan—"

"Have you been fucking Kristen as well as my daughter!?"

"Of *course* not!" Tobias denies vehemently, his eyes sliding to me with panic.

"It's not like that between Tobias and I, Daniel," Kristen insists too, her face flushing with color. "I swear."

"Oh you swear?" Dad laughs manically. "You *swear.* Because your word means something, does it? Jesus *Christ.*"

Kristen's lip trembles violently. "I know you're angry—"

"Angry? You ABANDONED us!" He points to me so aggressively that I actually take a step back. "You fucking held her in your arms, you looked at her perfect little face and you fucking LEFT! What kind of woman, what kind of *monster* would do something like that!?"

I feel as though I'm frozen solid and despite the fact that everyone is talking about me, no one seems to realize that I'm standing right here. A real flesh and blood person.

Tears well up in Kristen's eyes. "I'm sorry," she exclaims. And then—she turns to me. She looks me in the eye for a moment. I feel something shiver up my spine. What the hell is that? Some sort of deep-seated maternal connection? No, it doesn't feel like a connection at all. Just—recognition somehow. It's almost like my body remembers her. Even if I don't. "I'm so sorry, Ashley."

"Don't you dare fucking speak to her!" Dad yells. "Don't you dare fucking *look* at her!"

"Whoa," Tobias says softly, getting in between the two of them.

Dad's eyes bulge. He grabs the collar of Tobias's shirt and pulls him forward until they're practically nose to nose. "I *trusted* you. I fucking trusted you and you betrayed me!"

"I'm sorry," Tobias says with his hands in the air. "Fuck Daniel, I'm so fucking sorry."

Dad pushes him so hard that Tobias lands on the sofa. "Sorry? You think sorry is enough… after everything we're fucking been through…"

"This isn't Tobias's fault, Daniel," Kristen says desperately. She's hovering beside them, her hand outstretched. I can tell she wants to pull Dad away from Tobias but she's scared to touch him. "This is my fault."

"Of course it's your fault. Because everything you touch turns to shit, doesn't it, Kristen."

"Daniel, that's enough!" All three of us look towards Tobias who slowly gets up onto his feet. "I get that you're pissed and you have every right to be. But this shit is more complicated than you're making it out to be."

Dad just stares at Daniel as though he can't recognize him anymore. "I should have known," he whispers. "The two of you… it was always the two of you."

"Brother—" Tobias stretches his arm forward but Dad slaps it away.

I can't stand it anymore. There are so many emotions circulating in the space between all four of us that I can't breathe anymore. And since no one is paying any attention to me, I slip out of the apartment and head for the door. I can hear Dad's voice follow me into the corridor.

"Don't fucking touch me. Don't fucking speak to me. I'm done. The two of you deserve each other."

I hit the elevator button continuously, six, seven times before it opens. I rush inside and press for the ground floor. It's only when I'm out on the street that I feel like I can breathe again. It's painful but at least I'm getting some air in my lungs.

I start walking down the street, realizing that my cheeks are wet and I'm shivering despite how warm it is today. I'm not sure how but I end up in the park, looking out over the trees. There's nothing quite as calming as trees.

For a long time all I hear is white noise. My head is reeling and my body feels like it's in shock. I sit there and stare at the trees and wait for my heart beat to slow down. I wait for things to start making sense again.

I watch kids play and couples walk by hand in hand. I watch a dog walker try to reign in seven different breeds and a woman jogs past with her air pods in. It's amazing how the world just keeps moving, even when you feel like your world has come to a screeching halt. It's both terrifying and deeply humbling.

"Hey." I gasp when his hand comes down on my shoulder. "Shit, sorry," Dad says. "I didn't mean to scare you."

I sigh. "Do you mean now? Or back there?"

"Fuck," he mutters as he takes a seat on the bench next to me. "It was a real shit show back there, huh?"

That one almost makes me wanna laugh. "Do you have to ask?"

"You had me worried there for a second."

"Me? Why?"

"I've been walking around for the past two hours trying to find you."

I raise my eyebrows. "Jesus, has it been two hours since I left the apartment?" Dad nods and I let out a low whistle. "Feels like a couple of minutes."

"Maybe it's a good thing I took two hours to find you. Took me that long to calm down."

I smile. "I don't blame you."

"Well, I blame me," he says heavily. "I should have been focused on you. But all I could have in that moment was myself." He wraps an arm over my shoulders. "How are *you* doing?"

"Honestly? I'm not sure. I feel… numb right now." I glance at him. "That was really her, huh?"

He sighs. "That was really her."

"She kinda looks like me." He nods. "Did you ever hate me for that? Even a little. Because I would understand if you did."

He smiles. "Never. Not even for one second. I took one look at you and it was love at first sight."

I rest my head against his shoulder. "Can we talk about what happened before she walked in?"

I can feel him tense up underneath my head. "Did you mean it?" he asks softly. "When you said you loved him?"

"I don't love him, Dad. I'm *in* love with him."

"He's not good enough for you, Ash."

I raise my head and glance at him. "Would you think any man is good enough for me?"

He purses up his lips. "Of course no man could be good

enough for you. And those are just the ones that are age-appropriate. This is Toby we're talking about, Ashley! This is the guy I grew up with—my so-called best fucking friend!"

I nod. "Just to be clear, we met the night before I started at Ackerman's. I was at the bar with my fake ID and he was having dinner with a friend. He came up to me after his friend left and we got to talking. We didn't exchange names but we did share really personal stuff with each other."

"Personal stuff?"

I nod. "I told him about my struggles and he told me about his. It was clear that we were in the same place really. I understood him and he understood me. We *agreed* not to exchange names. At least not until the week after when we agreed to meet at the same time and place."

"Jesus," Dad breathes.

"I also lied about my age that night. I think I told him I was twenty-five or twenty-six. It wasn't until the next day when I walked into Ackerman Corp. to meet my new boss that I realized who he *really* was."

"And what happened then?"

"He chose you."

I look towards my father who holds my gaze tightly. "He chose me?"

I nod. "He actively resisted me for a very long time. I'm the one who pushed his boundaries and argued with his logic. I'm the one who refused to take no for an answer. I just didn't think it was fair that I be denied the love of my life because he happened to be my father's best friend."

"Well, when you say it like that..." he stops abruptly. "It doesn't change the fact that he's been lying to you."

I nod. "I know. He's been lying to you too."

"I know."

"Did you find out why before you left?"

He shakes his head. "I was too angry to hear either one of them out. I left shortly after you ran outta there."

"Will you hear him out?"

He raises his eyebrows at me. "Will you?"

I chew on my bottom lip and look out towards the trees. "I don't know yet."

CHAPTER 37
Tobias

"Coffee or coke?"

Kristen pulls her hands down to reveal her face. "Don't care."

I roll my eyes. "Uh-uh. *I'm* the one who just lost my best friend and the love of my life in five seconds flat. *You* don't get to mope around like the world's just shat all over you."

"Are we comparing wounds now?"

"I'm gonna make you a coffee."

"I want a coke."

"Jesus," I snap, grabbing a bottle of coke and sliding it across the marble countertop towards her. I grab a second bottle of coke and sit down beside her.

She eyes my drink as it sweats out onto the marble. "You can have a beer, I don't mind."

I actually really need one. No—I just really fucking want one. That's precisely why I resist. Over-dependency on alcohol is not something I want to add to my growing list of problems. My family has had its fair share of addicts and I certainly don't want to join the list.

"A coke is fine."

She takes a big swig of her coke. "So—you're in love with my daughter, huh?"

I glance at her. "You wanna take a swing at me too?"

She smiles sadly. "I don't have the right to."

"No," I agree. "You don't. But I would understand the instinct anyway."

"That's because you have a wealth of compassion that's almost inhuman."

I roll my eyes. "You're overstating things."

"I'm actually not," she says firmly. "You saved my life, Toby. You may not believe that but I certainly do. Which is why I'm so fucking sorry about what just went down."

"You don't have to apologize—"

"Yes I do," she insists. "I have no right to barge into your life whenever I need you. Whenever I need a crutch."

"Is that what I am? Your crutch?"

She smiles guiltily. "Yes. But you're also my biggest champion and my best friend." She kinda trips over her last few words. She's always hated crying in front of other people. I've watched her swallow her tears more times than I can count. The only time I ever saw her cry was when she hit her rock bottom.

That was about six years ago.

"Kristen—"

"You never made me feel like a piece of shit even when you could have. Even when I *was* a piece of shit."

I put my hand on Kristen's. "We're all assholes sometimes. It's part of our DNA. You've always been harder on yourself than you needed to be. Ashley must get it from you."

Her eyes flare slightly. "She's fucking beautiful. I can't believe I made her. I can't believe she's mine."

"She's not yours, Kris," I say as gently as possible. "She's her own person. And if there is any person who can take credit for who she is today, for who might have some modicum of ownership over her, it's Daniel."

She looks down and runs her hand down the coke bottle. "I know."

"Why are you here?"

She sniffs. "Had a bad break-up. His name was Chad. I guess I just wanted to be around a friendly face."

"You never mentioned a Chad before."

"I think I was expecting it to end from the moment it started. I was waiting for the other shoe to drop. For Chad to turn into an asshole. Or to find out that he had a wife and a family stashed away somewhere. Or that he was a serial killer or something."

"Jesus, please tell me it wasn't the last one."

She laughs. "It turned out to be none of those things," she admits. "In fact, he turned out to be exactly what he appeared to be. A good man leading a simple life. Hard-working, principled, sometimes boring."

"Oh boy..." she nods. "So *you* ended up being the asshole?"

"He wanted the white picket fence and the mini-van," she says with a sigh. "He wanted a dog named Boon and at least a couple of kids."

"Ah."

"You know the stupidest part?"

"Tell me."

"For a while there, I let myself believe I was capable of that kinda life. I tried to convince myself that maybe it was what I wanted. That I'd grown up, matured. That this was the next step in my evolution. Marriage, kids, house with a mortgage. The works."

"Didn't work out, did it?"

"He got down on one knee and proposed and I stared down at him feeling... *sad*."

"You said no?"

"I had to." There's definitely a glaze of tears over her eyes but she wipes them away before they have a chance to fall. "He's a good man. He deserves a woman who'll be elated when he gets down on one knee. He deserves someone who *wants* to have his babies."

"I'm proud of you."

Her eyes go wide. "You're *proud* of me?"

"I am."

"Didn't expect that."

I smile. "Seven years ago, you would have accepted his proposal, planned a wedding and then disappeared on him one day without so much as a note or an explanation."

"Fuck," she mutters. "I probably would have taken the ring too."

I nod. "You took ownership of your actions, Kristen. You were honest with yourself and Chad. You knew that it would be hard but you did it anyway. I call that brave."

She shakes her head. "It's not brave, Toby. It's exactly the opposite. I date people I know I don't have a future with because then there's no chance *I'll* get hurt. Problem is—I end up hurting everyone else."

"If it's any consolation, I don't think you mean to. At your core, you've never been a cruel person."

She doesn't look like she believes me. "Thank you for saying that."

We clink our coke bottles together. "I'm sorry for showing up on your doorstep unannounced."

"It's okay."

"It's okay? Really? Even if I've cost you Daniel and Ashley?"

"What happened today is not your fault, Kristen. I should have been honest with them from the beginning. This is on me. No one else."

"You didn't have to protect me the way you did."

I sigh. "Don't you get it, Kristen? I will always protect you. You're one of my two best friends. That's not gonna change just cause you made some bad decisions."

Her bottom lip quivers as she jumps off the bar stool and hugs me sideways. "I don't deserve you, Tobias Mason." She pulls away from me slightly. "What're you gonna do now?"

I take a deep breath and try and calm my chaotic thoughts. "I'm gonna do the only thing I can do in this situation. I'm gonna have to let them go."

∽

IT'S BEEN TWENTY-FOUR HOURS AND I HAVEN'T HEARD FROM either Daniel or Ashley.

Not that I expected anything else but hope is a hard beast to kill. Still, I wake up in the morning feeling some kind of internal peace. I know what I need to know. It just took me losing everything to figure it out.

Go figure.

"Morning," I say as I walk into the kitchen.

Kristen's sitting by the center island, nursing a cup of coffee between her hands. She looks tired. "Morning. How'd you sleep?"

"I'd say I got a good three hours in."

She smiles sadly. "Because of me?"

"Because of *me*, Kristen. I'm blaming myself plenty. There's no need to blame yourself too."

She sighs. "Why didn't you tell me they were in California?"

I frown. "I've never talked about either one of them before. Why would I start now?"

Ping.

I look down at my phone and realize it's an email alert. From Ashley. Except that it's not a personal email. She's sent it to my business account. With my heart beating fast, I open and read through it.

A resignation letter.

I've been expecting it and yet, it still stings. No—that's not the right word. It *hurts.* It physically hurts. And for a moment, all I can think is, *how am I gonna deal with not seeing her anymore?*

"Toby? Everything alright?"

I put my phone down and sit down beside Kristen. "We've been friends a long time," I tell her without answering her questing. "You mean a lot to me, Kristen. And I hope you know that."

Her eyes go wide. "Are you breaking up with me?"

I can see how she would think that, given everything that's happened lately. But I've spent the whole of last night thinking about my next move. I want to fix things with Daniel and Ashley. But I know that cutting off ties with Kristen is not the healthy way to move forward for any of us.

I smile. "No, that's not what I'm trying to say."

"What *are* you trying to say?"

"That I understand your demons. That I'm proud of the work you've put in to change the course of your life. That if nothing else, I applaud you for being honest with yourself. I don't like how you did certain things but I get why you did them."

She looks like she's close to tears. "I would understand if you never wanted to see me again, Toby."

"Remember the day you called me up for the first time in years?"

She nods. "Of course."

"I do too. I remember hearing the suffering in your voice. I remember how much pain you were in. How scared you were. How desperate. You have no idea how glad I was that you decided to call me that day."

A tear slips down her cheek. "You're a good man, Toby Mason."

I embrace her and she cries on my shoulder for a bit. When we finally pull away from each other she looks calm. Serene even. She wipes away her tears and takes a deep breath. "I'm moving to India."

My jaw drops. "What?"

She nods, smiling shyly. "The idea's been percolating in the back of my head for months now. The first seed was planted while I was still with Chad. I think I finally made the decision last night. I'm gonna across the world, see what Asia makes of me."

In some ways, her decision shocks me. In other ways—not at all. "Are you buying a return ticket?"

She smiles a little wider. "Nope. One-way for the moment. I don't know if I'll stay in India for one year or five. I just know that I won't be coming back to the US for a good, long time."

"And you're sure?"

"A hundred percent. This is the right decision for me."

"Well then—I'm happy for you."

I give her another hug and head to the door. "I've got something important to do now. How about we get dinner tonight? You're gonna be sticking around for a little while longer, right?"

She chews on her bottom lip. "I'm actually gonna take a flight outta here tomorrow afternoon."

"So soon?"

Her smile grows a little sad. "I need to figure out where I belong, Toby. One thing I think I've figured out—I don't belong here."

She reminds me so much of Ashley in that moment. Maybe that's why I can't stop loving her now. Maybe my love for her was what fueled my connection to Ashley. Everything feels interconnected in this moment. And it galvanizes my decision.

"See you tonight."

She blows me a kiss and I head out of the apartment. The adrenaline is pumping hard as I make my way through town towards their neck of the woods. I have no idea what kind of reception I'll receive when I get there but I'm prepared to be persistent.

~

I CAN HEAR THEIR VOICES FROM INSIDE THE APARTMENT WHEN I step up to Ashley's front door. It takes me a few minutes and several deep breathes before I finally work up the courage to knock. It's Daniel who answers.

His face turns cold the moment he sees me.

"Before you slam the door in my face, please hear me out."

"I don't know if I care to hear your explanations, Toby."

"That's fine because I'm not here to give you an explanation." Ashley stands up from the dining table slowly. When I try to make eye contact, she looks away from me immediately. "I just wanted to give you two things." I pull out the two white envelopes hiding inside my jacket and hand them over.

Daniel looks down at it suspiciously. "What is this?"

"I just want to make it clear—I'm not trying to buy your forgiveness. But I do consider you family. *Both* of you. I wasn't able to take care of my mother or brother the way I should have but I'm gonna make damn sure I take care of the two of you." Ashley takes a couple of tentative steps forward but Daniel still doesn't take the envelopes. "I don't expect anything in return. I don't even want your gratitude. All I want you to do is cash these cheques."

"Cheques?" Daniel repeats incredulously.

I look my best friend in the eye. "You should have told me you were struggling. You've worked too damn hard to still be struggling to make ends meet after all these years. Take the money, pay off your mortgage, live a little, brother. You deserve it." I glance over his shoulder at Ashley. "And Ashley." It's hard to swallow the lump in my throat. "You're fucking amazing. I mean that. You're beautiful and brilliant and you can be more in life than just some rich asshole's PA. Do whatever you want with this money—travel, go back to school, start your own business, it doesn't matter to me. Just as long as you do something that feeds your soul and makes you happy. That's all I want."

It doesn't seem like Daniel's gonna accept the envelopes. So I push my way into the apartment just enough to place the envelopes on the little console table where Ashley keeps her keys. "That's all I wanted to say," I mutter softly. "Thanks for not shutting the door in my face."

I don't look at Ashley as I turn from the door and start walking away. I know that if I look at her—I won't be able to leave.

And I have to leave.

After everything I've done—it's the least I can do.

~

I STARE AT THE DIRTY PIECE OF GLASS IN FRONT OF ME AND try to ignore the intimidating black phone that I'll have to pick up in a moment. I've been sitting here for nearly fifteen minutes, and there's still no sign of him.

Typical really. Even when he has nowhere to go, he makes *me* wait.

Instinctively, I reach for my phone every few seconds only to be reminded that I was forced to deposit it in a little locker box before I went through security. Weird how naked I feel without it. More so because I keep wondering if maybe Ashley has called or texted.

I try and shake her face from my head. *You promised to leave her alone and that's what you're gonna do. Now's the time for fresh starts.*

Just at that moment, the door opens and a detention officer walks my father into the room. *Jesus, is that him?* I used to see him as this larger-than-life figure. A man whose very presence made you want to cower in fear.

But all I see now is an old man. An old man with a greying overgrown beard and a hunch that's cost him several inches. His eyes have a rheumy look as they land on me. He takes the phone gingerly and I notice fresh cuts on his arms. Apparently, life in incarceration hadn't exactly made a pacifist outta him.

He picks up the phone on his side of the glass and I follow suit. "They told me it was you but I didn't believe them," he rasps.

He sounds different too, like every word is a struggle to utter. "Hi, Dad."

He flinches, shifting uncomfortably from side to side. "Why are you here?"

It's a fair question really. It's been years since he was convicted and this is the first visit I've ever made. "I'm here because… I wanted to tell you something."

He smacks his lips together and looks around as though he's worried he's being punked. "Well? Get on with it."

I take a deep breath and say the words before I chicken out. "I wanted to tell you I forgive you."

There's a few long moments of silence. "What?" he snaps.

"I forgive you."

He scowls. "I didn't ask for your forgiveness."

I nod. "Oh I'm very aware of that. I'm not forgiving you for your sake. I'm forgiving you for mine. I'm letting go of the past and I'm moving forward with my life. And if I have a chance of resolving any of my issues, I have to let go of my anger towards you."

The old man looks like he has no idea what to say to that. Maybe that's why he goes with, "I… I didn't know how to be a father." It's the most honest thing he's ever said to me.

"I know, Dad. Like I said, it's okay now. Time for me to move on."

"What does that mean?" he demands. "You're done with me?"

"I wouldn't expect you to understand." I give him a decisive nod. "And you won't have to worry about your commissary account anymore. I'll put in a sum every month for as long as you're in here."

His eyes go wide. "I knew I raised you right."

I feel only the smallest flash of anger. "No, you didn't raise me at all. But that's neither here nor there. I've said what I came here to say."

He says something as I put the phone down but I realize I don't care to hear it. I don't need anything more from him any longer. Not an apology. Not an explanation. Not even closure. I've given myself closure.

And maybe that means I can give myself a fresh start too.

I have no other choice.

CHAPTER 38

Ashley

I t's almost twenty-four hours since Tobias stopped by with two cheques and a speech that I keep replaying in my head over and over again.

Dad and I hadn't discussed it. In fact, neither one of us had so much as touched the two cheques that are still sitting on the console table next to my keys.

Dad moves past me towards the bathroom. "I'm gonna take a shower now. You wanna head in there before I go?"

I shake my head distractedly. "I'm good."

He disappears into the bathroom, and a few moments later, I hear the water start to run. My mug is empty so I head into the kitchen to pour myself more coffee. I barely slept the previous night, which is why I'm really feeding my coffee addiction this morning.

I'd hoped to wake up this morning with an idea of what I wanted to do but I'm still no closer to figuring it out.

Do I cash the cheque? Do I return it? Do I talk to Tobias? Do I demand an explanation from him or do I leave him to his life and try and get on with my own?

It feels like I'm wading through quicksand and there's no one around to pull me out.

Knock, knock, knock.

My heart beat races up. My first and only thought is— *Tobias!* It's pathetic how much I wish it was him. With my hands trembling slightly, I go to the door and pull it open. I freeze on the spot.

She stands there in dark jeans, a white t-shirt and the same ankle boots I saw her wearing the first time. She's also got a leather jacket thrown over the handle of her suitcase. *Suitcase?*

"Hi Ashley." It feels weird hearing her say my name.

"Hi."

"I know this is unexpected but I would really like the chance to talk to you. Just for a few minutes."

At first, all I feel is anger. Then this overwhelming sense of sadness. I keep looking at her suitcase. She's leaving again and even though it has nothing to do with me, it feels personal. "You have no right to show up after twenty years and ask me for anything."

She flinches. "You're absolutely right." She pulls out an envelope—*what is with people and envelopes recently?*—and offers it to me. "I've written down everything I want to say in this. It's totally up to you if you want to read it or not. But I hope you will."

I stare at the letter and instinctively, I know that if I turn her away now, I'll regret it later. With a deep sigh, I hold the door open a little wider. "Why don't you just come in?"

Her eyes go wide with surprise. "Thank you."

She leaves her jacket and suitcase in the hallway and follows me into the apartment. She sits down on the sofa and I take the armchair adjacent to her.

"Okay. Go ahead. Tell me whatever it is you came here to say." She's staring at me hard. *Really* hard. "Kristen?"

She blinks, her cheeks flushing with color. "I'm sorry. It's just amazing to be sitting here with you after almost twenty-one years." She fidgets uncomfortably. "I should apologize for that."

I raise my eyebrows in disbelief. "You *should* apologize for that?" I repeat incredulously, already losing my fight with patience. "I have no idea what the hell that means."

"Jesus, I'm doing this all wrong, aren't I?"

"Why are you here, Kristen? Because if it's to ask for forgiveness—"

"It's not," she says quickly. "I know I don't deserve your forgiveness. But you *do* deserve an explanation."

I draw in a breath. I've spent most of my life trying to figure out why she had left me—us. And now that she's here, a flesh and blood woman with pretty eyes and a dimpled smile, I'm not sure I really want to know.

"I really thought I could do it," she says softly. And even though I have no idea what she's talking about right now, I lean in, hanging on her every word. "When I got pregnant with you, I really thought I could be a mother." She looks at me with tears in her eyes. "There's no big reason, Ashley. There's no grand revelation apart from the fact that I was young and scared and it was just too much for me. I can't even say I regret leaving because the truth is it never changed for me. I never longed to be a mother. If I had, I would have come back."

It is hard to hear. But weirdly, it feels healing too.

"I don't know. Maybe I knew that deep down even back then. I could feel myself slipping away. I could feel my control and my will power disappearing. Daniel thought I'd stopped drinking and smoking during my pregnancy but I hadn't. I just got a lot better at hiding it. The truth was, I *needed* the alcohol to feel brave enough to handle what was to come."

My skin feels like it's on fire. But apart from that very tangible feeling, my emotions are stagnant. I feel almost numb.

"Then I gave birth to you and I was hoping that some switch in my brain would click and I would fall into mother-hood the way that Daniel fell into fatherhood. It just came so naturally to him. He was the first person to hold you after the doctor pulled you out of me. He looked down at you and I saw it in his eyes. The switch had flipped for him. He was a father. End of story. And me?" She clasps her hands tightly together. "I waited for something to happen, some big swell of emotion that would allow me to be your mother… it just… it didn't happen that way."

She falls into silence and looks at me cautiously. "Go on," I encourage.

"I don't say any of this to hurt you. I just want you to understand."

"I'm listening."

She nods. "I did love your father. I loved you too. But I knew I would erode the love that both of you had for me if I stayed. I'd seen enough bad parenting to know that I just couldn't do that to you. Or Daniel. It became more and more clear to me. I'd be a better mother if I left than if I stayed."

I grit my teeth. "So you just decided to leave without an explanation?"

"I was a coward," she says simply. "Every time I so much as touched on how I was feeling, Daniel started talking about postpartum depression and baby blues. He told me that it would pass, that I would get better. He told me I would learn to be a mother."

"It wasn't that, was it?" I ask. "You didn't *want* to be a mother."

She runs a hand through her hair. She looks so extraordinarily young. "No," she admits. "The truth is—I still don't."

Surprisingly, that doesn't hurt as much as I would have thought it would. I feel a tiny spike of resentment and bitterness. And then it's gone. This woman may be my mother but it's just biology. It's DNA. She's *not* my mother. Not really.

"I'm not trying to say 'I told you so' but right after I left town for good, I kind of... broke down. I suppose some of it was guilt, but the rest of it was loneliness, isolation and helplessness. I met a man who fanned my worst desires instead of tempering them. Instead of cutting me off after five drinks, he just kept on pouring. When I finished a cigarette, he lit me another. He also introduced me to cocaine."

My eyes go wide. "Cocaine?"

"The most I'd dabbled in before then was weed. Cocaine felt like weed on steroids. I got hooked. I stayed hooked for a long time."

"You look good for a drug addict."

She smiles. "I'm almost six years sober," she says triumphantly.

I'm actually very glad to hear that. "Good for you."

"Six years ago, I hit rock bottom. I was homeless, living on the streets after my boyfriend kicked me out of his trailer. I was drinking heavily and stealing to survive. I genuinely had nowhere to go and no one to turn to. I started squatting in an abandoned building that was scheduled for demolition in a few weeks. There were a bunch of other homeless people squatting there as well. I was so low that I genuinely thought that maybe dying in that building was the best thing for me. So, on the day of the demolition, I stole money, bought myself a couple of grams of coke and shot myself up. I passed out that morning and woke up almost two days later in the hospital."

"Jesus," I breathe.

"I guess you could say I had something of an epiphany when I woke up. I realized that I didn't want to die. In fact, I wanted to live. Really *live*. And that realization is what led me to call Toby."

My heart beats unevenly. I feel... light headed and exhilarated all at the same time. "You didn't have contact with him before then?"

She shakes her head. "I abandoned him the same day I abandoned you and your father. But when I came to that day in Saint Agnes Hospital, I knew that if I called him, he would come."

I nod. "He came."

"Of course he came. He paid for my hospital bills in full. He spoke to my doctors. He asked them to release me into his care. He drove me straight from the hospital to a rehab facility that he had already paid for. He told me that he would visit me every two weeks. And for three entire months, he was there every two weeks without fail."

"You stayed there for three months?"

She nods. "He was there to pick me up after at the end of my rehab stint. I stayed with him for two months after that. He got me a job and a place to stay. Even helped with my rent for six months after that."

I close my eyes for a moment. "Dad... um... he thinks the two of you—"

"It was *never* romantic between Tobias and I. Ever. We were always friends. Best friends. And he was there for me when I needed him. He never judged me, even when he could have. He never blamed me, even when he should have. He never made me feel worthless. Probably because he knew I was already feeling that way without outside help."

I finally understand why she's here. "You came to speak to me today for him."

"He's a good man, Ashley. And he loves you. And when Tobias Mason loves you, he never stops."

"Why didn't he just tell me all of this?"

"You'd have to ask him. But I think I know him well enough to take a stab at the reasons he kept silent. The first is, he's never been one to talk about another person's struggle. I had trusted him with the most vulnerable part of my journey and there's no way he would have betrayed that trust. The second reason is…" she sighs. "He knew how much I'd hurt you and Daniel by leaving. I don't think he wanted to risk alienating Daniel by telling him that he was looking after me."

Click.

Kristen and I both turn to the bathroom door. Dad stands there looking somber-faced but calm. I was so absorbed in the conversation, I hadn't even heard the water turn off.

"How long have you been standing there?" I ask.

He moves forward just a little. "Long enough."

Kristen gets to her feet. "I'm sorry, Daniel. For everything."

His gaze flits to me for a moment. "I don't know if I'll ever be able to forgive you, Kris," he says bluntly. "But I want you to know that I am grateful to you. You may have left but at least you gave me Ash."

I wipe my tears away quickly before either one of them looks away. I'm not sure how, but there's this deep instinct I'm feeling that's telling me that this is probably gonna be the last time the three of us are together in the same room.

"Thanks for hearing me out," she says softly.

She walks to the door and Dad moves to my side. He wraps an arm around me and I lean into him. Kristen pauses at the threshold and looks back at both of us.

"I never thought I'd see either one of you again," she admits. "I'm glad I did. It makes me realize I did the right thing by leaving."

The door shuts. The silence that unfolds is complicated, pregnant with all kinds of warring emotions.

The loudest of all is… acceptance.

CHAPTER 39

Ashley

"Are you okay?"

I turn to Dad with dry eyes. There were points during Kristen's story when I had felt close to tears. But strangely, as of right now, I feel completely calm and completely in control of my emotions.

The puzzle pieces have finally been put together. Most of them anyway. Enough that I can see the bigger picture. I can appreciate its shortcomings but I can also appreciate its beauty.

"I'm fine," I say, venturing a smile. "Better than fine actually. How about you?"

Dad nods and he seems as surprised as I am of myself. "I'll admit now. I always thought about seeing her again one day."

"Yeah?"

He nods. "I expected fire and brimstone. I thought it would be the show down of all show downs."

I smile. "You could argue that the first meeting was."

Dad scoffs. "Ha! I didn't say half of what I'd practiced in the mirror."

"Aw, you practiced?"

He sighs and sits down on the sofa. He pats the cushion next to him. "I'm not proud of it now but yes. I did practice. I cursed her out, told her she should be ashamed of herself, blamed her for everything that went wrong in my life. I made her my scapegoat and I guess I got used to keeping her that way."

"Is it still that way?"

He shakes his head. "Seeing her again made me realize something." He looks at me with his forehead creased and his eyes glazed over. "I never let go of my anger. I made myself a victim and blamed her. I had abandonment issues and I transferred them to you."

"Ah, so *that's* where I got it from."

He chuckles. "I guess this whole thing made me realize that I'm not sixteen anymore. I'm not the boy she left behind. I'm not in love with her anymore and I deserve the right to be happy."

I link my arm with his. "You do."

He kisses my temple. "I feel a lot lighter all of a sudden."

"I've heard forgiveness can do that to you."

"Jesus," he breathes. "Wish I'd done it sooner."

I lean my head against his shoulder. "Me too."

He pats my knee and gestures over to the two envelopes that are still sitting on the console table by the front door. "I've made a decision."

I raise my head. "You have?"

"I'm keeping the money."

My eyes go wide. I really hadn't expected that. "Wow."

"Yeah."

"Does that mean…" and suddenly, all that emotion I thought I had mastered was back again, clogging up my throat and choking me up again. "Um, does that mean you can see yourself forgiving Tobias at some point?"

He sighs. "That depends."

"On?"

"You."

I glance over at my envelope. Then I get up and walk over to it. I pick it up and turn it over. I break the seal and pull out the cheque. It's a big one. *Fifty* thousand dollars. He hasn't just covered my college education. He's covered living expenses as well.

A tear lands on the cheque and I push it back into the envelope before realizing that there's a small folded piece of paper in there as well. It looks like it's been hastily torn off a book. All it says is—

Ashley, you have been honey to my soul.—I'm sorry.

And that's it.

That's it?

And suddenly, I'm furious.

I grab my coat and slip the envelope into my jacket pocket. "Dad, I have to go. I'll be back for dinner, okay? There's something I need to do first."

His eyes go wide but to his credit, he doesn't ask me where I'm going. Probably because he already knows. Still, he doesn't stop me.

"Good luck," is all he says.

I wave goodbye and head out. I consider taking a cab but I then I figure a walk will do me good. Maybe I can work off some of the adrenaline pumping through my body right now. Half an hour later, I arrive outside Ackerman Corp., but still, the adrenaline is pumping. My anger is still peaked.

When I get to Tobias's floor, I blow right past his new temp and burst into his office. Except that he's not here. The office is empty.

"Excuse me!" the temp gasps, running in after me. She's got dark brown hair, bright red lipstick and a tight see-through blouse that strikes me as incredibly inappropriate. "You can't just barge in there."

"Where is Mr. Ackerman?"

She blinks at me incredulously. "Do you have an appointment?"

I push past her and head to her desk. Then I start rifling through her papers. "Hey!" she yells. "You can't touch those! Stop!"

"Ah-ha!" I exclaim when I find his schedule. "He has a board meeting."

"It's in progress," the temp snaps, grabbing the schedule from my hands. "And I'm afraid it's a closed meeting. Who the hell are you anyway?"

"I'm not sure right now," I fire back. "But I'll let you know." Then I start heading towards the meeting rooms where I know the board meeting always takes place. In fact, it's the same room where Tobias and I had torrid sex the night of Louisa's retirement party. I can hear the temp race after me, but thankfully, those high heels she's wearing are slowing her down.

I turn the corner and catch sight of Tobias. He's at the head of the table but his chair is swiveled towards the view. He looks as though he isn't concentrating on the meeting at all.

I burst into the meeting room. Every single head swivels in my direction, including that of Tobias.

"I'm *so* sorry, Mr. Ackerman!" the temp gasps as she *click-clacks* her way in after me. "I tried to stop her, but she—"

"It's okay, Hannah," Tobias says immediately before looking at me. "Ashley? Is everything alright?"

"Is that a serious question?"

He glances toward his board of directors, all of whom are staring at me with rapt attention. "Um, if this is about the envelope I left you…"

"*Why* didn't you tell me about her?" I demand.

He clears his throat. "Ladies and gentlemen, would you please excuse us?"

There's a mixed reaction to the request. Some look shocked and offended. Others look amused and curious. Either way, everyone leaves in a single file, including his snippy little temp who throws me a dirty look before she leaves.

"*That's* who you chose to replace me with?" I demand when the door closes behind us.

We might have the room to ourselves now but we're still very much exposed through those glass walls. I'm very aware that *everyone* is watching and just pretending they're not. Not that I care at this point.

Bring on the popcorn!

"Ashley," he says softly. "*No one* could replace you."

He's standing three feet away. The distance between us feels vast all of a sudden. "Tell me," I say softly. "Why didn't you tell me about her?"

"Because I would have had to tell you everything," he says. Which is pretty much what *she* had told me he would say. "And that was her story to tell, not mine."

"She came over this morning. Before her flight."

"I had a feeling she might."

"She didn't say anything to you?"

He shakes his head. Then he sighs. "I'm sorry, Ashley."

"What are you apologizing for?"

"I don't know. All of it. Sometimes, I think I should have just finished my dinner that night and gone home."

I really have to fight my tears on that one. "You regret being with me?"

"Selfishly, no," he says heavily. "But for your sake—"

"Don't you *for my sake* me. You don't get to tell me what's best for me and what isn't."

He falls silent and nods. "You're right. I won't."

I pull out the envelope and throw it onto the boardroom table. "I'm not cashing the cheque, Tobias. I don't want your money."

His eyes go wide, his nostrils flare. He even takes a step towards me. "Ashley, please. Don't do this. This is about your future. Be angry with me if you want. Hate me if you must. Just take the money and go back to school. You—"

"I've made up my mind!"

"Then unmake it!" he exclaims. "You're too damn smart to—"

"I thought you were done telling me what's best for me?"

He bites his cheek for a second before he shakes his head. "Well, *screw* that! Your future is more important."

"No."

"Ashley—"

"If I let you pay for everything, then we're never going to be on equal footing in this relationship. If I go back to school, I'll do it on my own!"

He stares at me in shock. "In this relationship?" he exclaims.

I take a deep breath and nod. "Yes, in this relationship. Our relationship."

"We have one?"

I raise my eyebrows. "We do. If you're done fighting me on that."

"Jesus," he breathes, looking completely shell-shocked. "You... still want to be with me... after everything?"

I walk right up to him and cup the side of his face with my palm. "Kristen told me everything, Tobias. How you were there for her at her lowest point, how you took care of her." My bottom lip trembles. "I don't know how you got this impression that you weren't a good person because as far as I'm concerned, you're the *best* person there is."

He shakes his head in awe. "This feels... surreal. Is it real?"

I smile. "Why don't you kiss me and find out?"

He grabs me so possessively I cry out. When his lips land on mine, my toes curl with pleasure. My heart beats hard, my pulse races. It's like I'm coming home. This is home. *He* is home. And finally, *finally*—I feel like I belong.

CHAPTER 40

Ashley

Eighteen Months Later…

"You're not going to give me a clue?"

Tobias laughs. "You'll find out soon enough. We'll be there in fifteen minutes."

I squirm in my seat. "I hate surprises!"

"No, you don't. You just don't like waiting for them."

I roll my eyes. "You think you know me so well." The irony is, he *does* know me well. The last year and a half have been a whirlwind. Between Tobias's job, my schooling and the move to our new penthouse, we've had a lot on our plates. I'm hoping for a little downtime before my graduation, which is coming up in a few weeks. After that, I've got a few job interviews lined up for next month.

"Are you taking me to a spa? Cause you know I don't like full-body treatments, right?"

He scoffs. "Hello? It's me. The kind of gift giving."

I laugh. "You have had an excellent track record so far."

Ring-Ring. Ring-Ring.

I glance at my call screen. "It's Dad," I tell Tobias before picking up. "Hey, Dad."

"Hey, kiddo, how's it going?"

"Not sure yet."

"What does that mean?"

"I came home an hour ago to find that my suitcase was packed. Now Tobias and I are in a car heading to God knows where for this 'surprise' he's planned for me."

"Is this an early graduation gift?"

I frown. "I think this is more of a *congratulations on surviving finals* celebration."

"Well, then you deserve it. You survived finals."

"The last paper was a tough one."

"Don't stress, kid. You've got this in the bag."

I take a deep breath. "You're right. I just… get in my head sometimes."

"That happens when it's important to you. But don't forget to pat yourself on the back too. I know this past year has been tough, but you did it!"

Smiling, I nod. "I know. I'm proud of myself."

"You should be."

"So, you're still coming down for my graduation, right?"

"Are you kidding? I wouldn't miss it for the world."

"Good."

He chuckles. "Did you really think I wouldn't be there?"

There's a tremor of concern underneath that chuckle and I kinda feel guilty for asking. The day I had stormed into Ackerman Corp. and confronted Tobias in front of his board of directors had marked a turning point. But not all turning points are smooth.

I'd left Tobias that evening to go back to my apartment and have a chat with my father. I told him that Tobias and I were together. That we were in love. That we hoped we had his blessing but we weren't asking for permission. At least, *I* wasn't.

He had taken the conversation in his stride. He'd barely said anything through my explanation, but in the end, he hugged me. *"You're a grown woman, Ash,"* he said. *"And this is your life. I'm gonna have to respect that."*

"What about Tobias?"

He hadn't replied immediately and I remembered feeling as though my heart was gonna burst outta my chest. I did say that I wasn't asking for his permission, but the truth was, I couldn't imagine a world in which my father didn't like or approve of my decisions.

"Give me time," was all he said. And even though it had been hard, I'd left it there.

A few days later, Dad had gone back to Arizona. He called me three times a week and he texted constantly. He never asked about Tobias, but I always threw his name around a little bit. About four months after Dad left, we were talking one night when he asked, *"How's Toby doing?"*

My jaw dropped. Tobias was lying on the couch, his head in my lap. *"H-he's good,"* I managed to stammer out. *"He's right here reading a book."*

There'd been a few seconds of silence. Then—*"Can I speak to him?"*

The conversation had lasted three minutes or so. It was more small talk than meaningful conversation, but it was a start. Now they spoke a couple of times every month. The conversations never lasted more than a few minutes, but as they say, baby steps.

I'd visited Arizona twice in the last eighteen months, but Tobias hadn't come with me either time. So, Dad coming for my graduation was significant. It would mark the first time in one and a half years that Dad and Tobias would be face to face again. No one mentioned it but it was the giant elephant in the room.

"Of course, I didn't think that," I say with an awkward laugh. "I was just…"

"Oh ye of little faith."

I glance at Tobias who's trying to pretend like he's not listening. "I can't wait to see you."

"Me too. Have fun, kid."

"Bye, Dad."

"Oh, and say hi to Tobias for me."

"I will." I hang up and glance at Tobias. "Dad says hi."

His answering smile is definitely self-conscious. "He called me this morning."

"Um, *what!?*" That one's a shocker. "As in, he called you directly? On purpose?"

"Ha-ha. *Yes*, it was on purpose. I think he's trying to make more of an effort. He asked if I wanted to see a game with him while he was in town. Just the two of us."

My eyes go wide. "Just the two of you, huh?" He nods and I exhale sharply. "Well *damn*, that's a big deal."

"He loves you."

"He loves you too," I point out. "He's just trying to navigate the whole *my best friend is also my daughter's boyfriend* situation."

"You know what? Fair."

Laughing, I put my hand on his thigh. "Seriously. *Where* are we going?"

"Look ahead."

I notice a plane taking off in the distance. "Huh? It looks like a private hangar."

"It is."

"Um, why would we be driving to a private hangar? You don't even own a private jet."

He winks at me. "I do now."

I gasp. "You *bought* a plane?"

"It was a practical purchase. I have a fuck ton of business trips coming up next year and we do wanna travel, don't we?"

"Sure but I just figured we'd fly coach."

Tobias rolls his eyes. "My girlfriend doesn't fly coach. No. From now on, you're a private jet person."

"Urgh, I don't think I have the personality of one."

"I know. It's what I love most about you."

We hit the tarmac and there's already a whole crew waiting for us there. Our suitcases are carried on board, and Tobias chats with the pilot while I stare up at the beautiful, sleek private jet.

"Come on, baby," Tobias says, leading me towards the plane. "We're ready for take-off."

"Where are we going?" I whisper in awe as we climb the stairs up to the body of the plane.

"You'll have to wait to find out."

"Tobias!"

He cracks up. "Oh, all right. Where have you talked about going since you watched Les Mis on stage?"

I gasp. "France!"

"Ding-ding-ding!"

I jump on him, practically tackling him to the ground. We almost topple over into the cockpit. "Sorry, Lewis," Tobias apologizes to the pilot. "The wife gets a little excited when we travel."

Wife?

That one takes me aback. He has never referred to me as his wife before. Which, you know, makes sense, considering I'm *not* his wife.

But boy do I like how that sounds. I like how it *feels* too.

"Can I get you anything, ma'am? We have wine and champagne. There's also a cocktail menu."

The air hostess is a pretty brunette in a pristine blue uniform. "Um…" I glance at Tobias distractedly. I'm still kinda hung up on the whole *wife* comment from earlier.

"We'll have some champagne, Taylor. Thanks."

I stare out the window as the plane takes off. A little while later, Taylor brings us two flutes of champagne and a whole plate of strawberries. When she leaves, she pulls closed two curtains, effectively cutting us off from the rest of the plane.

I grab a strawberry and stuff it into my mouth, trying desperately *not* to think of myself in a wedding dress.

"Are you okay, beautiful?" Tobias asks curiously.

"Hm?"

"Are you okay? You just seem a little distracted."

Don't bring it up. "I'm good. Just excited… Paris!"

"I can't wait to show you around. We'll spend three nights in Paris and then I'm taking you to Leon for four nights and we'll finish off in Marseilles."

An off the shoulder dress would make a pretty bridal.

NO!

Stop it, you big loser.

"Ashley?"

I raise my eyebrows, feeling like a complete idiot now. "Sorry, sorry. I know I'm being a spaz. I'm just… thinking about my last final."

"No, you're not."

"Excuse me?"

348

"You're forgetting again. I *know* you. That's not your exam stress face. Now tell me, what's got you so distracted?"

He looks so damn handsome right now. With all the light streaming in through the open windows, his eyes look teal and his hair has an intoxicating hint of auburn that borders on gold. "Um… nothing."

"Ashley." He sounds almost stern.

"You called me your wife earlier," I admit, feeling like a right idiot for even mentioning it. But I'm a little too flustered to bluff my way through this. He'd probably sense a lie anyway. This whole '*I know you*' business is lovely but it can be a little inconvenient at times. "I guess it just threw me a little."

"Oh."

Oh?

I wave my hands. "It's a silly thing to fixate on. It was just a silly slip of the tongue and I'm sure you didn't mean anything by it." Pretty sure my cheeks are crimson now. "Sorry, I'll shut up. Let's drink more champagne and forget that I said anything."

He arches one perfect eyebrow. "I don't think I can."

I cringe. "Tobias—"

"You're right. It was a slip of the tongue. I really didn't mean to say it."

Kill me. Kill me now. "Of course you didn't. Which is fine. It's not like I'm expecting anything… things are good right now and—"

"I guess you could call it a… Freudian slip." He slides out of his seat and onto his knee in front of me. I gasp as he pulls out a small Tiffany box from his pants pocket.

"Oh my God," I exclaim. "No way!"

He smiles. "Ashley Payne. I want you to know that we

can do this whenever you want to, whenever you're ready. This proposal in no way means that we have to get married soon. I know you have dreams, ambitions and plans. And I want to support them all. So I'll wait as long as you want to wait. I just need to know that *one* day, you will be my wife." He opens the box and sitting on a plush black cushion is the most perfect solitaire diamond that I've ever seen.

There are tears in my eyes as I stare down at it. I can almost see my reflection in it. It's that big. "Tobias... I... I don't know what to say."

"*Yes* would be a start."

I burst out laughing through my tears. "Yes! Yes! Yes! Of *course,* I'll marry you."

I jump out of my seat and right into his arms. We're kissing heatedly on the floor before Tobias stops me. "Hold on, baby, I wanna get this ring on you first." I push back the tears as he slides the ring onto my finger. "Perfect."

I shake my head. "I can't believe it. We're engaged!" I stare at the ring on my finger. It's heavy too. And then I realize something. "Oh my God, we're gonna have to tell Dad."

Tobias grabs me and pulls me onto his seat so that I'm straddling him. I wriggle uncomfortably. "*Tobias,* this is so inappropriate. I'll sit over here—"

"No way. You're my fiancée now. And you're gonna sit on my lap, where you belong."

I blush fiercely. "But the air hostess—"

"Don't worry, she won't disturb us. I asked for privacy. And in any case, we have the whole plane to ourselves. That's the benefit of a private jet."

I relax a little and slide my palms up and down his chest. "Okay then…"

"And as for Daniel. He already knows."

My jaw drops. "Seriously?" I think I might be more shocked about that than the actual proposal. "You're not kidding?"

"Remember my business meeting in Cairo last week?"

"Uh, yeah."

He shakes his head. "I didn't go to Cairo. I flew to Arizona to spend the weekend with Daniel."

My eyes feel like they're gonna pop right outta my head. "He didn't breathe a word to me!"

"Because I asked him not to. I went over there to look him in the eye and ask for his blessing. I was prepared to beg if I had to."

I still can't quite believe it. "And he said yes?"

He chuckles, his hands sliding down to my ass. "You don't have to look quite so surprised."

"I'm sorry. It's just… this is insane. You guys are hanging out, spending weekends together… and he gave you his blessing." I stop short. "He *did* give you his blessing, right?"

Tobias laughs. "He did. But not before he told me that if I ever hurt you, intentionally or not, he'd cut off my balls and feed them to his neighbor's rottweiler."

I smirk. "Aw, so sweet."

"I thought so too," Tobias says sarcastically.

I bend down and place my forehead against his. "Did he seem… happy to give you permission?" I ask softly.

"He just wants you to be happy, Ashley. And I think it's safe to say he wants the same for me too."

Honestly, I'm so happy I could cry. "I love you, Tobias Mason Ackerman."

"You're my whole world, babe."

"And just so you know… I don't want to wait ages before we get married. Ten months, maybe twelve. But that's it. I *want* to be your wife. I can't wait."

"Good. Cause I was bluffing when I said you could take your time."

Laughing, I lean in and kiss him until I lose my laughter in his breath. My pussy is throbbing wildly and my body is alight with tingles. Especially with the way his hands are squeezing my ass.

"Mile high club—here I come," I whisper in his ear breathlessly.

"Oh you're gonna cum alright," he promises firmly, pulling my skirt up and kneading me against his erection.

I start pulling at the buttons of his shirt as he rips my panties right off. Honestly, in the last few months alone, he's torn, ripped and shredded through most of my lingerie. Not that he doesn't replace them all tenfold, but still. Regardless, it's hard for me to care when we're in the throes of the moment. And right now, I'm high on excitement.

I'm going to marry Tobias!

I'm going to be his wife!

He's going to be my husband!

It's too insane for words. Which is probably why this is the exact right way to celebrate. His fingers slide up my wet pussy. I ride his fingers as I bite down on my bottom lip, desperate not to scream the damn plane down. But the closer I come to orgasm, the harder it becomes to keep my moans quiet and dignified.

"*Hmm*... fuck... yes baby... *yes!*"

"Look at me," he growls.

I force my eyes open and make eye contact. God, he looks amazing. He pulls his fingers out of me and pushes me down onto his cock. I love the way he looks when he pushes inside me. The slight flare of his eyes, the clench of his jaw, an expression that says this is exactly where he belongs.

I ride him desperately, bucking hard against his throbbing

cock. The seats are spacious but probably not spacious enough for two people. Still, it only adds to the heightened urgency of the moment. I cum twice before Tobias stands up and walks me to the back of the plane. He fucks me up against the back wall. Then he sets me down on my feet, twists me around and takes me from behind while I use the backrests as supports.

It definitely feels like a very thorough initiation to the mile high club.

After my third orgasm, I twist around and get down on my knees. I take Tobias's cock into my mouth eagerly and start sucking hard. I'm spent, my knees are weak and my hands are trembling slightly. Pretty sure there's a little turbulence outside but I don't care at this point. I suck on his cock until he cums in my throat. I suck every last drop of him until his body spasms with pleasure and relief.

"Wow," he says, cupping my face as I look up at him. "You are amazing."

Smiling, I get shakily up to my feet and wrap my arms around him. I'm almost blinded by the shimmer of my own ring.

"You're the one who's amazing. I couldn't have gotten through this past year without you."

I really mean it too. While I pulled all-nighters to write papers and stressed out about each essay I had to hand in, Tobias had been my rock through it all. He was always calm, always patient. He was the voice of reason any time I started to doubt myself. When I started to waver, he encouraged me to keep going.

In fact, he told me I was smart and capable so often that I actually started to believe it.

"You did it all on your own."

I shake my head. "No, *we* did it. Together. Teamwork."

He hesitates. "Okay, I'll acquiesce to that."

I laugh. "This is it, you know?" I say, half teasing and half serious. "You and me. Forever."

His smile is soft and filled with hope. "Promise?"

I lean in and press a kiss to his lips. "Promise."

Epilogue: Tobias

Ten Years Later…

Davidoff Cologne is fresh in the air when I walk into the master suite. I shut the door behind me and head inside. The television is playing re-runs of an old Cubs game to an empty room.

Where the hell is the groom?

Just before I'd left the family suite, Ashley had turned to me and said, "Go make sure the groom hasn't got cold feet."

She was joking, of course. I had laughed carelessly. But now I find myself looking at the windows. *Ridiculous—we're like ten stories up.* I walk over to the open windows that overlook the private balcony, which in turn overlooks the gorgeous gardens of the Grand Hyatt.

Today, the gardens are decked out to the nines. There's a long white carpet that leads down to the wedding arch where the ceremony will take place. On either side of the carpet are rows of Chiavari chairs, each of which is adorned with an intricate arrangement of flowers running through their backs and legs.

The floral arrangements are a mix of purple agapanthus, white roses, and baby's breath. It's all minimal and understated but so elegant. I would expect nothing less from my amazing wife. She'd really gone all out on the décor. If she weren't so in love with teaching, she could have easily pivoted into event planning.

I hear a door from the next room where the four-poster bed sits. "Daniel?"

He appears from the bathroom, looking slightly flushed. "Hey."

That 'hey' is slightly trembly. "I was worried you'd split."

He snorts. "You have so little faith in me?"

I hand over the flower that's meant to go in his coat pocket. "I just never thought I'd see the day. Daniel Payne... walking down the aisle for the first time."

He takes a deep breath. "You know what? That makes two of us." He eyes the boutonniere. "Could you do it? My hands a little shaky."

"Cold feet?"

He shakes his head. "I'm nervous for sure—but no. I'm ready for this. Katherine is an amazing woman."

"I agree."

I'd had a good feeling about her from the day Daniel had introduced her to Ashley and I, a little over five years ago now. She was our age, a history professor at The University of Arizona and a woman who had her life figured out by the time she met Daniel. She was divorced, childless, and completely uninterested in changing that fact. They were perfect for each other.

"I'm forty-seven and getting married for the first time," he breathes. "Is that weird?"

I chuckle. "Dude, what's weird is that your best man—" I point proudly to myself, "—is also your son-in-law."

He snorts with laughter. "Facts."

"So—do you need a pep talk? Cause I got one in the bag. I'm happy to tell you what's expected on the wedding night as well."

He punches me in the arm. "Fuck off."

Laughing, I back out of the room. "I'm gonna go check on Ashley and the kids. Pretty sure she'll need help getting the little monkey into his suit."

Daniel smiles, his eyes getting all crinkly in the corners. That happens anytime I mention either Noah or Haley. Nothing lights him up quite like those two kids. "Good luck."

I give him a wink and head down the hall towards the family suite. I can hear them before I've even opened the door. Haley's giggle is the most infectious sound in the world and Noah's having an imaginary swordfight with his imaginary friends. He also happens to be doing it in nothing but his underwear and his bow tie.

"Noah Daniel Ackerman!" I scold. "Why aren't you dressed yet?"

Those big blue eyes of his go wide. "I'm fighting monsters, Papa!"

"Fight them later. Your Grandpa's getting married soon and we need to rally. I walk over to the bed where Haley's still jumping in her pretty pink flower girl dress. I spread my arms out and she jumps right into them.

I kiss her cheek. "Where's Mama?"

"In the bathroom. She was not feeling well. She said you were in charge of getting Noah dressed."

I frown. "Not feeling well?" I give her another kiss and plop her onto the bed.

"Papa!" she cries, giggling some more.

The bathroom door clicks open. "Noah, you better be dressed. Where's Papa?"

"Right here," I call, heading to the bathroom. "What's this about you not feeling very—"

I stop short when I set eyes on her. "*Wow*," I breathe. She's wearing a soft, off-the-shoulder, champagne chiffon dress that hugs her body in all the right places. She's arranged her hair into a series of intricate braids that she's piled around her head in an elegant if slightly messy updo. "You look *breathtaking*."

"Thank you." I love that even after nine years of marriage and two kids, I can still make her blush with something as simple as a compliment.

I walk over to her and gather her into my arms. "Are you okay? Haley mentioned you were sick."

She shakes her head. "I'm fine. Just… over-excited. Did you check on Dad?"

I nod. He's doing good. Nervous but he's ready.

"It's about time too. I thought I'd never get him married off."

Smiling, I bend down to kiss her on the lips but she leans away from me. She *never* leans away from me. "What is that?"

She smiles awkwardly. "You don't want to kiss me right now. I've just been sick. I mean, I brushed my teeth twice but still."

"So you *are* sick?" I ask, immediately worried.

She dismisses it casually. "I'm really not. Like I said, it's just all the excitement." She twists out of my arms and directs her gaze at Noah, who's still battling monsters. "Noah Ackerman! Get your suit on right this minute."

"Aw, Mama," he complains, turning the full effect of those puppy eyes on her the way only a four-year-old can. "Do I have to?"

She claps her hands together. "*Yes*. Move your butt. Come on!"

I grab Ashley's hand before she can escape me. "Babe, if you're not feeling good—"

"I'm *fine*," she snaps. Again—she *never* snaps at me. "Can you please just get Noah ready?"

I grab my unruly four-year-old and bribe him into his suit. Then I charge his sister with looking after him. The kid may be only six but she's got an old soul that I'd like to think she inherited from me. I take both kids and walk them down the hall to the bridal suite. Once I've handed them off to Katherine's entourage of cousins and nieces, I run back to my suite, unable to believe Ashley's repeated assurances that she's fine.

"Ashley?" She's nowhere in the suite. "Fuck this," I mutter under my breath as I walk into the bathroom to find her bent over the commode.

She groans as she gets up and walks over to the sink. "I'm fine."

"You keep saying that," I say. "Clearly that's not the case."

She gargles her mouth out and then brushes her teeth vigorously. Once she's done, she turns to me with a resigned expression on her face. "I kinda wanted to wait to tell you until *after* the wedding."

"Tell me what?'

She bites her bottom lip and smiles guiltily at me. "Um... I'm pregnant."

My eyes go wide and my jaw drops. "What?" I gasp.

We'd had this conversation two years ago. Are we done having kids or not? In the end, we'd both decided that our family was complete. We had a girl; we had a boy. Ashley had a lot to juggle with school and the kids. And I had three businesses to manage. Not to mention the fact that I was forty-four at the time.

Now here I am, forty-six years young, my beautiful young wife standing before me, telling me that we're about to be parents again.

For the third time.

"Are you sure?" I ask slowly.

She nods, a smile cracking through her nerves. "I've taken four pregnancy tests since yesterday. They're all big fat positives."

"Jesus," I mutter, running a hand through my hair. "Three kids!"

She walks into my arms and kisses my jaw. "I know it's a lot," she admits. "I know we decided we were done. But apparently... fate decided otherwise."

I look down at those sparkling eyes of hers and I feel the excitement start to rub off on me. "You're happy about this little accident, aren't you?"

She nods. "I am. I really, really am."

I smile. "Me too."

Her eyes brighten further. "Yeah?"

"Fuck yeah," I nod. "Another baby? With you? Sign me up."

Laughing, she kisses me hard on the lips. When she pulls back, we're both breathless. "I love you, Tobias Mason Ackerman."

I'm so overwhelmed that I can't respond right away. I just pull her to me and kiss her again. I don't have to say I love her though. I know she knows that I do. She'd taken all the broken parts of me and made me whole again. And I'd done the same with her.

No wonder neither one of us ever felt like we belonged

anywhere. It was because we were searching without even knowing it.

And once we found each other, the answer was obvious. And the wait was definitely worth it.

We belonged to each other.

And we always would.

Untitled

The End

~

Did you enjoy this read? Then check out Faking it with the Damaged Silver Fox

Sneak Peek of Faking it with the Damaged Silver Fox

I only wanted a no strings attached fling with my much older boss—but our families caught us, now we have to pretend to be in love.

At least, *he's* pretending.

On my first day at Donovan and Sons Law, I didn't expect to see the guy I had a one-night stand with - David Donovan, a reclusive billionaire partner of the firm.

Though we both try to deny it, we are drawn to each other.

It doesn't matter where it is, we can't keep our hands off of each other, in the bed, on his desk, against the wall, and so much more.

He is damaged. His divorce, the car accident he never talks about, and his desire to be a better father leave him little time for love.

So we agree, no strings attached.

Though we promise it won't affect work, the intensity of our attraction keeps surprising us.

We're caught by his best friend, is also my older brother.

I pretend we're in a real relationship.

Only, the more time we spend together, the more I wish this was real.

As Valentine's Day approaches, things change.

David just got a job offer halfway across the globe.

So, our fake relationship is maybe coming to an end.

The only problem is I am in love with him, and I won't let him go.

Start reading Faking it with the Damaged Silver Fox *now:*
Faking it with the Damaged Silver Fox

Printed in Great Britain
by Amazon